RAVES FOR JOHNNY D. BOGGS

The Despoilers

"Boggs' historical asides are aided by a narrative style that drives the story along full gallop." —*True West*

"Boggs has once more written a humdinger of a book with wonderful characters, even the villains. *The Despoilers* tears at one's heart, which is what really good fiction should do." —*Roundup*

"Johnny D. Boggs tells a crisply powerful story that rings true more than two centuries after the bloody business was done." —*The Post and Courier* (Charleston, SC)

The Lonesome Chisholm Trail

"Boggs is among the best western writers at work today. He writes with depth, flavor, and color, all of which are evident in this rite-of-passage tale . . . Boggs tells the familiar story with authenticity and power." —*Booklist*

"Realistic dialogue, a little humor to lighten up the dramatic tension, a strong plot, and a sense of place that leaves one sneezing from the dust makes for one of Boggs's best novels." —*Roundup*

Ten and Me

"Informed by accurate detail in almost every regard . . . Boggs's narrative voice captures the old-fashioned style of the past and reminds a reader of the derring-do of western legends of yesteryear." —*Publishers Weekly*

"This is an entertaining western in the classic mold. The characters possess enough human frailty to be believable, the author includes interesting stuff on the weaponry of the times, and there is enough gunplay to satisfy genre purists." —*Booklist*

Once They Wore the Gray

"Another dramatic story by a finalist for the Spur award of Western Writers of America." —*Amarillo Globe-News*

"Well worth reading, especially as it treats . . . an aspect of the Civil War that is often slighted in the history books." —*The Shootist*

Hannah and the Horseman

"I think Johnny D. Boggs is well on his way to being a major western writer." —*The Shootist*

"This book displays an admirable sense of percolating pace and point-blank prose."
  —*The Post and Courier* (Charleston, SC)

"Johnny D. Boggs moves his narrative at a lively clip, and it never turns mawkish." *Fort Worth Star-Telegram*

This Man Colter

"Humor, action, and a wonderful character in Gwen McCarthy make this a delightful read." —*Roundup*

"If you're into the true wild west, you will enjoy this rugged tale set in west Texas." —*Rendezvous*

Foundation of the Law

"As is to be expected with a Johnny Boggs novel, *Foundation of the Law* is full of those authentic historical details that make his stories so rich and believable."
  —*The Shootist*

Law of the Land

"Making bad guys into sympathetic characters is not the easiest feat but Boggs succeeds." —*Southwest BookViews*

"It is an engrossing story, and is told with Boggs' meticulous attention to authentic detail and believable characterizations. If his characters, including the Kid, don't look like, sound like, and behave like Boggs describes them, they should have." —*The Shootist*

"Boggs' unique approach to the Lincoln County War's legal skirmishing is both eye-opening and memorable."
—*True West*

The Big Fifty

"While I was reading *The Big Fifty* sometimes I would forget 'my favorite son' had written it."
—Jackie Boggs, Johnny's mother

"Johnny D. Boggs has a keen ability to interlace historically accurate information amid a cast of well-described characters and circumstances." —*Cowboy Chronicle*

"A fine novel that will leave you with the taste of grit in your mouth, and the smell of spoiled buffalo carcasses in your nose." —*Roundup*

Spark on the Prairie

"Brilliant." —*Roundup*

"Stunning." —*Persimmon Hill*

"This . . . continues a long-needed look at those who brought law and order to the frontier—not with six-guns but with law books." —*True West*

"A finely crafted historical novel with fully developed characters playing out their lives against the backdrop of early Texas settlement." —*American Cowboy*

East of the Border

"This is an amusing glimpse at a decidedly different side of some of the Old West's most famous names."
—*The Denver Post*

"We need more books like *East of the Border*." —*Roundup*

"*East of the Border* is a fun, lighthearted look at the thespian deep within every cowboy." —*True West*

"Boggs takes the historical facts . . . and gives us a fascinating tale of West meets East." —*The Shootist*

Camp Ford

"Boggs' carefully researched novel boasts meticulously drawn characters and captures in a striking way the amazing changes America underwent during the span of one man's life. An unusual, very rich western that should attract not only genre readers but also baseball fans and Civil War buffs."
—*Booklist*

"As baseball stories go, *Camp Ford* by Johnny D. Boggs is a home run . . . Think *The Longest Yard* . . . about baseball and without the glamour . . . Timeless."
—*USA Today Sports Weekly*

Killstraight

"It takes a skilled author like Johnny D. Boggs to drive the genre into new literary railheads, as he does in his novel *Killstraight*."
—*Tucson Weekly*

Doubtful Cañon

"Boggs's quirky western doesn't take itself too seriously, making this a fanciful and fun ride into some dangerous business."
—*Publishers Weekly*

"Boggs delivers a colorful, clever and arresting tale."
—*Santa Fe New Mexican*

"Uses its non-serious side to appeal to younger readers . . . well-flavored tale."
—*The Tombstone Epitaph*

Walk Proud, Stand Tall

"The author's deft hand at characterization and the subtle way he fills in the blanks as the story progresses makes *Walk Proud, Stand Tall* a tender story hard to resist."
—*The Denver Post*

"Boggs deftly balances the bitter and the sweet, the harsh landscapes and the humanity. That he manages it entertainingly is our reward."
—*Santa Fe New Mexican*

The Hart Brand

"Though an ocean away, *Kidnapped* and *Treasure Island* come to mind when reading this Western; Boggs' tale nearly matches the quality of those written by Stevenson."
—*True West*

"Some consider William Dale Jennings' *The Cowboys* the best Western coming-of-age novel. Others would argue it's *All the Pretty Horses* by Cormac McCarthy or *When the Legends Die* by Hal Borland. With *The Hart Brand*, Boggs stakes his own firm claim." —*Santa Fe New Mexican*

"Boggs, who writes with a finely honed sense of character and a keen eye for detail, combines historical fact with fiction to create a Revolutionary adventure from the vantage point of an average participant." —*Booklist*

"Johnny Boggs has produced another instant page-turner . . . don't put down the book until you finish it." —Tony Hillerman

"The relationships and setting shine: Daniel—striving at once to solve the case and reconnect with Comanche ways—is a complex, winning protagonist." —*Publishers Weekly*

"A rousing story with an emotional and philosophical depth that will surprise readers who don't expect complexity from a Western. . . . Explores the clash between white and native cultures . . . fundamentally different and strikingly similar." —*Booklist*

Soldier's Farewell

"This is not a simple Western . . . Boggs' familiarity with the landscape . . . puts the reader right into New Mexico and particularly through the rugged landscape along the Río Chama. And while this may seem to be a fairly traditional Western, the conclusion is anything but. Another good read."—*The Roundup*

"Boggs . . . showcases his talent for period detail, atmosphere, complex characters, and the ability to evoke a stark landscape." —*Booklist*

"Ultimately, *Soldier's Farewell* is a tale of two brothers falling far short of what their father expects of them, and what they expect of each other. This is another fine novel by one of today's better writers of Westerns." —*Tucson Weekly*

MOJAVE

JOHNNY D. BOGGS

PINNACLE BOOKS
Kensington Publishing Corp.
www.kensingtonbooks.com

PINNACLE BOOKS are published by

Kensington Publishing Corp.
119 West 40th Street
New York, NY 10018

All Kensington titles, imprints, and distributed lines are available at special quantity discounts for bulk purchases for sales promotions, premiums, fund-raising, educational, or institutional use.

Special book excerpts or customized printings can also be created to fit specific needs. For details, write or phone the office of the Kensington special sales manager: Kensington Publishing Corp., 119 West 40th Street, New York, NY 10018, attn: Special Sales Department; phone 1-800-221-2647.

ISBN-13: 978-0-7860-3337-9
ISBN-10: 0-7860-3337-1

First printing: August 2014

10 9 8 7 6 5 4 3 2 1

Printed in the United States of America

First electronic edition: August 2014

ISBN-13: 978-0-7860-3338-6
ISBN-10: 0-7860-3338-X

For Jim and Lynne Vanderhider

CHAPTER ONE

The Mojave Desert ain't hotter than hell.

It is Hell, with a capital H.

Get stuck in that fire pit, without horse, canteen, or the good Lord's mercy (or some poor, dumb son of a bitch to rob) and, quite honestly, there ain't much for a sinner to do. Except stick that Spiller & Burr in your mouth, and let a .36-caliber ball put you out of your misery. Which is what I was about to do—would have done, in fact—excepting that I had no powder, balls, or percussion caps. Did I mention that a Spiller & Burr is an old relic from the late War of the Rebellion, and even way back then Rebels never had much use for them thumb-busters, and bluecoats knowed better than to shoot them? Least that's what the one-eyed cur told me after I won the pistol from him with one damned fine bluff, convincing him that I had a straight against his pair of kings showing when all I really had was queen high. Besides, tired and parched as I was, plumb out of my sun-fried head, I doubted if I had strength to cock that revolver even if I had the ammunition.

Like as not, you've likely read that story about that California Gold Rush gambler that this gent named Twain or Hart or maybe it was Dickens wrote where this gambler gets hisself caught in a blizzard and sits down beside a tree and puts a bullet through his own heart, saying his luck has run out. I ain't read it, but there's this gal from some hifalutin society who the warden fetches into Folsom, and she's read it a time or two to some of us more literary-inclined inmates not being punished on the rock pile. It's a right fair story. Only that gambler never had it so good. He was in a blizzard, where it's cold and wet. Wasn't frying in a furnace with vultures just waiting for fresh supper.

My luck really played out about the time I won that Spiller & Burr. I had sat down inside this bucket of blood near Beal's Crossing on the Colorado River. The Army boys still soldiered at Fort Mojave, and, seeing how I wasn't wanted for nothing in Arizona Territory, I had lighted out that way to make my pile.

The name's Bishop, Micah Bishop. The time I tell about, I was around thirty or thirty-one years of age. I've never been rightly certain on account that I got brung up and educated and my knuckles rapped by the Sisters of Charity in an orphanage in Santa Fe. Course, I can't go back to New Mexico Territory. Truth be told, if it weren't for a couple of nuns who figured my hide was worth saving, I'd be buried facedown in some potter's field in Las Vegas with a noose still wrapped around my neck. So I was done with New Mexico Territory. Same as I was shed of Missouri, where I'd also had to kill a body. And in the Indian Nations. And there was even those down in the great state of Texas who would like to see me hanging from what passes for a tree in that country. Not for killing. No, sir. No, the late Big Tim Pruett, a gent I rode with for a spell, once warned me never shoot no Texan, because there will be more Texans coming after you, and there's just too many Texans to kill. But I did admire the horses they breed down in that great Lone Star State, and I sometimes wound up selling some where the legality of a bill of sale I'd forged might could have been called into question.

Anyhow, since I got freed from that stinking dungeon in Las Vegas, I'd rode out of New Mexico and come to Arizona, and pret' soon set myself up dealing faro, Spanish Monte, and stud poker for them soldier boys at Fort Mojave. Won a right smart of money. Then a worthless Spiller & Burr .36. Only a short while after that, some of them infantry boys begun to question how come luck favored me so much and the methods I was using when I was dealing.

Well, you've heard that sad story. Least I have, often enough, here in Folsom. Honest gambler gets called a cheat. Harsh words get spoke. Some fools pull their pistols, and they ain't no twenty-something-year-old relics, but long-barreled, center-firing Colts, Remingtons, or Smith & Wessons.

Next thing I knowed, having gotten out of that stinking adobe gambling den with only a bullet hole through the crown of my hat, I was forcing the ferry man at the crossing to fetch me into California, *muy pronto,* while still trading lead with them infantry boys whose lousy shooting made a body wonder how in hell we had preserved the Union, freed the slaves, and whipped the Mojave and Paiute Indians.

Well, it was pitch dark. And, like me, them soldiers had been drinking a mite, and the misnamed Honest Abe Rohrbough didn't serve nothing but the worst forty-rod rotgut he brewed hisself at that gambling palace.

Suffice to say that I made it across the Colorado River and into California, and I don't think I'd killed nobody, so I reckon I could still make my presence known in Arizona at some later date. Not Fort Mojave or Beal's Crossing, but down south or somewheres. Besides, I'd been calling myself Corbin—nothing else, just Corbin—so I figured that Micah Bishop would likely be free from law-dogs, and if that son of a bitch Corbin—never caught his first name—who almost got me hung in Las Vegas, happened to ever show up at Beal's Crossing and got bruised and maybe even bloodied and possibly even killed, good for him.

Not sure how long it would take the ferry man to get his boat back to the Arizona side, and how angry them bluecoats was at me, I pushed the buckskin gelding I'd borrowed into a fast lope across the Mojave. At night, the desert gets cold. I'd never been to California, so I kept to the military road for a spell, then turned off toward the northwest, think-ing that might fool the infantry boys was they bound and determined to catch up with me.

I doubted if they would. Remember what I said about my luck playing out? I'd left most of my piles on that poker table—betting that Honest Abe Rohr-bough, the cheat, had already taken a healthy cut for his house percentage—along with the Reming-ton over-and-under .41 derringer, which was empty when I dropped it by my tumbler of Rohrbough's barleycorn. Gamblers would be wiser if they'd pocket something other than a derringer. I mean, two shots ain't gonna turn away five angry poker players. I'll have to remember that next time I set down at a layout and deal with a marked deck.

The only thing I'd managed to leave Beal's Crossing with—not including my hide, hair, and life—was my black hat, my vest, my boots, and that Spiller & Burr, which I had emptied along the path from Rohrbough's and then on the ferry.

But I did have a canteen hanging from the saddle horn and a good buckskin gelding.

Had, that is.

Turned out, shortly before dawn, I realized that them infantry boys had gotten some good training in marksmanship at Fort Mojave after all. Since turning off the military road, I had given the gelding some breathers, slowing down, easing my way through unfamiliar country. Now some of them boys at Rohrbough's, and even Honest Abe hisself, had mentioned this mining camp in the California desert, around something they called the Painted Hills, that was named Calico. Big silver strike there, and I was just dumb enough to try to find it. I mean, I didn't have much in the way of possessions, as I just told y'all, but I think I forgot to mention that I did have a deck of cards in my vest pocket. And them cards was marked to my liking.

Way I remembered it, Calico was about a week's ride from Fort Mojave, so with the sky lightening up in the east, I figured we might as well make a bee-line for Calico. How hard could them Painted Hills be to find? I'd been sitting in the saddle, letting the buckskin catch his breath, my left leg hooked over the horn, when I decided it was time to ride some more. So I lowered my leg, found the stirrup, and give the gelding a little kick.

Instead of moving forward, he started to fall. I leaped off the saddle, not wanting to have an eight-hundred-pound horse roll over me, and the horse just collapsed. Lifted his head once, snorted, and expired.

Well, I cussed that horse and cussed my luck and cussed them bluecoats from Fort Mojave. Turned out, a couple of them had aimed well enough to put two bullets through that buckskin. I'll say one thing for that horse, though. He carried me farther than he had no right to. Got me out of Beal's Crossing.

I looked up.

To this.

When the sun appeared, I got a good look-see at a spartan wasteland that stretched out in all directions. Couldn't see no Painted Hills, but, by jacks, I'd only covered maybe ten miles since the Colorado River. That left me a hundred and thirty or thereabouts to cover. Afoot. With one canteen.

Now, knowing what I know today, what I should have done was simple. Just backtrack my way to the Colorado River. I could have followed the river south, perhaps all the way to Yuma, a right far piece to walk, but I would have had water all the way down. Or even just wait a spell and sneak across the river at Beal's when the soldier boys was marching and drilling and sweating at the fort. What I done, of course, being the stubborn fool and thinking so much about plucking some greenbacks from dumb silver miners in a stupid town called Calico, was simple:

I just fetched that canteen, pulled my hat down low, and set out walking west.

Oh, there was hills. And washes. And rocks. And creosote and cholla. And one intense sun on my back.

But I'd lived in harsh country before, and I knowed that this being summer, monsoons oftentimes brought down real gulley washers in the afternoon. I also knowed that a desert might look lifeless, but you could always find a seep or a spring with some good water. Hell, even a Mojave rattlesnake needs water to live. You just had to know where to look.

Alas, I didn't.

I was also wise enough, experienced enough, to know that only a fool walks across the desert in the heat of the day. So when the sun got too high, I found myself a patch of shade, stretched my legs out, and taken a sip of water. A small sip. Figured I'd better save some of that water for the days to come.

Funny thing about taking a sip of water on a hot day in a barren desert. It makes you thirstier. So I had myself another sip. And then another. Before I made myself put the stopper back in that canteen.

Then I fetched my deck of cards from my vest and dealt a little one-handed *vingt-un*.

I slept some—being a gambler, I am used to sleeping in the day, but usually I sleep in a hotel bed or at least in a wagon yard, and not in a desert where all sorts of things might kill me. When the sun finally dipped behind them hills waiting for me out west, I got up, taken another sip of water, and started walking.

Made sense, you see, to wander through this country in the dark. You didn't have to worry about dying of heat stroke. Just stepping onto one of them green serpents. Folks say that the Mojave rattler is the deadliest snake you'll run into out west. Then there was man-killing scorpions. Or just stepping into a hole and breaking your leg, or neck.

That first day and night wasn't too bad. Second day fared passably well, too.

After that, though, things get a bit fuzzy. I recollect singing. "My Bonnie Lies over the Ocean" and "Home on the Range," two tunes I never really cared about. Maybe I disremember. Maybe my mind was gone.

Truth is, I don't know how many days I wandered out in the Mojave. It felt far. Felt like forever. Somewhere along the trail—if you could call anything around me a trail—I had shed my vest. I'd even tossed that deck down some hole, and it was a good deck. Hardly even the best sharper could have noticed how I'd marked them pastecards.

Water run out. Oh, I kept the canteen, for a while, that is. Must have dropped it, or pitched it, or just forgot all about it somewhere between where the buffaloes was roaming and the zephyrs was so free. Anyhow, at some point, in the heat of the day—reckon by that time I'd done forgot about walking at night and resting in the daytime—I savvied that I was done for, so I sat down, back against a boulder, and tried to put that Spiller & Burr in my mouth. But didn't have the strength, or a paper cartridge and copper cap.

Along about that time, sounds come to me. The squeaking of wagon wheels, the creaking of harness leather, and good, fine American cussing.

But I didn't care. Closing my eyes, I decided that this was a good place and time to die.

Only a short while later, or maybe it was a day or two, a shadow crossed my face, and I heard this voice say:

"Reckon you owe me one, mister."

My eyes fluttered open, and I spied this shadow that was speaking at me. The silhouette wore a flat-brimmed, low-crowned hat and held the longest snake I'd ever seen in his left hand. Course, it wasn't a snake, just a blacksnake whip, but I didn't know no better. Not as dead as I was. He certainly wasn't some angel, unless he was "The Angel of Death."

I tried to answer him, to tell him, "Yes, sir, I reckon I surely do owe you one, mister," but my tongue had gotten so fat, my lips so cracked, my face so blistered, I couldn't say nothing. Which is exactly what I said.

The shadow leaned beside me, and he yelled something to some *hombres* somewhere behind him, or in front of him, or maybe he was just talking to hisself, as far as I knowed at the time.

"It's your lucky day," the specter told me.

Turned out, it sure was. Because instead of dying alone in the middle of the Mojave, I was plucked back into the living world by a gent called Whip Watson.

Course, now that I have time—five to seven years, the judge told me—to think about how things played out, I've studied on that bit of fortune. How I was to ride with Whip Watson, how I was to come right smack between him and another freighter named Candy Crutchfield, how an Oriental princess named Jingfei, which means "Quiet Not," and a passel of mail-order brides, was to come into my life. How I was played for a fool, flayed, flimflammed, flummoxed, flaxed out, and, finally, incarcerated here at Folsom.

Hell, I'd have been better off had I just died out in the Mojave Desert.

CHAPTER TWO

Like I said, I didn't die. Now, them first few days riding in the back of one of Whip Watson's freight wagons is about as forgotten as my Moses-like wanderings across the Mojave Desert. Had me some wild dreams, rare for me, some disturbing nightmares, but I've never been one for remembering such things. I do recollect this woman in white with black hair and a huge Mojave rattlesnake hanging around her neck feeding me soup. Least, she called it soup. It tasted like dung. And I recalled floating on a ship, sailing the high seas, and then I'd wake up, fearing that I'd been shanghaied, and finding myself lying in that freight wagon next to crates and crates of tools and kegs of gunpowder. And I'd start to sit up, but then I'd just fall back onto somebody's bedroll, and I'd close my eyes and go back to sleep.

Till one evening, I woke up.

The wagon wasn't moving. I smelled a campfire somewhere beyond the canvas tarp, heard voices speaking Mexican and what some folks might even call English.

"Evening," a voice said.

I turned my head.

A candle had been lit, and sat flickering atop one of the crates—not the kegs of gunpowder, or course—so I seen the gent real good.

He dressed hisself in a fine Boss of the Plains, black as my soul but with a fancy horsehair-hitched headband. He wore a blue silk shirt, double-breasted black vest, black-and-white polka-dot bandanna, black-striped woolen britches with the thighs and seat reinforced with black corduroy, the legs of which was tucked inside high-topped stovepipe boots, blacker than the ace of spades except for the red crescent moons inlaid in the tops. It was a right fancy outfit. Especially when you got a gander at the two nickel-plated Colts shoved into a black sash, their ivory grips butt forward, facing me.

His eyes was black as night, too, like most of his duds, but his hair was white, like bones that've been bleaching underneath the Mojave sun for years. A real contrast, if you was to ask me, black outfit, black eyes, but white hair. Like there was good and evil in this man. I'd soon come to know better than think that. Sun and wind had bronzed his face, but there wasn't not a hint of beard on his cheeks. I knowed why. I could smell the soap on him. Here's a guy, in the middle of nowhere, who shaves before supper. Hell's fire, he probably shaved before breakfast, too. I smelled something else, too.

My eyes found the bowl he held in his left hand. Steaming hot. Smelling mighty fine.

"Where's . . . ?" My voice cracked. Had to swallow down some spit. "Where's the lady that's been feeding me?" I asked.

He laughed so hard he almost spilt the soup, which would have been a tragedy. Placing the bowl near my bedroll, he wiped his nose with the back of his left hand, and laughed some more. "I haven't seen a *lady* since Prescott," he said.

I give him the dumb look.

"I've been feeding you, mister."

"Oh." Sure couldn't hide the disappointment in my voice. Because he dressed real fine, kept hisself clean and shaved, but this guy, iffen you was to ask me, was uglier than sin.

"Brain must've been playing tricks on me," I told him. "I saw this woman feeding me soup. With the damnedest, longest black snake hanging around her neck."

"Like this?" He pointed at the floor.

Which is when I saw the whip. Well, they do call those whips "blacksnakes."

I laughed.

"It bites, sure enough," my savior said. "Kills like a sidewinder. Eat your soup, if you're able."

Well, knowing that this wasn't some goddess saving my worthless hide but an ugly man with two pistols and a whip, I managed to get myself into a seated position, back against the wagon's side, and tasted the soup. I've tasted better, but I smiled politely. And kept right on eating.

"That's good to see," the man said. He pointed a slim finger at me and the bowl and the spoon. "Thought you was gonna die on me. That would have set me back a spell."

"Maybe you won't have to bury me," I told him.

"Oh, I wouldn't have buried you, mister. Takes too much time. I would have just tossed your body to the buzzards. You would have set me back ten dollars had you croaked. Juan Pedro said you'd surely die before we reached Calico. I bet against that old Mex."

"I'm glad Juan Pedro lost his bet." Then his words struck me. I finished the soup, lifting the bowl and draining the rest. "You're going to Calico?"

He motioned at the crates and kegs. "That's where we're selling this." He took the spoon and bowl, tossed them through the opening in the back of the wagon. "Juan Pedro!" he shouted. "More dishes for you. And you owe me ten dollars, old man."

His black eyes lighted back on me. "You owe me, too."

"I'm your servant," I told him, and give him this slight bow.

With a grin, he moved back, taking his whip with him, sitting on one of the kegs.

"That's good to hear," he said. "Because I can use a man like you."

Which made me a bit nervous, more wary.

"You know me?"

"I know enough." He reached into his vest pocket, pulled out a fine cigar—not one of them two-cent jobs I was prone to smoke, but a real fat expensive cigar—and fetched the candle, lighting the smoke, and him sitting on a keg of gunpowder with six or seven more kegs well within reach of some random spark.

Didn't offer me one of them cigars, but I don't think I would've lit it up if he had. I'm a gambler, but I don't take chances that might get me blowed to perdition.

When the cigar's tip was glowing, he moved the candle back atop the crate marked "Hammers" and exhaled a long stream of smoke toward the top of our canvas roof.

"I find you half-dead, more like three-quarters dead, fried, soles of your boots worn to nothing, clothes threadbare, alone in the desert. No horse." He stared at me, waiting for some response.

"Had a buckskin," I told him. "Died on this side of the Colorado River." Figured there was no point in telling him how that horse had expired.

"Most people would have returned to Arizona Territory."

I smiled. "I've been to Arizona. Never seen California."

Which satisfied him, I reckon, 'cause he moved on.

"No canteen, either," he said.

I looked around, like this white-haired man dressed in black would have fetched my canteen and left it within my reach. Like I told y'all, I didn't remember shucking it, but it sure wasn't in with the hammers and pans and powder in this wagon.

Give up looking. I turned back to my savior with a sheepish look on my face. "I had one," I told him. "Don't know what I done with it."

"You've never been in the desert before," he told me, and puffed on his stogie.

Oh, I had. Had almost died in what, in New Mexico Territory, they call the *Jornado del Muerto*, the "Journey of the Dead," which is just as deadly, just as miserable, and just as barren as the Mojave. If I didn't have the canteen no more, I sure knowed why. Even empty, canteens feel heavy, and for a fellow afoot with no water, they weigh as much as a dead man's bloated body. But I didn't say none of this. Something about this guy's demeanor told me that he didn't cotton to arguments or getting hisself contradicted or corrected.

"So I ask myself, we found you lying against some rocks," the man in black with the white hair said. "What kind of man is it, who with no water, no horse, nothing except a ratty old hat. . . ."

I reached up for my ratty old hat, which sure wasn't as fancy as my rescuer's Stetson, and give him another one of my sheepish looks.

He had stopped to draw on his cigar, pushed the blue-gray smoke up toward the canvas roof again, and he finished his question.

"I ask myself, what kind of man is it, who alone in the desert, no horse, no gun, no chance . . . what kind of man is it who still carries a revolver?"

With that, his left hand snaked behind his back, and he pulled out that old .36. With a grin, he flicked the antique toward me. I ducked, let it slam into the wooden slats. Then I reached over and picked it up.

"A cap-and-ball antiquity that, by my guess, even empty—as it was—weighs more than an empty canteen."

"Sister Rocío," I told him, "always told me I had more luck than sense." Instinctively, I looked down at my knuckles, almost feeling the good nun's ruler rapping them hands of mine. She could wield a ruler like a sledgehammer.

"Your sister?" he asked.

I shrugged. Didn't see no need in giving him any information he might be able to use against me somewhere down the line. "Just a woman I knowed," I told him, "back when I was a kid."

Course, I was more interested in the revolver.

It felt different because it had been cleaned. I could feel the oil on the cylinder, the barrel, could smell it, too. It also felt heavier.

"It's loaded," my savior told me.

I shot him a quick look. He was holding the cigar with his left hand, dangersomely close to one of them kegs of powder, but the thumb of his right hand was hooked on that fancy sash, just a hop and a skip from the Colt near his left hip. Next, I studied that Spiller & Burr a mite closer.

Carefully, I laid the .36 between my legs.

"Yeah," I said, "but it don't work without caps."

He chuckled, slid the cigar into his mouth, and used his left hand to reach into another vest pocket. Something shiny come flying toward me. This one, I managed to catch.

It was a straight-lined capper, brass, fully filled with likely fifteen number-eleven percussion caps. Put them babies on the nipples on that cylinder, and I'd be ready to tackle some sore losers from Fort Mojave or set up another crooked poker game.

"Thanks," I said.

"Reckon you owe me," he said.

"Reckon I do," I told him.

He pushed himself to his feet, kneeling a mite, holding out his right hand. His left, I noticed, wasn't nowhere near none of his guns. Unless he had some hideaway derringer up his sleeve.

"Come on," he said. "Meet the boys. We've got food that's more solid than soup, and genuine Tennessee sour mash."

My rough hand took his soft one, and he pulled me to my feet.

"Name's Bishop," I told him—and yes, I thought

of using another handle, but hell, he had saved my life, so I reckon I owed him at least that much honesty. "Micah Bishop."

"Whip Watson," he said, and he was heading out the back of the wagon, and I was following him.

CHAPTER THREE

Outside, gathered around a right cozy fire, assembled the worst-looking bunch of ruffians I'd ever laid eyes on—and I once rode with Sean Fenn. And, well, Big Tim Pruett wouldn't have never gotten mistook for some handsome thespian. I'd expected to find teamsters. You know, mule skinners and freighting types, ugly, burly men handy with whips and cusswords. Well, they was certainly ugly, and plenty of them I'd call burly, and I suspected that all of them knowed more cusswords than Webster.

Only I wasn't so certain I'd call them mule skinners. No, sir, what I'd call them boys was . . . gunmen.

Squat assassins. Shootists. Man-killers. Vermin.

A thin, leathery graybeard rose from behind the coffeepot. I thought he might be fetching me a cup of that brew, which sure smelled better than the soup I'd just et, but he come with empty hands. I figured him to be Juan Pedro, and I figured right.

The sun had just set, so it was still fairly light outside, and that fire was roaring hot, so I got a good look-see at the Mexican. He dressed like a vaquero—or maybe one of them Spanish noblemen—

if you savvy what I mean. A dandified silk shirt, tight-fitting black jacket with pretty red and blue braid all up the sleeves and shoulders. Dark blue pants called *calzoneras* decorated with silver conchos from the hem to the knees. Black boots and spurs with large rowels. And a flat-brimmed, flat-crowned hat of the finest beaver, and a fancy-braided stampede string to keep his hat from flying off.

I never cottoned to stampede strings. They choked a body's neck, and too many folks already wanted to put ropes around my neck as it was. Big Tim Pruett always told me that the best way to keep a hat on your head in a windstorm was to buy one that fits snug. Mine, while not much to look at, fit me just fine.

Juan Pedro also wore a brace of Schofield revolvers in a red sash around his belly. There was a Green River knife stuck inside one of his boot tops, and I could tell by the way his left arm hung and from that bulging fancy jacket that he also kept a smaller revolver in a shoulder harness.

Juan Pedro, I decided, was a right careful man.

With a slight bow, he introduced hisself. His name was a lot longer than Juan Pedro, but Juan Pedro was part of that handle. Then his left hand reached into a pocket on his jacket, and he fished out a coin. I knowed it was gold. I could even see the word *liberty* on the gal's head, and them stars all around the coin. A gold eagle. Looked to be fresh-minted.

He spoke some smart Spanish, then started to extend the ten-dollar piece to Whip Watson, but quickly pulled it back.

"Ah," he said, switching to English, "but I believe

the bet was that this *norteamericano* would live to see Calico, Señor Watson. We are a long way from Calico, still."

Whip Watson stood a bit behind me, and after that introduction, I wasn't about to take my eyes off of Juan Pedro, but I heard Watson say, "That was the bet."

"So if I kill him now, you would owe me ten dollars."

"I reckon so."

Me? I'm thinking: *These are the guys you wanted me to meet?*

Juan Pedro was staring at me then, smiling. He had right pretty teeth. Real straight. Mostly white. Excepting for top front one with a silver speck in the middle. It glittered like a rattlesnake's eye. He was slipping that gold coin back into his pocket, but that pocket was right above one of them bit Schofield revolvers, and I wasn't the fool he must have thought me to be.

What I done was cocked that .36.

Don't know why—fate maybe—but I still held that newly cleaned revolver in my left hand. Course, what Juan Pedro and Whip Watson and nobody else knowed was that I can't shoot worth a nickel with my left hand. Even with my right, it ain't a sure bet I'll hit the target, though I had gotten lucky with Sean Fenn and some of his boys, and those other rapscallions I've already mentioned who are now roasting in hell. What Whip Watson and I knowed, however, was that I hadn't put percussion caps on that old relic, and a cap-and-ball gun don't work without the cap part. What I was gambling on was that Juan Pedro couldn't see that them nipples was empty.

Must have worked, because Juan Pedro laughed

and dropped the coin in his pocket real careful, then inched both of his hands away from both of his revolvers that I knowed he carried.

"This is a smart man you have here, Señor Watson." Juan Pedro was still grinning, but I was looking past him at those other, ahem, *freighters*. "Perhaps he will live to see Calico."

"He will." Watson walked to the fire, and squatted by the coffeepot.

Juan Pedro gave me another one of his bows, then stepped aside, extending his left arm in a friendly gesture that wasn't sociable at all.

"After you, amigo," I told him.

Laughing again, he turned and went back to his place. I taken myself a deep breath, let it out, and found that capper Whip Watson had give me back inside the wagon. Set that .36 on half-cock, and began putting those caps on them nipples—all six of them, deciding against safety for the moment— and stepped toward the fire to meet some of the rest of the boys, wondering if they'd be as sociable as Juan Pedro.

They wasn't the most talkative bunch. Mostly they just grunted, drank, and farted. I counted fifteen of them, besides Juan Pedro and Whip Watson, and I ain't that fast at ciphering but I do know how to count. Cards mostly. But seventeen mean-looking gents around a campfire didn't tax me none.

What struck me strange was that nobody was eating. There was food hanging from pots, and it smelled real fine, but the pots just steamed and bubbled, yet nobody taken nothing except the coffee. Didn't bother me too much, on account of all the soup I'd swallowed, and besides, I spied a jug making its way around that circle, and assumed that was the genuine Tennessee sour mash that Whip Watson had mentioned.

So there I sat, between Whip and a sour-smelling guy with a fat gut and arms that looked as solid as two-by-fours and a rough, black beard that was moving, not from the wind, on account there wasn't no wind, but on account of the bugs. I wanted to move, but didn't want to disrespect the gent none. So I just slid as far away from him, but not too close to Whip Watson, as humanly possible.

I looked at the jug. Then I looked at the fire. Then I looked at the Spiller & Burr, which I decided wasn't very sociable being in my left hand, so I slid it into my waistband. No one noticed. Also, I started to notice something. They wasn't considering me, wasn't even following that jug of liquor, and most of them wasn't watching the fire or the food. They stared out at some rocks, but it was getting darker by the minute, and I couldn't see nothing but the shadow that was some boulders.

It couldn't be Mojave or Paiute Indians. Couldn't be bandits. Because these boys I was sitting in a circle with certainly wasn't greenhorns and if there was something dangersome in them rocks, they wouldn't be sitting around a campfire waiting on a jug of Tennessee sour mash. Since I didn't find no interest in looking at boulders that was disappearing in the darkness, I stared at the wagons. It was an odd assembly. Not those big long-hitch freight wagons pulled by massive spans of mules or oxen that I'd expected to see with a freighting train. No, these was mostly farm wagons with rear wheels topping four feet high, some with canvas covers— like the one I'd rode in—and others without. There was two combination market and pleasure wagons, and four old Conestogas like they'd taken on the old Oregon Trail all them years before. I'd never even seen one in person, just woodcuts in magazines and such. But the damnedest thing of all was that I also counted four Columbus carriages. They were parked closest to the fire, so I could see them real good. And Big Tim Pruett had once stole a Columbus buggy and give this rich lady whose husband owned one of the mines in the mountains the ride of her life up and down Wyandot Street in Denver City till he got arrested, and I got conscripted by another lawdog to help carry the lady, who had fainted in pure terror, to the nearest pill-roller.

Now, you can hall freight in market and pleasure wagons, and certainly Conestogas hauled supplies from Missouri to Oregon or even California, and farm wagons would fill the bill iffen you didn't have freight wagons. But I didn't see no reason anybody would be taking four—that's right, *four*—fancy rigs that I'd seen selling for three hundred dollars and more in towns like Kansas City and Dallas.

The next day, I'd get a real close look at those buggies, and they all was top notch. Made of hickory, with full fenders, silver-plated glass lamps so they could go at night, and canopy tops of fancy body cloth with full back and side curtains. And two-seaters, all of them, with buffed leather that didn't look dusty at all. On account that Whip Watson had some of his burly men buffing that leather, getting out all the dust and grime, making those rigs look like they'd just come out of that factory in Ohio.

But that evening, before I even saw what care Whip Watson had his men giving them buggies, I was already wondering: *Why in blazes would you haul supplies to a mining town in the middle of the Mojave Desert in fancy carriages?* Then it struck me that Whip Watson planned to sell those buggies in Calico. Shrewd man, this Whip Watson. Miners get rich, and they want to show their wealth. A fancy conveyance like a Columbus carriage would probably bring six hundred dollars in a remote spot on the map like Calico, California.

I was just about to compliment Whip Watson on his capitalism when something caught my eye. Didn't come from those boulders where most everybody still was watching. It come from one of the Conestogas.

What drawed my attention was an orange dot that got brighter, then dimmer, then disappeared, then glowed all orange again. Somebody out there was smoking a cigarette. Then that somebody stepped around from behind the feed box on the back of the wagon, and I spied another orange dot that twinkled. I could make out their shapes now as they met near the water barrel on the wagon's side.

So there was nineteen men in this company.

No. More. Two other shapes of men came dimly into view beside the second wagon. I looked down the line, and, sure enough, there was a fellow sitting on the wagon tongue who must've been cleaning his fingernails with a pocketknife. I just guessed that there was another guard on the other end of that wagon, so I looked at the final wagon. It taken a spell, on account that the light was fading fast, but I saw another glow from another smoke. That led me to guess that there was twenty-five men.

Well, it's a handy thing to have guards posted at night in country such as this. The West ain't no place for careless folks, but those guards—iffen that

was the case and they was truly guards and not just
cigarette smokers who didn't feel like waiting their
turn for a taste of sour mash—appeared interested
in only those four big wagons. Which got me to suspicion that there must be something right valuable
in them wagons.

Ever seen a Conestoga? Not just a woodcut in
Harper's Weekly or some such. I mean in person.

They remind me of that big white whale that this
peg-legged Captain Ahab was chasing in another
one of those books that gal from that hifalutin society read to us boys in Folsom before we got real
sick of all that harpooning and avast-ing and whale
blubbering and guys named Queequeg and Quahog
and Ishmael and so we asked her to read something
from the *National Police Gazette* instead.

Those wagons are eighteen feet long and maybe
eleven feet high, curved *fore* and *aft* (I did pick up
them two words from that book nobody had heard
of about that crazy captain and that whale) with the
thickest white canvas covers you'll find anywhere.
The wheels' rims was made of iron. They looked
like whales, I mean to tell you, but they was built like
forts. Once I'd heard tell from some old-timer that
Conestogas could haul twelve thousand pounds.
So whatever Whip Watson and his boys was hauling
in those wagons, there must be a lot of it. I didn't
figure it was gunpowder, hammers, pickaxes, and
copper mining pans.

Twenty-five men. But by then it was too dark to
count the number of wagons.

Then my brain reminded me of something else.
It takes mules or horses or oxen to move wagons,
especially Conestogas. Those animals would be off
somewhere real close, but they would be guarded,

too. I'd put at least two men to make sure no animals wandered off or got wandered off by men like me who got attracted to good horses. Maybe four.

Twenty-nine men.

Make it thirty.

Somebody said something in our campfire group, and I looked back toward those boulders, or where the boulders were because now you couldn't see that far. Another orange glow. Too big, too bright, I figured, for a cigarette, so I decided this gent smoked cigars.

Everybody seemed taken by this cigar-smoker. A side glance even showed me that Whip Watson found the man coming from the boulders interesting. I started to look back at Cigar Smoker when the man with bugs in his beard jabbed my arm with the jug.

He said something to me. Or maybe he just farted. I took the jug, and he looked at the orange dot. That was just my luck. I got to drink after a man who stank worse than the rankest of farts and had bugs in his beard and probably everywhere else on his person.

I didn't want to be disrespectful, but I didn't want to be swallowing graybacks or ticks or whatever those bugs were, so I wiped the lip of the jug with my shirtsleeve, hoping that Bug Beard wouldn't find offense to this act and stomp my head into the ground. He didn't. Didn't notice me. Like everybody else, he focused on the man coming from the boulders.

The jug came up to my mouth, and I drunk. No bugs, no forty-rod whiskey, but pure, genuine Tennessee sour mash. Went down smooth as silk. Maybe that's what Whip Watson was hauling in those big wagons.

I savored the taste, but figured that Whip Watson wanted a snort hisself, but he would not begrudge me one more nip. The jug went back up, and came straight back down.

Thirty-one men.

As they neared the camp, the flames from the fire was so high, I could tell that there wasn't just one man coming from those rocks. Only one was smoking. The other, a slimmer shadow, trailed along a few feet in front of the big guy with the long nine cigar.

Thirty-one. Maybe more, maybe a couple less. But quite the crowd.

I started up with the jug again, and was drinking. Then I was spitting and spluttering and brushing the liquor off my face and clothes.

Bug Beard cussed me, Juan Pedro shot me the evil eye, and a few others glanced my direction, but none focused his attention for long on me. They looked straight at the slim person who didn't smoke a cigar as he come into camp, slipping between a guy in Levi's and a bowler hat and a guy in buckskins that was older than them Conestogas.

What had caused me to spit out good whiskey was the thirty-first man.

Who wasn't a man at all.

I doubted if she'd come up to my chin. Tiny, she was, and thin. She wore a robe—a *changyi*, I'd come to know it was called—the color of slate, but all embroidered into that dark satin was colorful silk of gold and red and green, butterflies mostly, but also bouquets of flowers, and the edges were a shiny gold trim that caught the light from the flames of the fire just right. Her feet were the tiniest things I'd ever seen. Maybe they weren't that tiny, but they was wrapped tighter than a tourniquet and with dark green silk bindings around the ankles.

Yet it was her face that drawed most of my attention. Hell's fire, that was what every b'hoy in camp had been staring at them rocks for, waiting for her to come back into view. Small, round, almost like a porcelain plate, dark hair parted in the middle and curved just above her ears, tucked up in a bun behind her head. She wore silver earrings. Her lips were thin, in a hard line. I couldn't see her eyes. She seldom looked up.

Cigar Smoker, who had an old Henry rifle tucked up under his arm, kept puffing on his long nine, and found a space to sit. The girl just walked straight to the fire, kneeling ever so royally, and finding one of the hooks to check on a pot of grub. She had real long fingers, meant for playing the piano or running through a fellow's locks who needed a haircut.

My fingers went to my hair, which was knotted like a crow's nest and dirtier than the guy next to me, only with no bugs . . . I hoped.

I wondered if she'd cooked my soup. What was heating over the fire sure smelled better than anything I'd tasted.

"How about that whiskey, Micah Bishop?" Whip Watson's voice finally reached me, and I realized that I still held the jug. I passed it to him, but didn't see him, just kept looking at that celestial princess.

Whip Watson took a swig of sour mash and passed the jug on down the line.

"Hey, Jingfei," he called out. "What's for supper?"

CHAPTER FOUR

"You got a mighty fine cook," I told Whip Watson after he passed me a good cigar to smoke after a great meal.

"First time we tried her out," Whip said as he struck a Lucifer on his boot heel and held the flame out for me to fire up my Havana. "Yeah, she did all right. She'll work out just fine."

I didn't know what all we'd eaten, couldn't name or identify much of the food except for the beef and the noodles, and some of them peppers would burn you like hell's hinges. But it was nourishing. And mighty filling. Truth be told, I hated to cleanse my palate as an educated, fancy Easterner might say, or Big Tim Pruett when he was in one of his moods, with that cigar. I found it hard to believe that the girl who'd cooked this great supper was the same one who'd served me soup that tasted like shingles.

"Tastes better than what Zeke's been cooking," Whip Watson said, and the fellow sitting next to him grunted, spit, cussed, and burped.

Leaning forward, I peeked over for a better look at Zeke. I thought he was wearing black gloves, only

I realized his hands was the color of charcoal, and he wasn't a black man, neither. Just dirty. Real dirty.

I leaned back. "He cooked for you?" I asked.

"It's not his strong suit," Whip Watson said.

I said, "It's not even in his wardrobe."

Whip Watson laughed and pulled the cigar from his mouth, jutting the hot end toward the Chinese girl who was now cleaning the dishes. "She's a good cook. Had I known that before we lit out of Prescott, I'd have had her do our cooking during our journey." He nodded his own approval at his own idea. "We'll let her keep at it. Till we get closer to Calico. Then I don't want her doing nothing. But looking mighty fine."

"She looks mighty fine already," I said.

"Reckon so. For a yellow-skinned gal. And I don't care much for those eyes, how they slant and all."

Zeke was standing, taking his empty plate to the wreck pan. Bug Beard was right beside him.

"You're one to talk," I said, "about beauty."

Whip shot me a cold glance.

I pointed the other end of my cigar toward them two cads dropping their tinware in a basin by the fire. The Oriental princess didn't even give them no notice, just reached into the pan, brought out Zeke's or Bug Beard's bowl, and went to scrubbing.

Finishing my thought, I said, "Considering the men you hire."

He laughed then, and pulled himself up. "I didn't hire them to look gorgeous," he said, and extended his hand toward me. I was sore and still a mite weak, so I was grateful for him to help me stand. "And I wouldn't say you're the prettiest thing I've ever plucked from the Mojave."

He give me a motion to follow, and, being the

good guest, I did. After all, the jug of Tennessee sour mash had been returned to him somewhere during supper. We went back to the wagon that had been my bed for a while. Once he'd taken a pull, he tossed the jug to me. I swallowed some. He tasted some. I drank more. He killed the last of the whiskey and pitched the empty jug through the opening in the canvas into the back of my wagon. Maybe he thought I could use it as a pillow.

Then he pointed toward the wagons, the buggies, all those conveyances that I couldn't see but a few on account that it was pitch black beyond the campfire.

"A smart man could make a small fortune in Calico," he said. "Maybe a large fortune. . . . If he can deliver what I got."

I wanted to ask, *What do you got?* But I just sucked on the Havana. I'd seen that he had some fancy carriages and gunpowder and tools for miners. And a bucket load of wagons.

He looked at me. "And get there first."

I said, "I reckon you're right," because I reckoned that he was. Hell, he'd know better than me. I'd never been to California until I'd crossed the Colorado River an eternity ago that probably hadn't been more than a week.

"Got some good men with me," he said, and his Boss of the Plains tilted over toward the campfire, where Juan Pedro and Cigar Smoker and Zeke and Bug Beard and some men I hadn't gotten around to naming yet warmed their hands and stared at the Chinese girl still cleaning dishes. I wouldn't call them good, but they was likely good at something. Robbing church collection plates come to mind. Rustling come to mind. Horsewhipping Quakers come to mind. Robbery, murder, and larceny come to mind. So did sodomy. I looked one or two of them over, but then my eyes lighted on the girl.

"What did you say her name is?" I heard myself asking.

He didn't answer. Not at first. I realized I was staring at that girl, who just focused on doing her chores, and I turned to see an orange dot real close to me. Then the dot disappeared, and smoke blowed in my face, and Whip Watson said, "Don't go getting any notions, Micah Bishop. You owe me one. I don't owe you anything."

I smiled, though that took some doing. "No notions, Whip," I said. "Just wondering."

The cigar went back to his mouth. The tip glowed once more. After a moment, he answered, "Jingfei."

I repeated the name. As best as I could.

"Means 'Quiet Not,'" he said.

This caused me to marvel over the man who had saved my life. "You speak Chinese?"

"No," he said. "Not Manchu not Canton not Japanese. And damned little Spanish. She speaks English."

I hadn't heard her say a thing, English or nothing else. Far as I could tell, Jingfei hadn't even burped or farted. Quiet Not sure didn't fit her, from what I'd seen over, hell, all of ninety minutes.

"I have twenty-eight men riding for me," Whip Watson said, which made me grin. My ciphering and guessing had been damned close. "They're good at what they do, and that's minding their business, doing what I tell them to do and when I tell them to do it. For that, if—and that's likely a big if—

we make it with this cargo to Calico, they'll get two hundred dollars."

I smoked. He smoked. He talked. I listened.

"That's what I can offer you. Two hundred dollars. I'm a bit of a gambler, and I'm gambling that you're good with that gun. Even if that gun isn't worth a damn. I'm guessing that you and the law don't always see things eye to eye. I'm guessing that you can hold your tongue. I'm guessing that you probably don't want to be going back to . . . let's say, Beal's Crossing, anytime soon. I'm guessing that you don't expect to walk the Streets of Gold when you meet your demise. I'm guessing that if Zeke or Guttersnipe Gary were to start a row with you. And they just might. Because they're earning the same money you'll be earning and you've only got a little ways to go before we reach Calico. I'm guessing that if those two blackhearts were to start a row with you, you probably could handle them both. Because they have guts, but you have brains."

That last part, I knowed, some people would disagree with, but I kept my poker face and kept right on listening.

"I'm thinking that you've killed before, and likely know you'll have to kill again. And it won't bother you. I'm guessing that you're like most men in this country, in that you don't care how you earn your pay as long as you get your pay. I'm guessing that you're also smart enough to know that if you were to try to cross me, I'd gut you like a fish." He paused, spit out the tobacco juice that one gets smoking cigars, and stared at me.

"Am I guessing right?"

I said, "I guess so."

He stepped closer, so I could see him better on

account that now he was more in the light from the fire.

"Remember you owe me one."

"I'm good at remembering," I said. And I was. I remembered cards, I remembered the little things folks did when they was bluffing, or when they had a good hand, or when they was sandbagging. I remembered words people spoke months later. That's how come I can write all this down in the library at Folsom prison, or in my cell, or on Sundays when they make us go to hear the preacher man and I'm supposed to be writing down what the preacher is saying but instead I'm writing these here words.

"Good." Whip Watson pitched the cigar into the desert. "Then remember this. Stay away from Jingfei."

"Oh." Quiet Not was his girl. That explained some things, I guess. Why she was traveling with a bunch of men—if you aren't particular on how you define *men*—who could give even Big Tim Pruett fits, had Big Tim not been dead and buried already. "You don't have to worry about me, Whip," I said. "I was just admiring her is all. Same as Zeke and Guttersnipe Gary"—whichever one he was—"and Juan Pedro and all your boys. I'm a lot of things, but I've never been known to do something as low down as chase after another man's girl."

Which was one of the most shameless falsehoods I'd ever told.

"Especially if that man's paying me two hundred dollars."

Which was gospel.

"Glad to hear it, Micah Bishop." He smiled, but he wasn't friendly. Motioning toward the wagon, he told me, "You can sleep in here again tonight.

Tomorrow, you and me will go for a ride. Get a good night's rest, Micah Bishop. Like as not, you'll need it."

Which wasn't quite the same as Sister Rocío tucking me in and telling me to have pleasant dreams and not to worry that if I died before I waked the Good Lord would my soul to take. Which Rocío never done, by the way. In some ways, she was worser than the jailers who'd made me sleep in my own vomit after a good drunk. But I certainly would have preferred that one-armed, blind nun riding alongside me than me joining up with Whip Watson and his thirty—I mean twenty-eight—hombres.

So I finished smoking my cigar, leaning against the rear wagon wheel, listening to the sounds of the desert night. Wondering what I'd gotten myself into, but, well, it's not like I had much of a choice. Hell, Whip Watson had saved my life. I could be feeding ants and coyotes somewhere out there in the Mojave. And two hundred dollars was a right smart of money. I could handle and tolerate and maybe not even have to kill cutthroats like Juan Pedro and Zeke and Bug Beard and Guttersnipe Gary, whoever he was. Besides, it wasn't that far to Calico, and, well, Jingfei sure was pretty to look at. Long as Whip Watson didn't see me do it too much. Because I figured Whip Watson knowed how to handle that blacksnake whip of his.

After a spell of thoughtful thinking and staring, I decided to turn in. Started climbing into the back of the wagon, but then I remembered what all my bedchambers held. I didn't gamble as recklessly as Whip Watson, so I pitched what was left of that Havana into the dirt. Got myself inside, tossed my hat down, and sat on a keg of gunpowder, and just looked through the opening in the canvas at that Celestial princess as she scrubbed and washed and rinsed and didn't say one word.

Zeke had climbed into his bedroll closest to the fire. Most of the boys had done turned in. Standing in camp, just close enough to the fire so that I could make out their persons, Whip Watson was conversing with Juan Pedro, Bug Beard, and a tall gent with a silk top hat adorned with a fancy headband of colorful beads—a man I'd soon learn was no gentleman at all but a real arse called Guttersnipe Gary—gesturing here and there, pointing southeast, then northwest, then at the Conestogas, then at Jingfei.

Losing interest in watching them boys, I looked over at where the Conestogas were parked. I had to be patient, but you learn that trait when you're playing cards for a living, or when you're hiding out from the law or sore-losing foot soldiers from Fort Mojave. Eventually, I seen it. Another cigarette glowing in the dark. Then another.

That confirmed my suspicions. Either they was real careless, or they weren't so concerned with some bandits or Paiutes or Mojaves or infantry soldiers from Fort Mojave attacking them. A good pair of eyes can see the light from a cigarette or cigar. So this notion hit me that those guards didn't care about with what might be lurking around in the desert. They seemed to be protecting what was inside them wagons from men like Juan Pedro and Zeke and Bug Beard and Guttersnipe Gary.

From what I'd seen over supper, that seemed like a real smart move. I wouldn't trust a man like Bug Beard as far as I could throw him, and I had no plans of throwing him anywhere because that would mean I'd have to touch him, and them bugs in his hair just give me the chills.

Wasn't much longer after them thoughts had crossed my mind that I saw some boys leaving camp, grumbling, dragging their boots across camp and into the darkness. First, I decided that they were going to answer nature's call, but they all carried long guns with them, and not newspapers or pages from magazines, but then they didn't strike me as the types that thought cleanliness was next to god-liness. They didn't go behind the boulders. They went to the Conestogas, and as a few of the orange tips started moving, it struck me that they was just changing guards.

Which caused me to take another peek at Jingfei. She had finished cleaning the dishes, and was now drying her hands with a dirty, wet towel. Sure enough, she had also set out eight more plates and eight tin cups. I hadn't bothered counting the number of boys who had walked out of camp, but I sure counted eight men walking back, all armed with rifles of all sorts and calibers and sizes.

They took their grub and coffee, sat down by the fire that was starting to die, and then Whip Watson was by them, pointing, and talking in whispers that I was too far away to hear. Juan Pedro was at Whip's side, and he was translating in Spanish, I figured, for them that didn't savvy English.

My eyes followed Jingfei as she left camp. She disappeared in the dark, too, but she wasn't alone. Guttersnipe Gary and Bug Beard walked with her, though they kept a respectful distance. The dark swallowed them, and the two men wasn't smoking, so I didn't have an orange tip to follow once I couldn't see them no more. But from the direction that had taken, I had a pretty good idea where they was bound.

They were making a beeline for one of them Conestoga wagons.

CHAPTER FIVE

Hopeful that I'd dream of Jingfei, I lay myself down to sleep, but my luck wasn't changing none, though I was alive and not dead. Nope, I didn't dream of that porcelain face and them long, slender, wonderful, flexible fingers. I dreamed of Whip Watson and Mojave rattlesnakes and getting my hide peeled off me by a blacksnake whip. That whip lashed me good, and pain blinded me, got me to screaming my head off. Dreams are funny things. Sometimes you know you're dreaming, especially if it's a real bad nightmare. This nightmare, I knowed that nothing wasn't real, that Whip Watson hadn't flayed off my hide, that I was dreaming, but I thought that I was screaming in my sleep, and that I'd wake up yelling and everybody in camp would know I'd been having a real bad nightmare, and then Bug Beard and Zeke would likely be mad as hell at me for waking them up.

That's when I jerked myself wide awake. Sitting up. Expecting to hear myself scream. Only I woke up in a cold sweat, certain-sure, but I wasn't yelling nothing, and I hadn't woken nobody up because it was already daylight.

Outside of that wagon, however, somebody was yelling. Real, real loud. Next, I heard something else. The sound of a blacksnake whip cracking in the morning air.

Grabbed my hat, pulled on my boots, fetched the Spiller & Burr, and climbed down out of that wagon. Didn't see Jingfei, and I didn't look over toward the Conestogas. I must have been the last one to wake in camp, because twenty-six hombres had made a wide loop around the camp. One of them was Juan Pedro, who grinned and motioned me to hurry and join the morning circle.

The whip spoke again. I caught a glimpse of it above the hats of the burly men.

A man screamed.

Juan Pedro motioned me and mouthed the words *Muy pronto.*

I didn't exactly run, but I stuck the .36 in my waistband, pulled down my hat tighter, and moved toward the men who wasn't saying nothing. Juan Pedro and Cigar Smoker made room for me.

Feet wide apart, hat lying on the ground, Whip Watson was retrieving the blacksnake.

Cigar Smoker wasn't smoking that morning. Nobody was. And nobody had started coffee or breakfast. Cigar Smoker whispered, "They don't call him Whip for nothin'."

The whip had been gathered up again, and flew again.

The man lying beside the remnants of the fire shrieked.

The man? I hadn't gotten around to naming him. He was on his hands and knees, his hat off, blood and saliva dripping from his torn lips, pooling in the dust underneath him, him crawling around like a dog. The whip lashed out again. He yelped, collapsed, and brung his hands up to cover his head. His hands were bloody heaps. The whip struck again, and he flipped over, arms now stretched out in front of his sweat- and blood-drenched long blond hair. His fingers flexed, pulled at the sand. What fingers he had left anyway. By my count, three was missing, recently sliced off by that blacksnake whip.

"I warned y'all in Prescott that the merchandise is forbidden," Whip Watson yelled. "Didn't I? I warned every single one of you sons of bitches what would happen. Don't you remember? Conrad here . . . he didn't listen. Didn't believe . . . *me*."

The whip cut into Conrad's back. He got up, tried to crawl away, but he wasn't making much progress. Fell on his face once when his arms collapsed, and it taken the strength of Hercules for him to lift his bloody face back off the ground. His clothes? Well . . .

It's like this. The shirt he was wearing hung in shreds. Sleeves drug behind his wrists, dirt caking on the bloody cloth as he crawled. And . . . well . . . well . . . you couldn't really tell if what now hung from his back and side was the remnants of his shirt—or slices of flesh.

Again, the whip struck. The man, all screamed out, groaned and fell into the dirt, and rolled over, faceup, eyes closed.

His britches had been cut to pieces, too. They was dragging behind his boots, and his dirty un-derwear had gotten ripped apart and hung in bloody tatters. Thankfully, the man now seemed to be unconscious.

"Where am I, Mister Clark?" Whip Watson yelled out.

"Thirty-one," Mr. Clark answered.

"Thirty-two," Whip Watson said, and the whip ripped at the cloth covering Conrad's groin.

Funny. I'm what most folks call a pagan, an unholy lout, a backslider, but even after running away from the Sisters of Charity and running away from the law for quite a spell, all those years in that orphanage in Santa Fe had an effect on me. Out here in the Mojave Desert, surrounded by strangers, and watching a man whip another fellow to death with a whip meant for oxen, I could hear Sister Rocío reading Second Corinthians to us wayfaring, abandoned young'uns. So right then I prayed—I mean I prayed—that this punishment was "forty stripes less one." And I hoped Conrad wouldn't get beaten with rods and stoned after those thirty-nine lashes.

"Back in my youth," Whip Watson said as he brought up the whip, "everybody bragged—only it wasn't brag, but fact—that I could knock a horsefly off an ox's ear without touching the ear." He leaned back, smiling, focusing on Conrad's exposed privates. "And the *cajones* on a *cabrón*?" The whip flew.

My head turned away.

"You watch this, damn you!" Whip Watson roared. "You watch, Mister Clark! All of you! Watch and learn!"

I spit out the gall rising from my gut, and somehow managed to turn back to the ugly scene. Wasn't the only one who had looked away. Even Juan Pedro wasn't smiling no more, but biting his lower lip and balling his hands into shaking fists. One fellow—no, it was two—had dropped to their knees and was heaving up last night's supper and Tennessee sour mash.

Six stripes later, it all ended. Whip Watson began calmly coiling his whip, then picked up his hat. Nobody else moved, especially Conrad. By my reckoning, he had breathed his last after the thirty-fourth lash.

"All right." Whip's voice seemed calm as he adjusted the Boss of the Plains on his white hair. "No breakfast this morning."

That meant one prayer got answered. I didn't even want coffee. Nobody could eat after that scene, excepting, possibly, Whip Watson.

"Hitch the wagons, and let's ride."

The men departed, excepting Conrad, who had already departed this world. Standing like a lummox, I watched Whip Watson, now grinning, walk to me.

"How'd you sleep?" he asked.

"Oh." Had to wait to make sure I wouldn't vomit into my new boss's face. "Fine. I reckon."

"Good." He stepped to his side, pointing at one of the Columbus carriages. "You'll take Conrad's buggy. You know how to hitch a team?"

"Yeah."

"Good. Juan Pedro will tell you which horses are yours."

I had been right about the livestock. Oxen pulled the Conestogas, big mules got hitched to the other wagons, except for one that got pulled by two bay Oldenburgs, and matched sets of fine horses were for the Columbus carriages.

My buggy had two short-legged Holsteins, brown, better than sixteen hands tall with deep girths and strong shoulders. Spent my time focusing on hitching the two geldings to the carriage, but every now and then I'd glance at one of the Conestogas. Didn't see Jingfei. Didn't spot nobody but Zeke and Mr. Clark as they busied themselves getting four ugly oxen into harness.

Beside me, a young whippersnapper who'd already hitched his two gray Percherons, pulled a rag from his pants pocket, opened a can setting on the front seat's passenger floor, and dipped the rag in that can. He looked at me and said, "Better hurry, mister, get that leather buffed so you can see your reflection."

Which is when I learned what a hard rock Whip Watson was for keeping his carriages clean.

Rubbing one of the Holsteins' neck, I said, "But we're in the middle of nowhere."

The fellow was already scrubbing. Kept right on working that greasy rag, but he lifted his head. He had startling blue eyes, reddish hair, and a fuzzy mustache that you could probably wipe off without a razor. I doubted if he was out of his teens. I decided to name him Peach Fuzz.

"Don't matter," Peach Fuzz told me. The head dropped and he kept on working.

Which is what I was doing about ten minutes later when Whip Watson rode a black mare up beside my wagon. I glanced his way, seen the whip coiled around his saddle horn, and got busier buffing.

"That's fine," he told me. "Looks real fine. But let's save some of that wax for later." I stuck the rag in the can and closed the lid, staring up at my boss, and wiping the excess wax off my fingertips and on my trousers.

Juan Pedro galloped over. He rode a nice palomino mustang.

"We ready?" Whip asked.

"*Sí, patrón.*"

"All right." Whip was leading his black behind my buggy, and I stepped back to see him tethering that fine animal to the late Conrad's rig. "Go steady, but not slow. You know what to do, Juan Pedro."

"*Sí.*"

"If anyone gets out of line, kill him."

Juan Pedro grinned. He hooked a thumb toward the late Conrad's corpse. "I think we will have no more problems of that nature, *patrón.*"

"I hope so."

Three mule skinners brought four-five sacks from one of the farm wagons, and another had a big bladder of water. These got dropped on the back floor of my buggy which had once belonged to the late Conrad. The skinners weren't thanked, weren't dismissed, just did that chore and skedaddled.

Whip started to get into the carriage, but then he stepped back, back a right far piece, and he cupped his hands over his mouth and hollered, "You men!"

Didn't take no time at all for all them men to finish what they was doing real quick to line up beside their wagons. I took a glance at the Conestogas, but Jingfei did not poke her head out of the canvas. Well, Whip had said, *You men.*

"That peckerwood"—Whip gestured wildly toward the late Conrad's body—"was to have been paid two hundred dollars upon reaching Calico. Since he's no longer with us, I will divide the wages

I promised him among you. Two hundred dollars divided twenty-eight ways."

Since there was no abacus in camp, I couldn't quite figure that out—less than ten dollars for certain—and while it wouldn't go far, these men, even Peach Fuzz, had probably killed men for less than that.

One guy called out, "Wouldn't that be twenty-seven? Since that peckerwood's dead?"

Damned mathematicians.

With an ugly grin, Whip Watson extended a long arm and long finger right at me. "Micah Bishop has joined us," he said. "He gets the same wages as all of you rowdies."

Now, if you was to ask me, since Whip Watson had just killed Conrad, it would have made sense just to pay me the dead guy's wages, and not provoke feelings of ill will among my fellow workers.

Whip grinned, and said to me and Juan Pedro: "That should keep them occupied."

"How so?" asked Juan Pedro.

"Trying to figure out the difference between two hundred dollars divided by twenty-eight and two hundred dollars divided by twenty-seven." Whip jutted his freshly shaved jaw at me. "That's how much you just cost them."

I didn't bother trying to cipher that equation. It couldn't be more than a few cents, but this crew appeared greedy.

"Get in," Whip Watson said to me, and I was happy to oblige. "You drive."

"Guttersnipe!" Climbing into the driver's spot, I saw the fancy-silk-hat-wearing fellow step from behind one of the Conestogas. He pulled his hat off and made a beeline for my Columbus beauty.

Got me a better look at that tall dude with the beaded headband as he hurried our way, and then crawled into the seat right next to me. He had to duck to keep his head from poking through the canopy, and he had already removed his Abe Lincoln hat—though our late president never wore no headband quite as fancy as the one Guttersnipe had. I figured him to stand six-foot-five without the hat. He was shaped like a telegraph pole, just a regular string bean, hard as juniper and full of knots. Had a thick brown mustache and goatee like the one on Buffalo Bill Cody's chin. Wore a green evening frock coat with red velvet patches on the elbows and outer pockets, tall boots with mule-ear pulls, and two holsters on shell belts strapped across his waist. Since one Colt stuck out one way and the other Colt stuck out the other, I guessed him to be a left-hander.

He settled in beside me and said, "Name's Guttersnipe Gary. But you can call me Guttersnipe Gary."

"Micah Bishop," I told him. "You can call me anything you fancy."

He grunted, pulled a pouch of chewing tobacco from one of the green pockets, and stuffed one cheek.

"Drive over the body," Whip Watson said from the backseat.

"What?"

"Drive over Conrad's body." His tone told me he wouldn't answer any more questions.

It was a mean-spirited thing to do, but, well, I had seen my boss work that whip, and I figured he knew how to use his revolvers, and he was behind me and I never fancied getting shot in the back. I released

the brake, clucked my tongue, and turned those
Holsteins right toward camp.

They weren't keen about the job, those fine
horses, what with the blood all fresh and all, but
they did it just the same. The carriage tilted a bit,
but nobody was for the worser, and them high-
stepping horses just went right along out of camp
and into the desert with the sun on our backs.

"That'll show them boys that I mean business,"
Whip Watson said from behind me and Guttersnipe Gary.

To my way of thinking, whipping the clothes off
one of the men, peeling off his flesh, then castrat-
ing him before he expired would have showed
everybody his definition of business. But what did
I know?

"Where we going?" I asked.

"Calico," Whip answered.

CHAPTER SIX

A few days later, I got my first look at Calico.

Late morning, we come to a crudely painted sign that read:

WEL-COM 2 CALICO
QUEEN OF THE DESERT FLOWRS

Well, maybe if all the flowers in the desert had wilted and died and been blowed over with dust, then, maybe, just possibly, Calico could've been queen.

First folks we seen come scurrying down the trail that led to town, raising more dust than our Columbus carriage was forcing up. I eased the Holsteins to a stop, set the brake, and just stared. Four men, bearded, dirty, but with massive arms, come up pushing an empty wheelbarrow. "Welcome," one of the fellows cried out, "welcome to Calico. Right this way, gents, to the Hyena House."

Another one said, "Best hotel you'll find in Calico."

"Yes, sir, this here's your bus," the first one went

on, motioning at the wheelbarrow, and he started to say more, but the third man poked him in his ribs with an elbow.

The fourth one spit a river of tobacco juice onto a beetle, which probably appreciated the moisture. He laughed like those proverbial hyenas.

The first fellow blinked, and stared, and blinked again.

"Why," he said after the longest pause, "you ain't the stagecoach."

"But," the second one said, "you still won't find a better place to hang your hats than the Hyena House . . . gentlemen."

I figured they'd all gotten the sunstroke. Right severely.

The fourth one shifted his quid of tobacco into another cheek.

"Drive on, Micah Bishop," Whip Watson said, like he was the Prince of Wales, and I clucked my tongue and flicked the lines, and the Holsteins carried us past the four guys. A few minutes later, we rode right past the Hyena House. Wasn't more than a cave in the canyon wall, though the four proprietors had built a wall of rocks out front. And the sign, painted the same color and probably by the same shaking hand as the sign welcoming us to Calico, hung above the cave's opening.

I sure hoped that wasn't the best lodging Calico had to offer.

Next, we passed lean-tos, and crudely built stone huts—no mortar—and dugouts, and, of course, caves. That's where some folks lived, and then we looked off and seen the cemetery.

"Well, now," Whip Watson said, "that boneyard reminds me of something, Micah Bishop."

"What's that?" I asked.

"Juan Pedro owes me ten dollars. You made it to Calico, and you ain't dead."

"Glad to be of your assistance," I told him.

Guttersnipe Gary spit tobacco juice into the street, mighty careful not to get any on Whip Watson's fabulous buggy, and a short while later we entered Calico proper.

Near as I could tell, the Queen of the Desert Flowers was a one-street town. Well, it was a long street, with high, barren hills off in the not too distant distance. I guessed that those were the Painted Hills I'd heard tell of. *Painted,* I said to myself, *four shades of brown.* Most of the mines lay beyond the town. I could see specks that was miners moving in and out of caves in those dark hills. Off to the south was a deep—and I mean deep—canyon. I reckon the only place you could put a town was where they put Calico.

Overall, however, Calico turned out to be not that bad of a burg.

I mean, we passed a couple of water wagons, so they had water here. Had to haul it from somewhere, and I don't know where they found the wood to build some of the businesses. Certainly not in the hills. Only thing that could grow in this desert was rocks. But, yep, some of the buildings were wood frame, although about every third or fourth one was dirty brown, made of what they called "rammed-earth adobe," which bared little resemblance to the adobe houses across New Mexico and Arizona territories. Reckon this was a California thing.

Miners and merchants walking along the boardwalks stopped to stare as I drove our Prince of Wales, Whip Watson, down the street.

"Where we going?" I asked.

His Highness said, "Just drive to the end of town, turn around, come back down. I want to get the lay of this place."

Hell, there wasn't much of a lay to Calico, but I was just the driver. Did some more tongue-clucking and more line-flipping, and the Holsteins kept high-stepping down the dusty street.

The lay of Calico, on the right side of the street, went something like this: More water wagons. A nicely built frame building with freshly painted (not even brown) wooden columns and a crowd of folks sitting on barrels and empty crates watching us go by. The sign, painted by someone who knowed what he was doing, read:

ISAAC NOEL

Dealer in
FINE WINES
LIQUORS
and
CIGARS

"That'll be our first stop," King Whip said.

Not much farther down the road, we passed a building, and the smells coming out of those windows made my stomach start growling because Guttersnipe Gary ain't much of a cook, but there ain't much anybody can do with hardtack, jerky, salt pork, and beans. Felt like a long time since I'd tasted Jingfei's chow.

"And that," King Whip said, "will be our second."

I made a note in my mind to remember the Globe Chop House. Like I'd forget that place, or them smells.

On the opposite side of the street I spied a

bridge, if you would call it that, that crossed the canyon, and there was more buildings that looked like dirt, and just caught a glimpse of someone running down into the canyon. Next to the bridge, on this side, stood a schoolhouse. Didn't see no one in it, and now that it struck me, I hadn't seen any kids anywhere in Calico.

Back on the right side of the street, there was more men in wool coats and black derbies who stared at us as we passed. On the other side, men in tattered clothes and thick beards stared.

We saw some more mines off behind the buildings, some privies, some holes, some narrow draws, a few smaller hills. Then we reached the end of town. Nothing beyond that but homes in holes in the rocks, decorated with barrel staves, and a crew of miners walking down a path like they was heading toward the gallows.

Guttersnipe Gary said, "Reckon that's the way to the big mines."

I said, "Reckon so," and got busy turning the team around.

"Stop," Whip Watson said, and I stopped.

He leaned over and said, "That's a nice building going up, ain't it?"

We looked. We agreed. Seemed to be a two-story frame structure, with even fancier wooden columns than those outside of Noel's watering hole. No glass yet, but two holes told me there would be two plate-glass windows on either side of some fancy doors. Six or seven carpenters kept busy pounding nails or sawing saws.

"That'll be the palace of Calico," Whip Watson said as he leaned back in his shiny leather seat.

"Beats the Hyena House," I said, and clucked at the Holsteins.

This time, I focused mostly on that side of the street. A rammed-earth adobe that called itself a post office . . . a rough-hewn cabin that said it was a grocery . . . some buildings that looked like they'd been standing here since the time of Adam, and some new ones, and dirt ones, and dirtier ones.

"How old's this mining camp, Whip?" Guttersnipe Gary asked.

"First strike was five-six years ago," Whip answered.

We passed a pile of garbage where some dogs was digging, and a couple of men, too, in rags. The garbage wasn't brown like most of the hills and most of the buildings. Mostly, I saw ash.

"Fire?" I said.

"Yep," Whip Watson said. "That's why some of the buildings look new. First fire swept through here back in eighty-three, I think it was. When they rebuilt, they made every third or so building be made of dirt, or adobe, or rocks. Something that would keep the fire from jumping from building to building."

"Did it work?" Guttersnipe Gary asked.

"I guess," Whip answered. "There was another fire the year after the big one, but it didn't burn near as much. And you can see for yourself . . . this place is booming. Stop here."

We wasn't at Isaac Noel's saloon, but I tugged on the lines and said, "Whoa," and the Holsteins whoaed.

"Wait here," Whip Watson said, and he leaped out of the carriage, with some writing papers in his hand, and he . . . disappeared on the other side of the street in a building with a sign that said:

SLATER & McCOY
Purveyors in Implements & Sundries

Guttersnipe Gary wasn't much of a converser, and I didn't feel much like talking, so we sat there in the front seat, nodding at some men who passed our way, not making eye contact with some of the other brutes.

Five minutes later, I heard barking, growling, then a savage attack of yipping and screaming. The Holsteins got a little skittish, and I got a better grip on the lines, wanted to look back, but didn't dare take my eyes off our horses. Whip Watson's dander would get up if I wrecked this carriage, and I remembered Conrad, and what Whip Watson was capable of when his dander—not to mention that whip of his—got up. Guttersnipe Gary leaned out his side to see what the commotion was about. The barking stopped, a yelping replaced it, and Guttersnipe Gary leaned back inside and fingered the brim of his fancy top hat.

"Dog fight back at the garbage pile?" I asked.

"Something like that," Guttersnipe Gary said. "Only it wasn't the dogs, but the men we passed."

"Oh."

I stared off down the street at the endless desert. It could drive a man insane, living out in a place like this for . . . what? . . . five or six years? A long time to be in a furnace with no trees and nothing at all but mines.

"You reckon mining silver's worth it?" I asked.

Guttersnipe Gary snorted and spit tobacco juice onto the boardwalk. Dust soon covered it. "Well," he said, "there's a bunch of borax nearby, too."

"Oh," I said, like mining borax made living in

this hellhole worth getting so addled that you think you're a dog and fight over scraps to be found in a mountain of ash and garbage.

About that time, Whip Watson stepped out of Slater and McCoy's mercantile, and climbed back into the carriage. He was smoking a cigar that wasn't a Havana, but wasn't no two-center, neither, and he passed one to Guttersnipe Gary and another to me. By the time we reached our next stop, Guttersnipe had thumbed that tobacco out of his cheek and was puffing away like a satisfied man.

I wasn't satisfied yet, even though I was smoking a cigar, too, because we weren't at Mr. Noel's saloon, but at the grocery store. Once again, we waited, and Whip Watson went inside. No dog fights this time, but a few rowdies standing in front of the hovel on our side of the street stared at us a most uncomfortable time. We didn't say nothing. They didn't, neither.

Whip Watson came out, and we continued our way back down the street, stopping at just about every business that wasn't a saloon or a café.

More men passed us. We nodded.

One even come up to us, the first sociable fellow we'd met, and put his left hand on the lamp on Guttersnipe Gary's side and said, "Fancy rig you boys got here. Interested in sellin'?"

"You'll have to talk to the boss man," Guttersnipe Gary told him.

"You tell him to look me up," the gent said, and he fished out a card and passed it to Guttersnipe Gary, who took it and slipped it in one of them green and velvet pockets. The gent told us his name, but I disremember what it was, and tipped his derby and went on down the street, whistling.

Eventually, Whip Watson had been inside most of the businesses, and we finally got to stop at Noel's saloon. I feared Whip might make me stay out with the Columbus carriage, on account every man we'd met seemed to fancy it. Or maybe they just admired the Holstein geldings and Whip Watson's trailing black mare. I surely did, and I know something about horses. At least, stealing them.

But whip in hand, Whip said, "Come along, boys, and let's cut the dust."

On the crowded boardwalk, he stopped a little waif—first kid I'd spied in town—and said, "Boy, do you know a Rogers Canfield?"

"Can't say I do, sir," the waif said.

Whip produced a half-eagle from his fingertips. He was good at magic, too. "Find him," he said. "Send him here." He let the boy take the gold coin. "And there's another one of these for you when you fetch him."

The boy's eyes growed like mine was probably doing, and he took off running. Whip laughed, rose, and noticed—like me and Guttersnipe Gary already had detected—that the crowd of men had given us a berth, and everyone who wasn't eyeing Whip Watson was watching that kid run down the street.

"If something happens to that boy," Whip told the waif-watchers, "something happens to every mother's son of you."

He grinned that scary look, told me to fetch his black horse to the water trough, then join him and Guttersnipe Gary inside. Which I done real quick.

The saloon was crowded, but I made my way to the corner table where Whip sat with Guttersnipe Gary, and I slid into the vacant chair as Whip filled a long-stemmed glass with wine. I would have preferred whiskey, Irish if they served it, but a beer would have tasted good, too. Still, I accepted. Guttersnipe Gary lifted his goblet in toast.

"To Calico," Guttersnipe Gary said.

"Calico," me and Whip said.

Glasses clinked. Wine wasn't bad at all.

"What did you notice about Calico, boys?" Whip said, and set his glass down on the table.

"Not big," Guttersnipe Gary said, "but plenty of people."

Whip nodded. "More than twelve hundred, Max Slater told me. And that don't count miners in the district."

"What else?" This time, he trained them mean eyes on me.

Well, I'm not blind. Didn't think I'd be interviewed about it, but I've trained myself to study things like towns and gamblers, and I've spent enough time in dungeons and pits and stockades to know when one's missing.

"There's no jail," I said.

Guttersnipe Gary slammed down his goblet. He hadn't noticed, but Whip Watson looked pleased. Until this guy with brown-stained teeth sitting at the table across from us dragged his chair against the floor—which made all of our skin crawl—turned around, and spoke directly to Whip Watson.

"Don't need no jail."

That wasn't all he said. "Don't need no jail," he repeated, "because Calico is as pretty as a girl's calico skirt." Which, ask me, was a bald-faced lie. "We're peaceful. No murders. No robberies. Not even a marshal. Now we do have some vigilance committee, but they haven't even met since we tarred and feathered Bart Marcy and sent him up to Utah back in eighty-four."

The way we had seated ourselves was that Whip Watson sat with his back against the wall. Superstitious, I guess. Like Wild Bill Hickok, he wanted to see who was coming in the saloon. Wild Bill hadn't done it once, and he was dead. Whip Watson still breathed. From Whip's seat, he could see the front and side door to Isaac Noel's saloon. He could see who was passing by the window that was behind my head. He could even see the long mirror that stretched behind Isaac Noel's mahogany back bar. I sat on Whip's right, where all I could see was Whip, Guttersnipe Gary, and the backs of seven miners crowding along the bar, plus an overflowing spittoon. Guttersnipe Gary sat on Whip's left, where all he could see was me and Whip and the window and the people outside staring inside and likely wishing they had money for a fine wine, a fine liquor, or a fine cigar.

Whip Watson leaned forward, and his eyes got darker, and his right hand let go of his glass of wine, and he reached for his whip, which lay atop the felt-topped table like a rattler.

"Mister," he told the man with the brown teeth, "who in hell invited you to join our private conversation?"

I glanced at the man. He got all pale, and his eyes growed with fear—and, criminy, he hadn't even witnessed what had happened to Conrad a few days back. So he muttered his apology, and slid his chair, careful not to make anybody's skin crawl, and got back to the conversation he had been invited to listen to at his own table.

After letting go of his blacksnake, Whip Watson

drained his glass. I refilled it because that's the kind of guy I am. Then I needed a drink myself, so I filled my glass and slid the bottle to Guttersnipe Gary.

"That's right." Whip had lowered his voice. Just so some other fool wouldn't think he was invited to join our private conversation. "No jail. No law."

Guttersnipe Gary emptied the bottle into his own goblet. "My kind of town," he said.

"Not quite." Whip Watson straightened, sipped his wine, all pleasant again. "What else is missing?"

I sipped my wine and thunk. Guttersnipe Gary sipped his wine, but I don't think he had a brain to think with.

My brain drew pictures of what I had seen. There was an apothecary . . . and Whip Watson had spent considerable time inside J. M. Miller's store, which had a powder depot attached to one side . . . and I recollected the barber shop on account that I needed a haircut . . . and another mercantile on account that I needed some new duds . . . a doctor's office . . . a newspaper called the *Calico Print* (I remembered that because the editor's name was stenciled on the window, and Guttersnipe Gary had told me how he'd hate to be called Overshiner, which told me that Guttersnipe Gary knowed how to read) . . . a couple of picket homes that said they was boardinghouses . . . and the Applewhite Livery and Lodging House.

"Come on," Watson said, just a trifle louder. "We rode up and down Calico. What didn't you see?"

Right then I knowed, but turned out that Guttersnipe Gary had a brain and could think and had noticed the same thing that I hadn't seen.

"Petticoats!" he shouted.

Actually, he used another word that begins with a P.

CHAPTER SEVEN

Don't misunderstand me. There was women in Calico. A town five or six years old with a population of twelve hundred, there had to some petticoats, and after our bottle of wine and our rye whiskey chasers at Noel's place, we discovered some. Like that prostitute named Betty who had a crib behind the privies behind one of the worser grog shops, but she was, as Guttersnipe Gary described (mind you, to her face), "a dried up ol' whore," which wasn't polite but did describe Betty to a T. Denver Dotty run the South Saloon, where we'd stop for another drink, and I'd hate to tangle with her. She'd stitched overall pockets onto the front of her dress, wore a cap made for a man and boots made for a miner. Her whiskey wasn't fine. Another lady, if you ain't too particular about who you call a lady, we found at another watering hole, where we stopped for another drink, but this Madame De Lill wasn't much to look at, neither. Later that afternoon, I got a fleeting glimpse of a dressmaker who had an office above the bank. Not to mention, as we saw a few more kids, we figured there had to be a schoolteacher who might be a school marm, and some of these businessmen likely had wives, or at least concubines, and a drummer at the South Saloon said a couple of gals run a couple of the boardinghouses.

Say ten to twenty women. In a town of more than twelve hundred. And probably another two thousand men in the mining district that stretched all through this desert.

"You know what you're doing, Whip," Guttersnipe Gary said.

"That I do," Whip Watson agreed, and we entered the Globe Chop House for some real good beefsteaks and fried taters.

We were finishing our slices of cherry pie—the cherries come from airtights, but it wasn't like you'd find fresh fruit in Calico—when the dirty little waif poked his head inside the restaurant, and before the man in the black evening duds with tails who'd sent us to our table could toss the boy out, another fancy-dudded man came in, said something to the guest-sitter, and slid the fellow a coin. Dirty Waif kept pointing at us, and him and the dude eased their way to where we was sitting.

Whip Watson laid down his spoon and pushed back his chair a mite.

"I found Canfield, sir," the kid said.

"I see you did," Whip said, and tossed the boy another five-dollar piece. The waif was gone before you could say thank you, sir, which the kid didn't say. All the patrons eating seemed relieved that the dirty tyke wasn't spoiling their dinners.

"Have a seat, Mister Canfield," Whip told the newcomer, who settled into the empty chair.

He was a dark man. Dark hair. Darker eyes. Dark

suit. Dark hat. And, as I'd soon learn, an even darker soul.

Whip didn't introduce us to Rogers Canfield, and Canfield had no interest in us.

Canfield said, "So you are Whip Watson."

After a slight bow, Whip said, "And you are Ronen Kanievsky."

His dark face got a bit lighter, and he was leaning back in his chair, and I thought he might either suffer an apoplexy or get up and leave. But another man in some more fancy garb had stopped by and was asking, "Would you care for a cocktail, Mister Canfield?"

Mr. Canfield, or Mr. Kanievsky, stuttered and stammered and finally spit out that a Tom and Jerry would be just fine, so the waiter in the black duds said, "Very good, sir," and walked away.

For a while there, nobody said anything until Guttersnipe Gary finished licking the crumbs off his plate.

Finally, Mr. Canfield/Kanievsky, said, "What's in a name?"

Which, considering as many names as I'd used in my life of devilment, was something I could relate to, and I figured so could Whip since I allowed how his mama and daddy likely hadn't named him Whip.

The drink arrived, and our guest took a fair-sized swallow, set the glass on the table, and straightened, doing his damnedest to look dignified again. "Names are not important," he said, "but business is. And by business, my name is *shadchan*."

Now, I know Micah Bishop ain't much of a handle, and some of the other names I've used— John Smith, John Jones, Smith Jones, and Big Tim

Pruett mightn't be all that clever—but Canfield and Kanievsky and Shadchan sound a bit ludicrous, if you ever ask me. Even Guttersnipe Gary said, "Shadchan sounds like you're a damned Chinaman."

Which got me to thinking about Jingfei.

"You don't look like no Chinaman." Guttersnipe Gary had consumed quite a lot of liquor, and the canned cherry pie and all its crumbs hadn't sobered him up none.

"Shadchan isn't his name," Whip said. "It's his occupation. It's Hebrew. He's a matchmaker."

Canfield/Kanievsky the *shadchan*/matchmaker lifted his Tom and Jerry and toasted the air across the table toward Whip Watson.

Then Whip Watson dipped his left hand into his coat pocket, pulled out a leather purse, and fished out more coins. Two he slid to me, and they was by-grab double eagles. The other, which I took pride in the fact that it was only a ten-dollar piece, he pushed over toward Guttersnipe Gary.

"Canfield and I have private business to discuss, boys," Whip said. "Making arrangement for our delivery in a week or so. Isn't that right, Canfield?"

"Indeed," Mr. Canfield said.

"Guttersnipe Gary." Whip eyed him. "You need a bath. And a poke." Although he didn't seem pleased with either chore, Guttersnipe Gary took the gold coin. Whip then turned toward me, and I sure hoped he didn't say I needed a poke because I'd seen that dried out ol' whore named Betty and really didn't want to come down with one of them painful diseases in my manhood. Again.

"Micah Bishop," Whip said, "you need some new clothes. A bath. And a shave." That was it. I let out a sigh of relief. "If you're going to be my lieutenant," Whip said, "I want you to look like a man and not a bum."

I thanked him, sent a nod Canfield's way, and rose.

So I was Whip Watson's lieutenant. I'd always figured his *segundo* was Juan Pedro, and wondered how that graybeard would feel now that he'd lost ten dollars to his boss and might soon be taking orders from me. Looking at Guttersnipe Gary, who was standing and giving me a cold, cold stare, I knowed he wasn't too pleased with my promotion.

"I'll meet you in an hour at Noel's saloon," Whip told us.

That afternoon, I wandered down the streets and boardwalks of Calico, gripping those double eagles tighter than a miser. Walked to the end of town, where the carpenters stayed busy as bees building what was to become the palace of this town. Next door was Miller's store and his "Giant Powder Depot," where a guy in sleeve garters was directing some hefty gents as to how to load kegs of blasting powder onto the back of a wagon.

Went inside the store to get duds that would befit a man of my new stature.

Black boots, with seventeen-inch tops, fit me just fine. As I'd always been partial to striped britches, I found a pair that were brown—Calico's favorite color, seemed to me—with navy stripes. Some suspenders, too, new socks, and a pretty blue band-collar shirt that even come with a pocket over my heart and mother-of-pearl buttons. A double-breasted vest of burgundy brocade. A fine Seth Thomas watch with a bird and a tree and a farmhouse and some other pretty designs on the hunter's case so I'd have something to stick in one of the vest's pockets. Gun belt, brown, and holster, brown, and pouch, also brown, for my percussion caps, capper, and some .36-caliber paper cartridges. New bandanna, brown again, only color they had except for pink polka dots. Socks. Unmentionables. And a real nice Stetson, not a Boss of the Plains, but a fancy hat with tan bound edges, a curved brim, and side dents.

Been a long time since I'd paid for store-bought duds, and I'd never spent Calico prices. I walked out with my new clothes wrapped in brown paper and my fancy hat in my hand and what little change I had in another one of my vest pockets, thinking that Whip Watson would make a fortune on his carriages and hammers and gunpowder, and wondering if I had enough money for a haircut and bath and shave.

So there I stood, listening to the hammering and sawing next door and a whistle whine way up the canyon at one of the big mines. Trying to recollect where the barbershop was.

That's when Lucky Ben Wong stepped into my life.

First words he says to me was: "Need bath? Need shave? Yes. Yes. You do. You do."

I looked down to see this Chinese gent, not even as tall as Jingfei. Black cotton shoes, black cotton pants, and a fairly fancy black cotton shirt that wasn't tucked in. His ears stuck out, his mouth was too long for his face, and he wore a silly little wool cap on his mostly bald head. I say mostly, because this little pigtail—called a *queue,* I'd learned in all my travels—come out of the back of his noggin.

He even held a black umbrella. Like it had rained in this place in the past fifty years.

The man in black repeated his words, making me wonder if he could read my mind—or just smell me. Then he said, "Lucky Ben Wong take care of Mister American Gentleman, yes, yes, yes. Follow me."

Seeing how I figured a dude from China maybe wouldn't charge as much as a J. M. Miller or a barber on Calico's Main Street, I followed the little fellow.

Which took some doing. Lucky Ben Wong moved like a cat chasing a rat. Couple of times I was tempted to reach out and grab his pigtail, but thought that would be rude, and I had my hands full with all my new duds and such. He turned down that alley I'd spotted on our tour of Calico, run past the schoolhouse, and was bounding across the bridge.

That's where I stopped, hearing that bridge rattle, and watching it sway. I looked down, seen how far of a drop it was off this shelf, and wasn't entirely certain that bridge would hold Lucky Ben Wong. There was people living down in the canyon. More rammed-earth adobes, smoke coming out of chimneys, some kids playing in the dirt. Chinese kids.

"Come! Come! Come now!" Lucky Ben Wong was beckoning me to cross. "No worries." He read my mind. "Bridge safe. Come. Come. Come."

I come. Reluctantly, but I come, and followed the man in black as he weaved his way between other earthen buildings. Clothes dried on lines. Good smells from another building reminded me of Jingfei's supper. There was buildings with signs with chicken-scratch marks that I knowed was Chinese.

An elderly woman smiled at me, and I tried to lift my hand to tip my old hat that I'd soon be rid of, but couldn't quite make it without dropping my packages and such.

Finally, I come to Lucky Ben Wong's bathhouse.

Give him this much: He was enterprising. He held open the black India rubber tarp that served as the door to his place of business, which wasn't frame, and wasn't stone, and wasn't rammed earth. It was made of coal oil cans. Empty ones, I assumed.

Didn't like it none, but I went inside.

Funny thing is, the water was hot, and the soap lathered up real fine, and all in all, turned out to be a fine bath. I scrubbed and scraped and got all the Mojave Desert off me, and here's something I didn't consider until after I paid Lucky Ben Wong a dollar for a hot bath, a shave, and a haircut.

There's no source of water in Calico. I didn't know where the Calico Water Works Incorporated got its water, but, like the wood, it certain-sure wasn't close. They hauled water in wagons, and sold it. The board of directors was likely richer than the mine owners. Only there's no way a water wagon could cross that rickety bridge, and the canyon's too steep for a wagon to make it down and up. That meant that Lucky Ben Wong hauled all that water hisself, dumped it in a cistern out back of his place. You figure how much work that takes. And he charged me only a dollar—in a town where I'd just paid $2.50 for a sixty-five-cent shirt.

"Need grubstake for mine?" he asked after handing me a cup of hot tea. No charge for the tea, neither. It come with the price of the bath, haircut, and shave.

"How's that?" The tea burned my lips, but was tasty.

"You come strike rich in Calico, right?" He smiled. I took back what I said about his mouth being too long for his face. He had a real nice smile.

"No," I said. "I'm not a miner."

On account that mining's real grueling work.

"Got a job," I added. Thinking: *But wish I didn't.*

"Good. Good for you. But if change mind. If need stake. See me." He tapped his fancy black shirt. "I stake everyone." He smiled again, and as I was thinking that for a man who lives in a shack made of coal oil cans, that grubstaking line of his wasn't paying too much, he tells me:

"Made six hundred dollars already."

"Not bad," I said, thinking if he got here in 1881 or likely '82, that would figure out to be about . . ."

"This month. Yes. Good month. But last month even better."

I lowered the tea. "You made six hundred bucks this month?"

He give a real sheepish shrug and smile. "Month not over yet."

Laughing, I pushed up the brim of my new hat, having given my old hat and my old clothes to Lucky Ben Wong to burn, shook my head, and said, "I'm in the wrong line of work."

"What work you do?" Lucky Ben Wong asked me.

Dishonest, said me to myself, but just returned one of them sheepish shrugs and smiles back at Lucky Ben Wong.

Then Lucky Ben Wong says to me, "Opium?"

I blinked. I said, "Huh?"

He pointed behind the washtubs toward a black table and some cots and some long pipes on the table, and somebody was on one of them cots who I hadn't noticed before, and he appeared to be sleeping real sound.

"No," I said. "Thanks."

His round face bobbed. Maybe that, and not grubstaking miners, was how Lucky Ben Wong earned better than six hundred dollars a month. Or probably that's how he could afford to charge a buck for a bath and grubstake miners.

I finished the tea, set the cup on the saucer, and stood up to shake my savior's hand. I was clean, properly outfitted for a lieutenant of Whip Watson's, with a full belly, sober head. He reached up to shake my hand.

"You see me soon," he said, "but don't wait long. Lucky Ben Wong soon be married. Soon be living in San Francisco. Be gone from Calico."

"Don't blame you," I said. We shook. "Congratulations and good luck."

I was stepping toward the door when the canvas flew open. The flash of a gunshot blinded me, and I cussed as I felt a bullet tear a hole through my new six-dollar hat.

CHAPTER EIGHT

I ducked right before another bullet punched past me and poked a hole in one of them cans of coal oil.

Then I was lying flat on my belly behind a tub of dirty water, trying to get my Spiller & Burr out of my new, stiff holster. A bullet sang out, whined as it ricocheted off the tub, and dirty bathwater splashed on the sleeve of my blue shirt.

The opium addict behind me muttered something that I couldn't catch.

Another shot flew wild, knocking the entire can out of the wall, creating a window that sent light and dust down on me.

My watch was still ticking. Even better, I was still breathing.

Lucky Ben Wong yelled, "Murder! Murder! Murder!"

One of the gunmen snapped at him, "Shut up, Chinaman!"

Another voice said, "Or I cut off your pigtail. Once we're done here."

That told me some things. First, there was two

killers. Second, I figured these guys had come gunning for Lucky Ben Wong, after all Lucky Ben Wong made a lot of money in these parts, and if you were going to rob someone, you'd rob him and not a bum like me. But those boys had come after me.

Me?

Would've made sense if they'd robbed me before I'd made it to J. M. Miller's store. After all, I had forty dollars before I stepped inside the mercantile. Once I'd left, I had $6.19. After bath, shave, and haircut, I was down to $5.10, having tipped Lucky Ben Wong nine cents before I knowed how much he earned a month.

All right, somewhere out in the Mojave Desert, in a wagon train led by a Mexican named Juan Pedro, I could count twenty-five men who'd likely kill for that bit of money. But in Calico? Where there were silver miners galore and Chinese men pulling in more than six hundred dollars a month? Kill a man for five bucks and change? Didn't make sense.

I pushed myself up, lifted the .36, and squeezed the trigger.

"Murder!" Lucky Ben Wong yelled. "Murder! Murder!"

One of the assassins cursed. Fired again.

The opium addict yelled, "I am trying to sleep!"

Now, I really hated to do this, but two men with guns was closing in on me. Later, I told Lucky Ben Wong that I did it to protect him, what with him crying out *murder* and all, I didn't want those boys to shoot him since it was me they come after. But that was just a falsehood. I done what I did to save my own hide.

In Calico, men built stone houses without mortar, and I could see streaks of afternoon light shining through the walls, so Lucky Ben Wong didn't use mortar in his construction, either, and if a bullet could create a window by knocking out a can, well, I wasn't sure it would work, but the next bullet bounced off the tub behind me, and hit in front of me as I crawled along the dirt floor.

After snapping off another shot, I got to my feet and ran straight for the wall.

Lucky Ben Wong hadn't put a rear door to his place, so the only way out was through the wall. Didn't know if this would work, but it did. Lowered my shoulder, said a *Hail Mary Full of Grace,* sent another bullet at a figure rising from behind the barber's chair in the corner, and smashed into that wall.

The cans collapsed, and I was bouncing outside off cans, smelling the coal oil, rolling over, kicking an empty can out of the way, aiming the Spiller & Burr through the hole I'd just made, but didn't see no gunmen coming out because the roof was collapsing and dust was rising thicker than the walls of Jericho, and over the rattling of tin and the ringing in my ears, and the shrieks of half the population of the Chinese section of East Calico, I made out Lucky Ben Wong's "Murder! Murder! Murder!" Only now, he was likely expressing what he'd like to do to me for ruining his home/barber shop/bathhouse/opium parlor.

The boys inside seemed learned enough to know better than to go through the hole I'd made, and the dust wouldn't stay there forever, so I got up, damned near tripped over two more cans, and moved away from the rubber front door, running behind the building of cans, gun in hand.

As I ducked behind some laundry, I heard more

cans rattling, and somebody cussing, and figured the two assassins had made it outside and was coming after me. Long underwear slapped my freshly shaved face. I went through it, ducked underneath a pair of Levi's, and turned a corner, leaning against one of those adobe houses to catch my breath.

After I inched my way to the western edge of the shack, I raised the gun, already cocked, and listened. Folks were screaming, hens kept squawking, and a few dumb people across the path stood in front of their homes or businesses pointing at me, yipping like gossips in their foreign tongue.

Unless those two killers were blind, it wouldn't take them long to figure out where I hid.

I could see the bridge across the canyon, but I'd have to run down this footpath to get to it, and that would invite a bullet to my back. Stay here, and some innocent folks was bound to get hurt, possibly killed. Hell, even more important, stay here and I was guaranteed to get dead.

That's when I seen another Chinese person, a small woman carrying two babies in her arms, run beyond the houses and the café and the finger pointers. Run straight for the canyon's edge, then started down, she did, and I recollected those buildings and people on the canyon floor.

Of course, I gave the woman and her two kids plenty of time to make it down those steps or ladder or whatever the hell it was because I sure didn't want them to get hurt on my account. Well, maybe I didn't give them that long, because I ran across the street, looking back toward Lucky Ben Wong's place. Caught a glimpse of one of the man-killers.

He wore a Mexican sombrero and a pink shirt.

Almost caught a bullet in my gut in addition to a glimpse of that bad man.

I fired back, then was behind the brown wall as a bullet struck the corner and kicked up brown dust.

"I seen him, Paul!" Pink Shirt talked like a gringo, not a Mexican. "He's heading for the canyon."

Which was exactly where I was going.

At the edge, I looked down, seen the steps carved into the canyon wall that dropped to a ledge about six feet down. Perfect. I jumped. A bullet sang above me, and I landed on the shelf, knees buckling, pitching forward flat on my face. I almost went over the side myself, which was a fifty-foot drop and would have killed me, but somehow stopped myself from sliding off to eternal damnation.

Unfortunately, the Spiller & Burr went over the edge.

Spasms of pain shot through my knees and legs, but I couldn't worry about that now. I came up, and found the ladder that led to the pit.

Ladder. Built like that rickety bridge.

Great.

Ever clumb down a fifty-foot ladder? With people above you wanting to shoot you dead? And no friend waiting down below gripping the ladder to hold it steady so it don't tip over and send you flying?

Not something I recommend, but I had no choice. I grabbed hold, lowered myself, felt the rungs where I'd planted my feet groan and bend. The ladder was built by Chinese and for Chinese and I was an American, not fat but sure not skinny, and certainly heavier than any person who'd gone down this death trap—even a woman with two kids.

Halfway down the ladder, I thought: *How in hell did a woman climb down this rickety death trap with two little babies?*

Lots of Americans don't think much of the Chinese. Oh, they like their food and their laundries, and maybe their opium, but they don't care much for their culture, their pigtails, their pagan ways of thinking. But they are some people. As I hurried down, I kept thinking that Jingfei could have done just like that Chinese woman with the two babies. Chinese women are a wonder.

I slid the last fifteen feet, burning my hands, hitting the ground hard, and falling to my left. Right beside the Spiller & Burr.

A bullet kicked up dust a few inches from my feet, and rolling on my back, I spied Pink Shirt and the other fellow, a man with a brown hat—what other color could he be wearing in Calico?—and a Winchester rifle.

Pink Shirt had fired his pistol. He was leaning against the top of the ladder, trying to get a better aim. I was picking up my revolver, blowing dirt from the cylinder, and trying to cock the .36 without busting my thumbs. Not that I'd be able to hit a man, or two men, or a damned elephant fifty feet above me with a pistol. What did I have left in the chambers? Two shots? Three? Paul With The Winchester fired. The bullet slapped between my legs. Pink Shirt was leaning, cocking his pistol, but he had as much of a chance of hitting me as I did of shooting him.

Didn't matter, though. 'Cause soon as I cocked the Spiller & Burr that ladder was moving off to the right, and Pink Shirt was yelling like a girl as he went over with it, and Paul With The Winchester had stopped cocking his rifle and was reaching out for Pink Shirt's extended left hand, but not too far, because Paul With The Winchester didn't want to get pulled into the abyss hisself, and I scrambled up and run toward the west side of the canyon, causing ducks and chickens to squawk and cackle and a couple of dogs to bark, while Pink Shirt screamed all the way down and Paul With The Winchester yelled, "Artemis! Noooooooooooo!" Behind me come the crunch that ended Pink Shirt's life.

Then I heard Paul With The Winchester yell, "You son of a bitch!" A bullet killed one of the ducks in front of me. Blood and feathers landed on the left leg of my new $3.79 striped woolen britches.

Keep this up and I'd have to find a Chinese laundry.

Which I'd just run past.

Another round sent brown dirt from the side of that hovel into my eyes, but I got to the back and stopped, catching my breath, rubbing the dirt so I could see better, thinking how lucky I was to still be alive.

I smelled the smell then. The stink of human waste.

The trash pile Guttersnipe Gary and I had seen where the dog-men had been fighting wasn't the main dump for Calico. That was here. In I guess what you'd call Lower Chinatown. They simply dumped their chamber pots and other refuse over the side.

The ten or twenty Chinese who lived here had to live with this smell. The other twenty or thirty who lived at the top of the ridge had things better, especially if you were Lucky Ben Wong and earning all his money.

After I spit the taste out of my mouth, I laughed.

Said to myself, "Now you've really stepped into a pile of sheep-dip." Or something similar.

Paul With The Winchester couldn't climb down to where I was since the way down was smashed alongside the smashed Pink Shirt's body, but I'd have to find the ladder that led up to Calico proper. I blew more dirt from the Spiller & Burr. I could see that ladder. It stood right next to the bridge. I took a chance and looked behind me. More of those finger-pointing Chinese men and women stood atop the far ledge, showing everybody where the late Pink Shirt had landed and died. Paul With The Winchester was nowhere to be found.

To the north, the canyon seemed to widen and then curve. Once the Chinese settlement ended, though, so did all cover. Go that way, and I'd surely get killed. Stay here, and I'd be a sitting duck, and I'd already seen what Paul With The Winchester could do to a running duck with his rifle.

I could just wait here. But didn't like the smell, or the thought of dying in a pile of . . .

So I looked back west and south. Saw the ladder. Nobody—I mean nobody—was up top near the bridge. I guessed how people in Calico didn't care if the Chinese killed each other in East Calico or Lower Chinatown.

Crouching, I leaped across the path to the next building. No one shot me dead. I put the revolver in my left hand to wipe the sweat off my right palm, then bent over and plucked the two duck feathers off my $3.79 pants. The .36 returned to my right hand, and, still squatting, I looked up to see an old Chinese woman sitting in front of a kettle that was smoking over a fire. She stared at me. At least she didn't point no fingers.

I said, "Morning, ma'am."

She said, in perfect English, "It's afternoon, idiot."

I thanked her anyway, and moved to the next building.

Looking behind me toward the eastern shelf, I saw buildings and smoke and some people running this way and that. The finger pointers was gone, and, for the moment, the bridge was empty. I looked off toward the north. No Paul With The Winchester anywhere.

The lucky thing, appeared to me, was that on the west side the canyon wall wasn't more than forty feet high. Ten feet shorter than the east. All I had to do was climb up without getting killed.

A couple of buildings stood next to the canyon wall, but I had to cover about thirty yards with nothing for cover but a few piles of turds and trash.

Then come a sound from Calico proper, and I looked up at the backs of buildings. No longer did I catch the sounds of saws and hammers from the soon-to-be palace of Calico. There were shouts, barking of dogs (or men who thought they was dogs), and even a scream or two. A moment later, I heard it again. Gunfire. Three shots. Four. Five-six-seven-eight. Maybe a few more.

Out loud, I said, "And this town don't need a jail?"

Then I ran.

Well, I didn't expect to make it. The way I figured things, Paul With The Winchester was sitting on a chair in the shade in East Calico, maybe smoking some opium, but likely just waiting to find me. Bring up his rifle, jack a round into the chamber, and put me out of my misery.

Didn't happen. I made it to the first shack. Tried

to steady my breathing. Waited. Waited. Waited. Finally, I hopped over to the next building and still wasn't dead. From the inside of the shack come voices yacking at one another, talking back and forth, man and woman, bitching like husband and wife. Didn't want them to get hurt by Paul With The Winchester when he started blasting.

The ladder was right there. Ten yards away, forty feet high. I sucked in a deep breath, figured it to be one of my last, and run for the ladder. I got there, turned around, looked up toward the east, didn't see no assassin, didn't feel no bullet. Keeping the Spiller & Burr in my right hand, I reached up for the highest rung I could reach.

"You killed Artemis, you peckerwood."

I sighed. It was over. My hands come down, and I turned and looked up. Paul With The Winchester, at some point, had walked hisself mostly across the bridge. He stood about ten feet from the west side, somehow balancing himself, Winchester's stock braced against his shoulder, drawing a fine bead right on my middle.

"Actually," I told him, "Artemis killed hisself."

"Well, I'll kill you."

One eye was closed. The other, the one he was using to sight down on me, just disappeared.

CHAPTER NINE

Never heard the shot. One second I was looking into the eye of the man who was going to kill me, and the next moment there was a hole where that eye had been. Then blood started spurting out of that hole, the Winchester was flipping over the rope rails toward the ground fifty—I mean forty—feet below, and Paul Without The Winchester was staggering over the other end, and he was falling, too.

The Winchester hit first. It bounced a few times. Paul didn't bounce at all.

I backed away from the ladder a little more, still holding the Spiller & Burr, and a man in black with a rattlesnake coiled over his left shoulder appeared at the bridge. Because the sun was right in my eyes.

"Get out of that cesspool, Micah Bishop," Whip Watson said. "Those yellow devils aren't clean."

I started for the ladder. Whip Watson said, "Get that Winchester."

This I done, after shoving the .36 in my holster, and then I was up the ladder, and Whip Watson was shucking out the empties from one of his nickel-plated Colts. The .45 casings dropped to the dirt, and Whip was finding fresh loads from his pockets and refilling the chambers. Finished reloading, he looked at me.

"You owe me one," he said. "Again."

That was twice he had saved my life. I nodded my appreciation.

"That Winchester working?"

I looked at the barrel, and sent a .44-40 shell that landed on my head and bounced off my newly shorn, freshly washed locks.

"Yeah."

"Where's your hat?"

"In a bathhouse across the bridge," I said. Thinking: *With a brand-new hole in it.*

"Get it later. Let's go."

I pointed at Paul Lying Dead In The Dirt. "He was trying to kill me," I said. "So was another man. Never seen either one in all my days."

"Shut up," he said, like I was stupid. "Let's go."

He walked, and I followed, the late Paul's Winchester in my shaking hands.

Folks crowded the boardwalks of Calico, but the street was practically empty. Except for a dead man lying spread-eagled out in the center of the road in front of the Globe Chop House. Four men in brown suits and brown boots and brown bowlers stood over the body, which was dressed in tan duck pants and a yellow shirt except for the two big patches of red in the belly. One of the men, wearing the nicest bowler and a red tie, stepped over the dead man's legs. He said, "You'll answer to this—"

"Later, Slater," Whip Watson said, and he stepped over the dead man's legs, too. I done the same, chancing a look-see at the man who had blue eyes that stared straight into the blue sky. Didn't know him, neither.

A couple stores down was the second dead man—unless you count Pink Shirt and Paul With The Winchester That Was Now Mine, which would make him the fourth. He was propped up against a cracker barrel in front of Slater & McCoy's business, gripping a Remington in his right hand. He had two holes in his shirt, too, but a bit higher up and spaced closer together than the dead man in the street.

"Where was Guttersnipe Gary going?" Whip Watson asked.

I tried to get enough spit in my mouth to speak. "You told him to get a bath and a—"

"Never mind," he said, and we made a beeline across the street to where Betty, that dried up ol' whore, stood in front of the alley that led to her crib, screaming her head off.

She was yelling the same words Lucky Ben Wong had been yelling.

"Murder! Murder! Murder!"

People stood near her, but either they was deaf or they just didn't give a damn. Not that I could blame them, since two people lay dead on the streets, two more dead in Chinatown, and another man dead right behind Betty's feet.

Don't know if I'd seen him before or not, on account that he was facedown in the dirt, with one hole in the small of his back and the back of his head blowed off.

Whip Watson walked right past him. I done the same. Past the privies, we come to Betty's crib. The front door was open, but outside there was a big copper washtub.

"Damn," Whip Watson whispered.

He stopped walking.

I said, "Son of a bitch."

Reckon it happened something like this. Guttersnipe Gary had decided to get his wash and his poke at the same place. I don't know how much Betty charged for a bath, and I hope I never learn how much she charges for a poke, but I doubt if the combination would have cost Guttersnipe Gary even close to the ten dollars Whip had give him.

So he'd been sitting in the bathtub, scrubbing away, when two men happened down the alley.

He was still in the soapy water that was now fairly dark with blood. His right hand floated on top of that water. His left hand reached all the way to the ground, still gripping one of his revolvers. The two assassins had figured he'd be an easy target in a bathtub, but Guttersnipe Gary was a lot more cautious that even I had thought.

There was a dark hole over his left eye. He had sunk into the tub, so that his head rested against the copper rim, and I figured from how red the soapy water was there'd be two or three more bullet holes somewhere in his belly.

He'd managed to kill one of his killers who had tried to run away only to catch two bullets and fall at the end of the alley. I knowed there had to have been another assassin because even Guttersnipe Gary wasn't tough enough to kill somebody after catching a bullet in his brain.

"Let's go." Whip Watson turned.

I was glad to get out of that alley, even if it brought me right past Betty, who screamed, "Murder!" right in my ear as I passed by.

Sometimes I don't think too clear, or fast, especially after diving through a wall of empty coal oil cans, getting some new, expensive duds all dirty, and almost getting shot to death by two hombres I'd never laid eyes on before. But as we turned down Main Street and headed toward the end of town, I understood something.

"Sons of bitches," I told the back of Whip Watson's head. "They tried to kill me and Guttersnipe."

"They didn't try to kill Guttersnipe Gary," Whip said. "They did."

Another bit of genius struck me as I glimpsed the dead man by the cracker barrel and then the dead man surrounded by the brown suits. "They tried to kill you, too?" I asked Whip Watson.

"Tried."

I was about to ask a damned fool question about why anyone in this town wanted to kill all three of us strangers. But Whip saw something that interested him more, and he yelled, "Boy!"

The waif who'd brung Rogers Canfield to our dinner table was sitting on a box in front of a freight office. He saw Whip Watson with his whip and revolvers and me with Paul With The Winchester's Winchester, and he leaped from a sitting position, cleared the boardwalk and the hitching rail, and hit the dirt of Main Street running. Boy was angling toward an alley between a saloon and the assayer's office, and Whip was stepping onto the street, unleashing the blacksnake, then letting it fly.

Almost but not quite I'd forgotten all about Conrad, but the crack of that whip brung images that caused a roiling in my belly which was already in a tenuous state after nigh getting shot to death. My eyes closed, I heard a groan and some gasps and some shouts from the boardwalk, and my eyes opened.

Whip hadn't struck the boy hard. The leather had wrapped around the kid's feet, and tripped him up. He was trying to crawl away, but Whip was reeling him in like a trout. One of the women who ran one of the boardinghouses got all indignant at mistreating a child, but none of the menfolk done nothing about it. Even Mr. McCoy and Mr. Slater just stood with two other brown suits by the body of one of six dead men.

The dirty little waif yelled as he got drug. Dust rose in the air. The kid tried to use the palms of his hands as brakes, but Whip was right stronger than a puny little punk.

Eventually, Whip had pulled the kid close enough.

"I'm not going to hurt you, boy," Whip said, as he loosened the whip around the kid's ankles. He jerked the blacksnake away, then fished a coin from his pocket. It was just a Morgan dollar, not gold or nothing, and the kid, by my way of thinking, was already rich.

"Rogers Canfield," Whip said. "You found him."

"Ye-s-s-s . . . s-s-s-ir."

"Where?"

"In . . . his-s-s . . . off-ice."

"Which is where?"

The kid rolled over, got to his dirty knees, and pointed a dirty finger at one of the few two-story buildings in town.

"C-c-c-corner," he said.

A sign on the whitewashed frame structure said BANK, but lots of banks rented rooms in the top floor to various businesses. Provided the banker some income in case the bank went bust.

The dollar dropped in the dirt, and Whip was coiling his whip as he crossed the street. I didn't need him to tell me to come along. I came along.

Up the outer staircase we went, because walking into a bank with a man in black with a whip and me carrying a dead man's Winchester repeater seems like a good way to get killed as bank robbers. Upstairs, I opened the door, and Whip walked in, stopped. I come in right behind him, and we stared down a long hall.

The inside staircase came up in the center. Four doors on each side of the hallway. I looked down, made sure the Winchester was cocked. Whip kept the whip in both hands, and we walked toward the muffled voices coming from inside the street-corner office, past an attorney's office on the left . . . a mining headquarters on the right . . . a bookseller on the left . . . and the door opened on the right.

"If I were you," Whip Watson told the dressmaker, "I'd get back to stitching."

"And keep your head down," I advised as the door slammed in my face.

We passed the stairs. Didn't look down at any business going on in the bank. Passed a land office on the left, and a office for rent on the right.

Then we stood in at the end of the hallway, with a haberdashery on the right, and on the left, the corner office, where those voices were coming from.

"Where's Paul, damn it?" came a voice I recognized as belonging to Rogers Canfield/Ronen Kanievsky the *shadchan*/matchmaker.

I mouthed an answer: *He's dead.*

"Damn it," Canfield went on. "Paul and Gates . . . Patton . . . Dirty Lou . . . they should all be here by now. Damn it. Damn it. Damn it. This better have gone down the way it was supposed to have."

"The way it was supposed to have gone down," another voice said, "wasn't with Bernie gettin' his brains blowed out."

Canfield squealed and cussed, and Whip Watson put his hand on the knob to the office. I read the sign on the door.

ROGERS CANFIELD
MATRIMONIAL AGENT
MARRIAGE BROKER

And below that in real fancy script:

I Deal in Wedded Bliss

The second voice said. "I did my job, Canfield. Just give me what I got comin'."

That's when Whip Watson pushed open the door, making me realize that Canfield was an idiot, or maybe too damned confident, because he hadn't locked the door.

Whip went in first, and I followed him, having to duck as that whip sailed slightly over my head.

What I saw was Rogers Canfield standing and sweating in front of a rolltop desk. I saw the butt of a small pistol lying on some papers on that desk. A big Bible. I saw a bunch of parchments framed hanging on the wall. A painting of Jesus. Next to a painting of Cupid. Lots of mail piled up in a chair. Saw Canfield reaching for the pistol, choking out a scream. Then I turned to the second man.

Big cuss, with no front teeth, reaching a gloved hand for a Remington .44 stuck in a mule-ear

pocket. He wore a brown slouch hat and a buckskin
shirt. The gun had cleared his pocket, and Whip's
whip had snapped, and Canfield was screaming and
Whip was cussing, and No Front Teeth was thumbing back the Remington's revolver.

Then I saw a bunch of white smoke, and felt my
eyes stinging and heard my ears ringing and
smelled burned powder. I stepped to the side, jacking another shell into the rifle I'd just fired, and
shot again. But I didn't have to. No Front Teeth
wasn't there no more. There was a bunch of broken
glass and the curtain rod had been pulled down.
The curtains was gone. Just like No Front Teeth.

Turning, I saw Whip Watson coiling his whip.
The little pistol lay where it had been atop the desk.
Rogers Canfield lay on the floor, gripping his throat
and gagging. Whip was leaning, jerking the matrimonial agent to his feet, and shoving him into the
chair that wasn't full of mail.

I moved to the window and looked down. No
Front Teeth lay atop a water trough, legs bent on
one side of the trough, head hanging on the other,
one arm resting on the ground, the other floating
atop the water, a big, bloody hole in the center of
his buckskin shirt. The curtains lay in the street.
Good thing no horses had been slaking their thirsts,
I thought, and shrugged at the brown suits staring
up at me.

A lot of screaming and shouting was going on
outside, now that the ringing wasn't so loud in
my ears.

I turned, watched Whip Watson slap Rogers Canfield's face.

"This how you pay your partner, partner?" Whip
asked. Then slapped Canfield's left cheek.

"I—"

Whip slapped Canfield's right cheek.

"We had a deal."

"Yes . . . but . . ."

Another slap.

"So you're double-dealing."

"No . . . Whip . . ."

Slap.

"You wouldn't kill me . . . not without somebody else backing your play." *Slap.* "And I don't mean those five idiots you sent to kill us." *Slap.* "They're dead."

"Six," I said, now that No Front Teeth had departed this world.

Either Whip didn't hear me or didn't care. He was too busy slapping Rogers Canfield.

"Who's behind this?" Whip asked. "Who wants me dead? Besides you? Who wants my merchandise?"

"I . . ."

Slapped again.

Whip Watson backed away from the blubbering Canfield, picking up his blacksnake whip.

"One way or the other," Whip told the marriage man, "you'll talk. How's it gonna be?"

"You'll kill me anyway." Rogers Canfield sobbed.

"Maybe, but this way"—he gestured with the blacksnake—"you won't have any skin left on you. Ain't that right, Micah Bishop?"

The Winchester felt heavy in my hands. I swallowed down more bile and said, "Better tell him."

"You won't kill me?" Rogers Canfield begged.

Whip cracked the whip, just a little.

Canfield slid back in his chair, raising his hands over his face. "All right!" He wet his britches. "Please. It wasn't my idea."

"Never figured it was. You deal in *wedded bliss,* not assassinations."

I didn't know nothing about what they was talking about, but I did know that Rogers Canfield had tried to get me killed. So I didn't care much for him. I moved away from the window, away from Whip's whip, and stepped into the open doorway. I looked down the hallway, half expecting the law to come racing up those stairs, but then I recollected that Calico had no law. No jail. Just seven dead men.

I tried to recollect where the undertaker's office was in this town. He'd have a right prosperous day.

"Who?" Whip Watson's voice jerked my attention back into the marriage broker's office.

"But . . ."

"Who?"

"I can't . . ." The whip cut a slice off Rogers Canfield's left knee. Wailing like banshees are always wailing, he gripped his knee and said, "All right! All right. It was her idea."

Her? That caused me to straighten. It caused Whip to even step back a couple paces as he gathered up the blacksnake.

A moment of silence. Then Whip said, "Crutchfield?"

Rogers Canfield's head bobbed slightly.

"Son of a bitch." Whip turned to me. "Candy Crutchfield," he said. "Should have figured on her."

I nodded. Just to do something. I didn't know Candy Crutchfield from Adam's housecat.

"Figures. Does she have merchandise, too?"

Whip had turned back to Rogers Canfield.

"She said she did. And . . ." Canfield's Adam's

apple, raw and puckered and bleeding a mite from the whip, bobbed.

"And what?" Whip said.

Canfield's head turned, as if he expected the whip to slash again. "She said she'd take yours, too."

Whip swore. "And you figured what the hell, more money for you."

"No, Whip? I mean—"

"Stop it. You've told me all I need to know. Now I'm telling you something. I'll take care of Candy. But there are seven dead men, Canfield," Whip said. "You're paying for the funerals. I don't give a damn about the six you sent to kill us. Throw them over the canyon wall with the rest of the garbage and let those China devils deal with them, but Guttersnipe Gary gets a pine box and at least four mourners."

"Of course." He pushed himself to his feet, leaning over, gripping his bloody leg. "I'll get the money right now." He moved toward his desk. I saw the little pocket gun. So did Canfield. So did Whip. Figured the fool would make a try for it, but he went to a far drawer, pulled it open, withdrew a money box.

This got set on the desk, and he found a key, unlocked the box, pushed it open, and pulled out a handful of greenbacks.

"How much?" he begged.

"Hold it!" Watson snapped.

The paper money floated to the floor. Rogers Canfield done something else in his pants.

"I see that pistol." Watson had put the whip over his shoulder, but his right hand had drew one of the Colts, cocked it, aimed it at Rogers Canfield's chest.

"I wasn't . . ." the broker stammered.

"Just so you don't get any notions," Whip said. "Pick it up. Gently. And toss it into that spittoon."

"Yes, Whip. Yes, sir." Rogers Canfield done just like he was told. Well, almost. He never got to the tossing the pistol into the spittoon because as soon as he picked it up, Whip Watson shot him dead.

CHAPTER TEN

"He had a gun in his hand," Watson said as he walked past me in the doorway, slipping the smoking .45 into his sash. "That makes it self-defense."

Which is what Whip told Mr. Slater out on the street. And since one of the other Brown Suits went upstairs to find the late Rogers Canfield/Ronen Kanievsky lying in his own waste and blood with a hammerless .32 in his right hand, the vigilance committee ruled the death of Mr. Canfield, plus those six other killings, as self-defense, and poor Guttersnipe Gary as a murder in which the culprits were now roasting on a spit in hell.

Mr. Slater was satisfied. Justice had been served. What's more, his brother happened to be Calico's undertaker, and there was enough money on Canfield's office floor to pay for eight funerals, especially since only Guttersnipe Gary would be given any mourners.

Me and Whip wouldn't be around to pay our last respects.

"Take the carriage to the livery," Whip told me as we walked to where we'd left the buggy and Whip's black mare in front of the Globe Chop House. "Know the one?"

"Applewhite's?" I said.

"That's right." He handed me a wad of greenbacks. "Leave the carriage there. Tell the owner that I want the leather spotless when we get back. And the horses grained and rubbed down every day. Then pick out the best mount he has. One that can carry you hard, fast, and far. Get a good saddle." He glanced at the Winchester I held. "With a scabbard. And a saddlebag. Fill one bag with boxes of cartridges for that long gun."

I hoped I could remember all that.

"I'll meet you inside Noel's saloon. Then we ride." He said, "You want to speak to me, don't you?"

Which I knowed wasn't directed at me. Whip turned to look at a guy with gold-rimmed spectacles and ink-stained fingers.

"Yes, sir," the man said. "If you don't mind. If you're up to it after all this . . . ahem . . . er . . . well, I'm with the *Calico Print*."

Whip stepped onto the boardwalk. "Always have time for the press, sir. Let's talk in the saloon. I'll buy you a whiskey."

The fellow at Applewhite's sold me a four-year-old zebra dun that he swore had some Arabian in him and wouldn't let me down. Course, the horse was actually six years old, but knowing what I knew about horseflesh, I figured he was right about this gelding's stamina. We haggled a mite, and I reminded him of Whip Watson's instructions for carriage care, and we finally come to an understanding and a price.

I sat on the top corral fence while he had one of his boys saddle the dun for me and made out my bill of sale. Then a voice called out right behind me, "Mister American Gentleman. Mister American Gentleman."

Cringing, I dropped on the horse side of the corral, and saw Lucky Ben Wong bowing slightly, looking up apologetic. I figured he'd be mad as hell for me disturbing his place of business, leaving two dead men in Chinatown, and, well, doing some remodeling of his abode.

I pulled out some greenbacks from my vest pocket, stuck them between the rails of the corral, and said, "Sorry about your wall." Which was true. "I didn't want you hurt, killed maybe, so that's why I left like that and . . ."

He shook his head. "No. No. Not your fault. Bad guys shoot at you. No. No money." He shrugged. "Plenty money I make."

Lucky Ben Wong's hands had been behind his back. As he brought them into view, I reached for my .36, but he didn't hold no weapon but my new hat with the new hole through the center. He stuck it toward me, and I thanked him as I took it, pulled it between the rails, and settled it on my head.

The man who may or may not have been Applewhite brought over the zebra dun and the bill of sale. I'd already given him the cash, and he said, "Pleasure doing business with you."

"Likewise," I said, and took the reins.

He frowned at the hole in my hat, then give an even more distasteful look at Lucky Ben Wong, and went back to talk to his boys, not even opening the gate for me, but Lucky Ben Wong did that, and I led the dun out of the livery.

"Is it true?" Lucky Ben Wong asked as I walked my new horse back toward the center of Calico.

"Is what true?" I said.

"That Mister Canfield, dealer in matrimony, now dead?"

I stopped to give Lucky Ben Wong a different kind of look. Then I remembered him telling me that he was going to get married.

"It's true," I said. Adding a bald-faced lie: "Self-defense." And walked some more.

"Lucky Ben Wong no lucky," Lucky Ben Wong said, still walking alongside me. "Feel sad."

I wet my lips. We were approaching a gun shop, where I could get some boxes for the Winchester in the scabbard, but stopped, and looked again at Lucky Ben Wong, waiting until he looked up at me.

He did. Tears filled his eyes. He sniffed.

"Lucky Ben Wong," I said, "just what in hell is going on in this here town?"

He stepped back, and I feared he might run off, but he motioned to a ton of hay—didn't know where they found hay in this desert, either—in an empty lot between the livery and the gun shop. He went halfway down, then sat on a bale. I tethered the dun to the fence so he could eat for free some of Applewhite's hay, since Applewhite had tried to sell me a four-year-old horse that was really six.

Lucky Ben Wong sat, head down. I leaned against the picket wall of the gun shop, bending my left leg, resting the sole and heel of my boot against the wall. Then the little Chinese dude looked up.

"Rogers Canfield," he said, "deals in mail-order brides." Only when he said it, he didn't sound like most Chinese dudes I've heard talking. That pidgin English—which some folks accuse me of speaking—

had a Chinese accent, certain-sure, but it wasn't broken. And Lucky Ben Wong didn't look like he was about to cry. He looked mad. I dropped my leg, and hooked my thumb in my new $7.33 gun belt, next to my holstered Spiller & Burr.

"What happens," he asked me, "to me and everyone else now that Mister Canfield is dead?"

That's when I knew what kind of merchandise Whip Watson was hauling in those four Conestogas.

One time me and Big Tim Pruett had wintered in a cabin high up in the Sangre de Christo Mountains in Colorado, on account that the law was chasing after us down below, and the only thing we had to read was a copy of the *Matrimonial News,* Kansas City edition.

All right, we didn't read too much. Mostly looked at the pictures.

Of the girls. Not the men.

There was folks making twelve dollars a year, and folks making five hundred thousand dollars (which me and Big Tim Pruett figured was an exaggeration, like the Applewhite guy's judge of a horse's age). Folks of all ages, with lonely hearts, just wanting human companionship. Pretty girls, young and old, ugly girls, young and old, wanting to marry. And men, young and old, handsome and wretched-looking, wanting . . . well, you know.

So, say Big Tim Pruett saw a picture of a girl he fancied. He'd write a letter, send it to the *Matrimonial News* office in Kansas City, with the number of the advertisement he fancied wrote down on the envelope. The editor would forward the letter, I guess, to the gal. Maybe the gal would reply. Anyway, before you knowed it, the girl would show up and Big Tim Pruett would get hisself hitched.

That's one way to do it. My preference was to find a soiled dove who didn't charge too much and who was cleaner and prettier than Betty and then be gone next morning or maybe after ten minutes. The other way to do it was the way Lucky Ben Wong done it.

"I paid Mister Canfield five hundred dollars," Lucky Ben Wong said. "He found her for me. He said he was bringing her into Calico. We would be married, and then I'd sell all my interests, all my claims, even my place in East Calico. We would move to San Francisco."

"And live happily ever after?" I said with a smile.

He smiled back. Yes, sir, he had a real pretty smile for a Chinese man. "Not in California," he said. He pulled his pigtail around so I could see it. "This is why I have my queue. It is a sin to cut your queue. In the old days, you could be killed for cutting your hair."

Which struck me as odd, since Lucky Ben Wong had just cut my hair for $1.09.

"But that's in China," I said. "You're in America."

"But like most people from my country, we do not wish to remain in America. We hope to return after we have made our fortune."

"And you have?"

The pigtail went behind his back. "And I have found love."

"Why the phony broken English?" I asked him.

As he reached inside his shirt, he shrugged and answered. "It's how you Americans expect us to talk." He pulled out a locket that hung on a rawhide cord, pulled it over his head, and passed it to me. I turned the locket over, and sucked in my breath.

"My Jingfei is very beautiful," Lucky Ben Wong said, "is she not?"

"She is." I could only whisper.

"Jingfei means . . ."

"Quiet Not," I whispered, still staring at the image.

When I handed the locket and thong back to him, he was giving me a cold, calculating stare. I said, "You pick up things in my line of work. Names and such." And bullet wounds . . . and jail sentences . . . and the clap . . . "Where is she from?"

"Trinidad, Colorado," Lucky Ben Wong said.

"Never been there," I lied.

That satisfied him, and he slipped the thong and locket over his head, and I watched Jingfei disappear inside his black silk shirt.

I got a little more curious. "Did she have to pay Canfield, too?"

His head bobbed. "Two hundred dollars."

I whistled. Had I known all the money that could be made dealing in wedded bliss, I might have chosen another line of work.

"Canfield promised to bring your intended here?" I asked.

"Yes."

"He'd pay expenses?"

His head shook. "No. I sent Jingfei the money to get to Prescott." He even pronounced it right. Presskit. Instead of Press-cot. "That's in Arizona."

"Why not all the way here?" I asked.

"Because Mister Canfield said he had enough brides that his wedding present to us would be to arrange for transportation from Prescott to Calico. He was a good man, this Mister Canfield."

He was a boil on my butt, I thought. Then I said, "Enough brides?"

He nodded. "I am not the only one who found his true love through the late Mister Canfield."

"How many other . . ." Had to stop myself from saying *suckers*. Instead, I said, " . . . gents here are expecting brides from Canfield?"

"Does it matter?" Before I could answer he said, "But one man who came to partake of the opium, when he was in a deep state of delirium, he said, 'Two dozen brides are coming to Calico.' Then he said some very things disrespectful about women in general. And Mister Canfield."

I tried to savvy and sort all this out. All I got was a headache, so I started rubbing the bridge of my nose.

"With Mister Canfield dead," Lucky Ben Wong said, "I fear Jingfei will not come to marry me. Our deal—"

"She's still coming." I dropped my hand, and give Lucky Ben Wong the best smile I could muster. He looked back at me like he didn't understand. Course, I wasn't sure I understood anything at all. Still, I told him, "Watson's bringing her." He didn't know Whip, and I wished I didn't. "Man I work for. The man who killed Canfield . . . in . . . self . . . defense."

He blinked. Stood on weak knees, and said to me, "But I still owe—"

I cut him off, all incredulous: "*More money?*"

His little head bobbed quickly. "Yes. Yes. The money I paid Mister Canfield was a down payment."

A down payment on a wife. Hard to figure. I was pushing up my new hat with the hole in the middle, and now my head was really hurting. Lucky Ben

Wong kept right on talking. "The contract I signed with—"

"You signed a contract?"

"But of course. It is how business is done in America."

Hell, I hadn't asked Whip Watson for no contract. Wasn't even certain if I'd shook his hand.

"How much do you owe?"

He told me he owed $250. That made a bride in Calico, California, worth $950. Lessen the expenses the late Rogers Canfield had paid Whip Watson to haul his *merchandise* in from Prescott.

Only thing I could do was put my hand on Lucky Ben Wong's shoulder, give it a squeeze, and tell him, "Don't fret. I'll bring Jingfei in. That I promise you." Like my word was good for anything.

But the little man accepted it, bowed, thanked me, spoke some Chinese, then, since a couple of fellows was coming down the street toward the gun shop and in earshot of us, went back to his busted-up English.

"Lucky Ben Wong feel lucky. Me thank Mister American Gentlemen. Must go. Must go. Must fix house." Some more Chinese, and he was running, down the street, and I was moving to the bale of hay, and gathering the reins, and leading my new gelding the few feet to the hitching post.

As I stood at the counter of Wechsler's gun shop, waiting for my boxes of .44-40 cartridges for the late Paul's Winchester, I done some studying.

Whip Watson was delivering twenty-four brides to Rogers Canfield, and various other sundries to other merchants. Rogers Canfield, however, had also entered an arrangement with some witch named Candy Crutchfield. I tried to recollect that conversation Whip was having with Canfield before Whip had ended the conversation with a .45 slug through Canfield's heart.

Whip had asked Canfield if she had merchandise, too, and Canfield had said, "She said she did."

So maybe that meant Candy Crutchfield was bringing in her own load of brides. And she had bribed Canfield into hiring some worthless man-killers to put Whip Watson and his employees—in this case, me and Guttersnipe Gary—out of business. Hadn't worked out quite the way Crutchfield and Canfield had figured, thanks to Whip Watson.

Then another part of that conversation run through my memories, and I said, out loud, "Son of a bitch."

I looked up, saw Klaus Wechsler giving me a cold, mean, arse-whupping stare, which Germans is good at giving. "Not you," I said as meek as I could make it. He slid the boxes toward me, and I looked at all the money I still had. I pointed at the glass case. "That long-barreled Colt there?" I said. "It shoots the same rounds as the Winchester, ain't that right?"

His eyes still threatened an arse-whipping and he said, in that harsh Hun brogue: "If caliber of Winchester is forty-four-forty, *ja*."

"How much?" I asked.

He told me thirty-eight dollars, which was practically double what a Colt cost anywhere outside of Calico, California. But Whip Watson had given me a passel of greenbacks.

"I'll take it. And that shell belt hanging on that rack."

Now, I'd never thought much of men who packed two revolvers and fancied themselves as pistoleers, but I expected I might have need of as many pistols as I could carry, and a Colt Peacemaker sure seemed more reliable than a twenty-five-year old relic from the War of the Rebellion.

So I walked out of Wechsler's gun shop with two guns on my hips, a Winchester in my scabbard, and plenty of ammunition in my saddle bags. Mounted the horse I named Lucky and kicked him into a gallop over to Noel's fancy saloon.

Whip Watson would be in a hurry, and I wasn't gonna burn no more daylight. Because we both knowed what Rogers Canfield had said about Candy Crutchfield. She was bringing her own merchandise into Calico.

And she was planning on taking Whip Watson's, too.

CHAPTER ELEVEN

We left Calico with extra canteens—two dollars for a full canteen, ain't that criminal?—grub and grain. Pushed our mounts hard, but Applewhite hadn't lied about Lucky's pluck, and Whip Watson's black mare come full of grit.

I don't think Whip and me exchanged more than a dozen words as we rode back into the Mojave to find our wagon train and Whip's "merchandise." Then, early one morning, we reined in our already lathered mounts. While Whip stood in his stirrups to make sure he'd heard what he thought we'd both heard, I was already pulling the Winchester from the scabbard. More gunfire sounded beyond the next rise.

With a salty cussword, Whip spurred that mare into a gallop, filling his mouth with the reins and his hands with them two Colts. I was right behind him, slapping Lucky's side with the Winchester barrel.

Topping that knoll, we found Juan Pedro and the boys and them wagons and those four Conestogas, and we also found Candy Crutchfield and her killers and women-nappers.

Juan Pedro had made camp at the bottom. Nice place. Out of the wind. Apt to be a mite cooler. Good place to keep fires concealed, especially if you burned dry wood. On the other hand, it was a bad place to be if you happened to get attacked by thirty villains and one woman, armed with repeating rifles, which was happening when me and Whip rode down into the affray.

The boys I bunk with here at Folsom say that I'm full of horse apples, that this story I'm about to relate to you is something out of some blood-and-thunder, but I ain't writing no five-penny dreadful. This is bona fide. Happened exactly as I'm putting it down. More or less.

Candy Crutchfield's gang had come charging down the eastern side of the hill about the time Juan Pedro and the boys was finishing hitching up the teams. Me and Whip topped the ridge a few minutes later, then rode down the western slope.

Let me tell you about Whip Watson. He wasn't just good with a blacksnake whip, he knowed how to ride. I don't recommend charging down a hill with reins held by your teeth, and guns in both hands, into a fracas like that which had commenced. Man can get killed doing such a fool stunt.

Yet there I was, right off to his left, holding a heavy .44-40 repeating rifle. Granted, I had no intention of shooting from horseback, especially coming downhill, but when I seen some guy in buckskins shoot down one of our boys, and jump onto the lead ox pulling one of our Conestogas, I got riled.

Brung that Winchester to my shoulder, dropped the California-style reins over Lucky's neck, jacked a shell into the chamber, let a bullet fly. While riding downhill.

Missed, of course, and then I was cussing Bug Beard for more than he was worth, because that dumb idiot begun firing his pistol at me.

Not that I blame him none. After all, he knowed he was being attacked by some killers, and here come two guys riding like the devil's on our tails down toward the camp, guns blazing.

"Stop shooting, you damned fool!" I yelled at him, and levered another round. "It's me, you . . ." And I called him every word you won't find in Mr. Webster's book.

He shot at me again.

Then his pistol was empty, and he had to take time to reload, and I got out of his range, galloping toward that man who was getting those oxen to going, and taking one of those wagons right up the hill.

Next thing I knowed, I was flying.

Here's something a rustler here in Folsom told me after I'd related my story of the attack to him. If you're standing in your stirrups and have your pony going at a gallop, he said, that pony is more apt to stumble. He didn't believe my story, neither, but I believe what he said because he is a rustler so he knows horses probably even better than me even though I've been knowed to appropriate other people's horses, and besides that, Lucky stumbled while I was standing in my stirrups and running that gelding at a full gallop, and I went sailing past Lucky's neck.

Luckily for me, I landed in a soft bit of sand, breaking my fall by landing hard on my right arm, but somehow didn't break that arm. Busted my bottom lip, though, and bruised that arm considerable. Come up spitting out gravel and seeing orange dots. When my vision cleared, I seen my Winchester lying a few rods from where I'd struck, and Lucky streaking up the eastern ridge.

Several other horses, a few mules, and one ox bolted after Lucky.

Came up to my knees, and crawled, stumbled, flew, and dived for the Winchester, which I taken up. One of the Conestogas was gone. Cleared the rise off to the north. The other one, the one with the guy on the ox I'd taken a shot at, was clambering. I was aiming at that guy, and figured I might have a chance at hitting him, even though it would be an uphill shot at a moving target and twenty orange dots still clouded my vision.

Didn't get to shoot that dude. A bullet, you see, spanged off a black rock near me, and I jerked away, fell to my side, and cussed Bug Beard again for shooting at me.

The next shot tore a gash in my already perforated fancy hat, which, by some stroke of miraculous intervention, was still fitted on my head. Which, ask me, is another reason you don't need stampede strings, just a hat that fits.

I came up, but my next cuss at Bug Beard died in my throat, because the body shooting at my person wasn't Bug Beard at all, but was a guy in duck trousers and a patch over his eye, and two bandoliers of cartridges crisscrossing his chest. Having never seen him before, I deduced, even under the stress of battle, that he was one of Candy Crutchfield's women-nappers and aimed to kill me.

The Winchester roared, and Bandolier grunted, gasped, and dropped his Spencer repeater, and gripped his belly, which was spraying blood like water from an artesian well. But only for a few moments, because then he wasn't bleeding at all on account that his heart had stopped pumping on account that he was dead.

Whirling back around, I cocked the rifle, but what I saw turned my stomach, and, transgressor that I was, I prayed.

The fellow that had been on the ox rolled down the incline, dead. The team of oxen moved over the hill, but not with the Conestoga wagon. It stood there on the edge of the hill, but just for a moment. Then it began toppling over, and from underneath that canvas cover, I heard those terrifying screams.

"Jingfei!" I shouted, though she couldn't hear me. Nobody could hear me, because there was a lot of shooting going on. I didn't think, *Poor Lucky Ben Wong*. I thought, *Poor Micah Bishop*. Then, despite bleeding lip and aching head and throbbing arm and the occasional orange dot still flashing in my eyes, I sprinted toward the wagon as it rolled over and over, the canvas top flattening, the water barrels rolling off, the tool box breaking open, spokes of the busted wheels flying here and there, and the body of a woman catapulting out of the back, like she'd gotten spit out by the great whale, Moby-Dick.

Was a horrible thing to see. Makes me sick even to write down these words.

As I run, I glimpsed the rest of Crutchfield's men lighting a shuck back over the ridge. One of the Conestogas was gone. Two more remained where they'd been parked. One hadn't moved on account the two lead oxen lay dead in their traces. The other hadn't moved on account that it had been protected by Zeke and Mr. Clark and Juan Pedro.

Dust rose from the wreckage of the last Conestoga as it settled against some rocks. Dreading what I'd find, I stopped a few rods from that shattered mess, and looked at the girl who'd gotten spit out. I seen her blue calico dress, and her yellow hair, and I knowed she wasn't Jingfei. And from how her legs was jutting out from the skirt, and how her head was tilted, I could tell she was dead.

I cussed. Hell, ain't ashamed to admit it, I cried. Turned back toward that mess of wood and axel grease and dirt, and I said, "Jingfei . . ."

"Here I am," this voice called behind me. I turned and there she was. She'd come out of the Conestoga with the two dead oxen, lifting the bottom of her *changyi,* her feet not wrapped, but bare, her hair not bound but flying behind her like a horse's tail. Her eyes blazed with concern, and she dashed right past me, standing there stunned because I'd figured, the way my luck was going, that she'd be dead, but Jingfei exclaimed, "Help me, please!" She hurried right to that crushed wagon, and I dropped the Winchester and followed.

"Oh!" She stopped, bowed her head, turned her head even, then somehow mustered up all that courage it took, and moved closer. She was reaching down when I got to her, and gripped the muslin cloth we spied sticking out of the canvas. Together we dragged out a chubby redheaded gal with green eyes that was wide open, except the one that was covered with sand. A trail of sand-coated blood come from both nostrils and the corners of her mouth.

Me and Jingfei pulled her body from the wreckage, carried her a few yards, and laid her down as gently as possible on the eastern slope of the hill, so the sun wouldn't shine in her eyes.

I rose, looked around me, saw and heard Whip Watson barking orders, cussing his boys as damned fools. Seen some fellows cutting the dead oxen from the harness. Seen others walking around in a daze, some bloody, some helping the wounded, a few dead.

When I turned back to Jingfei, she was folding the dead gal's arms over her ripped dress, pushing a lock of red hair off the forehead, then closing those green eyes, even the one full of sand.

A moment later, she turned to me. "Her name," she whispered, "was Aibreann Halloran. She was to marry a miner named Conchobhar O'Flannagáin. She came all the way from New York City."

I thought that I'd hate to hear what names they'd saddle with their kids, then I felt real bad because that was a terrible thing to think, and then I knowed that she'd never have no children, and that in Calico, Conchobhar O'Flannagáin would be devastated, and then I was wiping my eyes, and Jingfei was telling me, "Come. There is no time for tears. Perhaps someone is alive."

But nobody was.

We hauled four other girls from that wrecked Conestoga—Annie Mercer, a widow from Liberty, Missouri; Darlene Gould, who had been married twice and had left two kids with her ma in Topeka and would send for them once she got settled with Husband No. III, who ramrodded a borax mine down in Mule Canyon; Chris McGover, who was trying to teach the girls in the Conestoga how to deal faro, which she'd learned from her late husband in Fort Worth, Texas, before he'd gotten shot dead at the White Elephant Saloon; and Molly Reid, jolly and blond and plain and coming from Terre Haute, Indiana, to find her betrothed who was, like her, interested in missionary work—and laid them all beside the late Aibreann Halloran while Whip Watson hollered at Mr. Clark to round up the horses that had scattered, and Juan Pedro barked orders in Spanish at the Mexicans in our bunch.

Finally, we brought down the body of Maud Fenstermacher, the blonde who'd gotten spit out of the wagon, and laid her beside the petite Darlene Gould. Maud's ma and pa had died in St. Louis, leaving her all alone at seventeen years old, and she was to marry a fellow who said he was the marshal of Calico and made three hundred dollars a month, and I thought: *Maybe it's for the best that Maud died here, and didn't get her heart broke because there ain't no marshal in Calico.* Then I got riled and promised to find this Jürgen Baader when I got back to Calico and whup him to a frazzle because if not for him and his lies, Maud Fenstermacher might still be alive in St. Louis.

"It is not fair." Jingfei reached out her tiny, slender-fingered left hand, and I understood that she wanted me to take it, and I done that. And we bowed our heads, a Buddhist and a backslider, and she squeezed my hand, and she thanked me, and let go, and straightened, and looked real hard and real angry at Whip Watson, who was leading his black mare right toward us, flanked by six other men.

"Are they dead?" Whip shouted.

Didn't think my voice would work, so I just nodded.

Whip took the Lord's name and Candy Crutchfield's name in vain, whipped off his black hat and slammed it to the ground. "That bitch killed six of my girls, made off with six more!" He cussed some more, dropped the reins of the mare, shook his head, and walked over to inspect the dead.

Had his blacksnake whip not been fastened to the horn on his saddle, Whip might have flayed the skin off my back, or anyone else who was handy, just so he'd feel better.

"We have twelve ladies left," Juan Pedro told Whip. Juan Pedro had been crossing himself and saying a prayer.

"Ladies!" Bug Beard snorted, and I give him a cold stare not for almost shooting me dead, but for being a rude, unclean son of a bitch.

"I want twenty-four!" Whip looked up with those freezing eyes, causing Bug Beard to stare at his dirty boots, then Whip glared at me. Suddenly, he was grinning, looking off to the north, the way Candy Crutchfield's gang had rode off. "No," he was saying, "I want forty-two." His head bobbed in agreement with hisself. "Candy's concubines. The six she stole. And the ones we have left."

Which would actually make it forty-one, but that's because I had turned around and seen Jingfei. She'd moved right around the Whip's boys, who was staring at their boss, and she had gathered the reins to the black, found a handy rock so she was high enough to reach the stirrups, and then she'd swung into the saddle.

Tiny porcelain doll that she was, she give that

tired mare a savage kick with her bare heels, and the black responded.

Whip's boys started cussing and scattering as the black mare like to have run over half of them, and even I was jumping off to one side. Zeke had retrieved my Winchester, and he was aiming right at Jingfei, and I stepped up, and caught the barrel with my already bruised right forearm. The rifle boomed, but the bullet went toward a cloud, and I cussed Zeke as a damned idiot.

"You might hit Jingfei!" I shouted.

"Or Whip's horse!" Bug Beard was trying to get back on Whip's good side.

Whip, of course, was yelling louder than anyone else. Then he shrieked like a girl. "Get her. Get that Chinese girl! Get her! Get her!" He punctuated his orders with a lot of cusswords. "But don't kill her!"

The problem, of course, was that Mr. Clark and three of the men had yet to round up any of our horses, including my Lucky, and Jingfei had already topped the ridge. I figured we wasn't getting Jingfei no time soon, but then Peach Fuzz was whipping those two gray Percherons with a whip that wasn't as fancy or as black and wicked as Whip Watson's. Peach Fuzz's Columbus carriage angled down the hill, and he had to pull hard on the lines to keep from running over those six dead girls.

I heard him yell, "I'll fetch her, Mister Watson! I'll fetch 'em all!"

I've never been one for planning nothing. I just go on instinct, or foolish notions, and that's what I done. Having some practice at running to catch moving boxcars as the train leaves a station, I run ahead as the Columbus carriage raced by, and I gripped one of the little bars that come down from the canopy, and it just so happened that it didn't break, and somehow I didn't go dropping underneath the wheels and getting killed, and I even managed to swing myself into the back floor, and bounced around some before coming up to my knees, and then, as the buggy started uphill, I got slammed down into the rear leather seat that smelled of fresh wax.

CHAPTER TWELVE

Ain't sure which hurt more, getting tossed over Lucky's neck at a full gallop, or almost breaking my neck as I got tumbled and bruised trying not to get chucked out of that buggy being driven by Peach Fuzz. Got a look-see behind me, once I got jerked off the seat, onto the floor, and almost into the Mojave, but spied only dust. Then I was jostled back inside, felt the rear wheels of the coach come off the ground as we went over a hill, or boulder, or something, hit the floor, the seat, then managed to grab hold of the back of front seat, and found myself sitting in the center of the backseat, watching Peach Fuzz whip those grays.

Now, for all you stampede-string-wearing proponents, here's another true statement: My hat was still on my head. Flattened a bit, and the brims bent and one side even torn, but it hadn't come off.

"Slow down!" I bellowed at Peach Fuzz.

He didn't even look at me, and sure didn't listen.

I repeated my instructions, and hollered, "Jingfei can't get far. Whip's horse is worn out."

Got flung back against the seat, but it was a

comfortable seat, yet I wouldn't expect less from a coach that cost three hundred dollars in Dallas.

Peach Fuzz's whip popped the air.

"I don't give a damn about that yellow-skinned girl!" he yelled back at me. "It's Bonnie I'm a-savin'!"

Wanted to ask him *Who the hell is Bonnie?* only my teeth was already hurting from the pounding I'd taken, and I was already howling on account we had started down another hill.

About then, at the bottom of the hill we was barreling down, I spied the other Conestoga. The oxen was still hitched, but the wagon wasn't moving. Didn't see Jingfei, didn't see Whip Watson's black horse, and I didn't see none of Candy Crutchfield's vermin.

Thinking about all that I didn't see, I was trying to reach some conclusion as to what it all meant, or didn't mean, but then Peach Fuzz was bracing hisself, tugging hard on those lines, even setting the brake, and we slid to a stop without wrecking or killing the Percherons or ourselves. Peach Fuzz had a better grip, though, and unlike me he didn't bounce off the back of the front seat, and then off the backseat, and didn't land on the floor.

Heard him jump out of the rig, heard him running around the desert, crying out, "Bonnie? Bonnie? Bonnie?"

I fell out of the carriage, and tried to find my land legs. I weaved this way, then that, managed to grip the side of the carriage as the grays blowed real hard, and Peach Fuzz kept calling out that girl's name. He jumped up, peered through the canvas cover, then ran to the front. While he was running like them chickens is always doing when they get their heads cut off, I started moving—real gingerly—toward the picket line that I'd spied and the mounds of horse apples that had been left behind.

"She ain't here!" Peach Fuzz wailed. "Bonnie's gone."

Lots of horse tracks I seen. And some small prints that would likely have been made by women.

"What are you lookin' at?" Peach Fuzz rubbed the tears out of his eyes with his fists, and staggered over to where I held a fresh horse turd.

My jaw jutted toward the team of oxen. "A wagon like that, hauled by a team of oxen," I said, "don't move fast. They knowed they could never outrun Whip Watson. So they left some boys here with horses." I pointed at the picket line they'd left. "Kind of a relay station. Got the girls out of the wagon. Mounted them up. Took off." I flung the turd toward the north, the way the tracks headed.

"Who?" He knelt beside me. "Who kidnapped Bonnie?"

"Candy Crutchfield, appears to me," I said, and looked for some recognition in his eyes. There wasn't nothing in them except tears.

"Who's that?"

"Hell if I know." I pointed at another set of tracks. One that had whipped right past the Conestoga and hardly even slowed down.

"Candy Crutchfield?" Peach Fuzz asked, his eyes following the tracks.

"Jingfei," I said. Hell, I even smiled. The girl whose name meant Quiet Not had plenty of gumption. She wasn't trying to escape Whip Watson. She was going after the girls, her friends—or maybe even they was just acquaintances—that Candy Crutchfield had woman-napped.

Peach Fuzz was already moving. "I'm a-goin' after her," he said, and I knowed that he did not mean Jingfei. I also knowed that I was, and that meant tagging along with him. Besides, it suddenly struck me that Peach Fuzz wasn't all that bad of a sort, and that maybe he could get his Bonnie, and I could get Jingfei, and we could get away from Whip Watson, Candy Crutchfield, Calico, and the whole Mojave Desert. Hide out. Forget all about Lucky Ben Wong, even if I had give him my word that I'd bring Jingfei to him. Settle somewhere peaceable. Tombstone, Arizona, maybe. I'd heard it remained a top place for a gambler.

As Peach Fuzz got into the wagon, and put his hand on the brake, I put both my hands on the harness between them two big gray horses, and watched his eyes get rid of the tears and harden over with the look of the reaper, or maybe of a lovesick fool. His right hand picked up that horsewhip.

"Get some sense, boy," I told him. "You got any water?"

The whip rose.

"You run these horses to death, and you'll never find Jing—I mean, Bonnie."

The whip reared back.

"And if Whip catches us . . ."

He lowered the whip. I pointed to the Conestoga.

"It'll take a while before our *friends* have gathered the horses Crutchfield run off," I said. "We got some time. We can take some oats from the wagon, water. Just enough to get by."

His head nodded like I was making sense, and, for once, I was. Then he said, "Do you know where they's a-headin'?"

"No. But there's too many of them so they can't hide their trail."

Course, that also meant that, once they got them horses, Whip Watson and company could follow us real easily. Maybe he already had, come to think on things. I mean, if Peach Fuzz and I had pursued the bad guys in a Columbus carriage, they was two more of them conveyances back at the camp. Course, if Whip happened to catch up with us, I could just tell him that we was after that women-napping woman Candy Crutchfield, and he'd likely believe me. As long as Peach Fuzz didn't blurt out that he was in love with a gal promised to some idiot in Calico.

"You know what Whip will do to you if he finds out you're sweet on one of his girls," I told Peach Fuzz as I brought a sack of grain and dropped it in our buggy.

Peach Fuzz, pretty strong for a kid his size, slung over a bladder of water. "I remember Conrad," he said, and returned to the big wagon.

Wished to hell I could forget Conrad.

As we come back with another haul, I told Peach Fuzz: "Best thing would be for you to let me go, you stay behind, forget all about that girl." On account that the way I had things figured, I could likely catch up with Jingfei on a hard-blowing black mare that had already covered a lot of ground, then load that Chinese princess in the buggy, and skedaddle. That plan wouldn't likely get me killed. But if I had to go with Peach Fuzz and try to sneak a girl named Bonnie out of a camp run by the notorious Candy Crutchfield, whoever the hell she was, and with maybe thirty or forty gunmen . . . well . . . that plan didn't appeal much to me.

Peach Fuzz didn't answer. He was climbing into

the driver's seat, and I had the brains this time to get right beside him.

I pointed.

"Just follow the tracks. Steady pace. The horses have had a rest, and they shouldn't be as winded as the ones we're after. You don't drive like a lunatic, we can catch up with Jingfei, then Crutchfield and your Bonnie."

He was gripping the whip in his left hand, and staring at me like he couldn't believe what I'd said. He wet his lips after a spell and said, "You sound like you know what you're doin'."

I grunted. Not many folks ever said that about me.

"I've had some experience," I told him.

"Chasin' bandits?" he asked.

"Being chased," I answered.

Hazel-eyed Bonnie Little was five feet, four inches tall, twenty-two years of age, fair-skinned, honorable, brown-haired, modest, liked the opera, grew up as a Methodist in Fort Smith, Arkansas, amiable, her pa had gotten struck by lightning and her ma had succumb to diphtheria, had never been married, was a virgin, and only wanted to live a respectable life and be remembered as an ornament to society.

"She told you all that?" I asked when Peach Fuzz finally stopped long enough to suck in some oxygen.

He shrugged. "Some of it was in the *Matrimonial News* advertisement she showed me."

"Even the virgin part?"

He glared at me. "That," he said stiffly, "she mentioned to me."

"No takers?" I asked.

Peach Fuzz glared harder.

"From the ad?" I explained.

He shrugged. "Rogers Canfield."

"I see."

I didn't, not really, but Peach Fuzz flicked the lines, and I glanced out behind us. Only dust I saw was our own, so I turned back and looked at the tails of the two grays. Peach Fuzz was talking again.

"Canfield says that he's found the right man for Bonnie, but he ain't. Do you think a whiskey drummer is right for a girl like my Bonnie?" I hadn't even finished my shrug when Peach Fuzz said, "Of course, he ain't right. Whiskey drummers don't like the opera, do they?"

Which got me to singing:

> *"I'm a hardy sailor, too;*
> *I've a vessel and a crew*
> *When it doesn't blow a gale*
> *I can reef a little sail.*
> *I never go below*
> *And I generally know*
> *The weather from the lee,*
> *And I'm never sick at sea."*

But all that did was get Peach Fuzz to glaring again, so I stopped singing. Hadn't seen many operas, but one time in Leadville, me and Big Tim Pruett had snuck into the opera house to see *Our Island Home,* and I sure liked that pirate chief named Captain Bang.

"She don't love him," Peach Fuzz told me.

"Hell." It was my turn to glare at him. "She ain't even met the guy."

"That's right. But she has met me."

I shrugged, about all I could do in a conversation with Peach Fuzz, settled back into that comfortable, clean, shiny, well-waxed leather.

"Besides," Peach Fuzz said, "she comes with her own dowry."

I give him one of my looks that wasn't a shrug.

"Five hundred dollars," he said, and flicked the lines again.

"Not too fast," I told him. Then I asked, "She's bringing five hundred dollars with her?"

"In a money belt. Beneath her corset."

Which got me to thinking scandalous thoughts that maybe Bonnie wasn't no virgin no more. As Peach Fuzz was holding that buggy whip, I didn't voice my thoughts. His glares was bad enough.

"She paid her own expenses to get to Prescott, right?" I asked.

He didn't glare, just give me a funny look.

"And Rogers Canfield said he'd pick up the rest of the expenses from Prescott to Calico. As a marriage present." That I didn't ask. Just said it like I knowed it was true, because I did know it.

"Who are you?" Peach Fuzz asked.

"Micah Bishop," I said.

"Did Bonnie tell you all this, too?"

I laughed. Peach Fuzz was all right as a buggy driver and Columbus-carriage-seat-waxer, and maybe even as a rescuer of damsels that is distressed by Candy Crutchfields, but he weren't much when it come to brains. And that's coming from me.

"Never even seen her, Peach—son."

"I ain't your son."

"Hope not. I ain't that old."

I waited for him to tell me his name, or whatever name he was using this summer, but he didn't. Just glared some more, and kept the Percherons and the Columbus carriage moving at a good but not too taxing pace.

Maybe I've mentioned this before, but if not, let me put it down in pencil that I ain't one much for planning. It's kind of like how you play poker some-times, let the cards fall where they fall. As we drove deeper into the Mojave and as that sun climbed up higher and got real hotter, I taken a drink from a pot we'd found in the Conestoga and had filled it with water from the barrel, and let Peach Fuzz have a drink, and then I looked at Peach Fuzz's waist.

"Where's your gun?" I asked him.

He shrugged. "I was a-fryin' up a mess of bacon when they hit us. Hadn't gotten around to gettin' full dressed."

"You got any weapon?"

"Barlow knife." He tapped his trousers' mule-ear pockets.

"You planned on rescuing Bonnie from thirty or forty gunmen with a pocketknife?"

He shrugged. That boy was smitten.

Me? I'd left that Winchester rifle with Zeke. So I had a Colt Peacemaker with a shell belt full of bullets, and a Spiller & Burr with a pouch of caps and paper cartridges. No long guns. Not a hell of a lot of water. No food, unless the two Percherons didn't mind us sharing their grain. I pushed my hat up. Well, the buggy would seat Bonnie and Jingfei.

All we had to do was get them, and go for a Sunday drive in a fine carriage.

"Stop," I said.

He was perfecting his glares.

"Damn it," I said, "stop this buggy."

Could tell he didn't cotton to the idea, but he tugged on the lines, and the Percherons was glad to take a rest. I pointed. Peach Fuzz stared. Ahead of us was a canyon, a right tight fit, but we could make it.

Peach Fuzz leaned out, looked at the path, then snapped at me, "Them tracks lead right into that canyon."

"That's what Custer said," I barked back, even though I doubted if Custer had said anything like that, but my words sank through Peach Fuzz's thick skull.

"Oh." Right then, he looked like a boy. He said, "You reckon that's an ambush?"

"It'd make sense." I pointed at all them rocks, the holes, the cracks. "You put ten, twelve men with repeating rifles"—I recollected the man I'd shot dead had been armed with a Spencer—"that's all Crutchfield would need to stop a whole posse." Or, I thought, Whip Watson and the boys.

"Who the hell is this Candy Crutchfield fellow?"

"Ain't a fellow, I said. He's a woman." I rubbed the stubble on my chin. "Yeah. Not hiding their tracks, just racing their horses. Makes sense. Yeah, if I was wanting to ambush Whip Watson, that's what I'd do." Pointed again at the canyon walls. "Just sit up in them rocks, and wait."

Problem was, somebody had thought of something different. Because almost as soon as them words had left my mouth, I heard a rifle being cocked right behind me and Peach Fuzz and the Columbus carriage and the two gray Percherons. That's when I recalled the dead shrubs and little sinkhole we'd passed right on our right.

A voice said, "Step out of that buggy, you two, or I'll blow you both to hell."

CHAPTER THIRTEEN

Luckily, I recognized the voice, and I reached over to stop Peach Fuzz from trying to get that Barlow knife out of his pants pocket, which would have taken quite a spell since his pants was too tight and he was sitting down.

"Jingfei," I said. "It's me."

She said, "I said get down."

Loved her voice. It had a hint of the Oriental princess that she was, but unlike her betrothed, Lucky Ben Wong, she didn't try to fool nobody by speaking that broken English. She spoke plain.

"Now," she said.

We got down. Hands up. Turned around real slow.

The porcelain face softened as she recognized me. Didn't lower the rifle, though. Appeared to be studying us, and I hoped that Peach Fuzz wasn't doing no more glaring.

Instead, he asked, "Where's Whip's horse?"

She answered, "Dead."

That was Whip's rifle she was holding. Whip's two canteens hung over her left shoulder.

Peach Fuzz shook his head. "Whip'll be mad."

She said something rather indelicate about what Whip could do.

"You shouldn't speak like that," Peach Fuzz said. "It ain't a-fittin' for—"

"Shut the hell up!" me and Jingfei both told Peach Fuzz, and for once, he complied.

"Back away from the buggy," she said. "I'll be taking it."

I backed, but said, "What about us?"

"Watson'll come along."

Even I didn't fancy having to explain to our temperamental boss how a mail-order bride from Trinidad, Colorado, by way of the Orient, had gotten the jump on me and Peach Fuzz and had stole his Columbus carriage after she had ridden Whip's fine mare to death.

So I pointed toward the canyon pass. "You try to go through that," I said, "and you'll get killed."

She said, "I already rode through it, then that black died, and I walked back through it." She motioned with the Winchester's barrel that she was tiring of our conversation. "And I'm still alive."

"You're going to get Bonnie, ain't you?"

When Peach Fuzz said that, his voice all whiny like the love-struck boy he was, I seen a softening in Jingfei's face. She took her eyes off me, and locked on Peach Fuzz, and she told him, "You're a nice boy. Bonnie really likes you." Her head bobbed. "Yes. I'm going after Bonnie and all the others." She turned back to me. "This isn't what we agreed to."

Didn't know what she meant, exactly, but I wasn't sure about nothing, so as I eased away from the carriage, and Peach Fuzz reluctantly came with me, and Jingfei moved cautiously toward the buggy, I said, "Rogers Canfield's dead."

That stopped her, and she and Peach Fuzz both echoed, "What?"

"Watson killed him," I told them. "It was . . . er . . . self-defense. Aw, hell, Whip shot him down like a dog."

"He was a dog," Peach Fuzz said, and I couldn't dispute that sentiment. "I told Bonnie he was a dog."

"It doesn't matter," Jingfei said. "My Lucky Ben Wong will be waiting for me."

"It matters to me," Peach Fuzz said, "because that drummer ain't fit to get hitched to my Bonnie."

Jingfei was trying to figure out how to get into the carriage without taking the rifle off me, 'cause she was smart. I mean smart because she didn't trust me. She did manage to sling Whip's two canteens into the back, but that was about all she could do for the moment.

"That carriage," I pointed out, "won't hold all the girls bound for Calico."

"Six will fit," she said, still trying to figure out how to get into that buggy.

"There are twenty-four others," I told her. She give me a look I can't quite describe, and I could feel Peach Fuzz's eyes boring into me. I gestured south. "Plus the twelve you left back in Whip's camp."

"Eleven," she corrected, which was another reason I admired Jingfei so. She could do ciphering real well. I'd forgot to take her out of the equation of the number of mail-order brides back yonder.

"Candy Crutchfield," I said, and explained to her, "the gal who led the attack on your camp and made off with six of your pals. She struck a deal with Rogers Canfield, too."

She didn't care for none of what I was saying, but Peach Fuzz appeared interested because he was asking things like "What?" and "Why?" . . . but Jingfei had leaped into the carriage while I was trying to talk some sense into her, and she done it real graceful, slicker than I can deal from the bottom of a deck. She cradled Whip's rifle in her lap, the barrel still pointed at my direction, and her hand that wasn't on Whip's Winchester reached for the brake.

So I sighed. "You need a plan," I told her.

Which stopped her. Now she give me the look that suggested that she really thought I had a plan, but that's on account that as a professional card sharp, I know how to bluff.

"Get in," she told both of us.

This time, Jingfei drove, I rode shotgun, though I didn't have a shotgun and Jingfei wouldn't let me hold Whip's rifle, but I did have my two revolvers holstered on my hips. Peach Fuzz bounced around in the big backseat. His Barlow knife remained inside his trousers pocket.

Course, I bit my lip, ground my teeth, and sweated a whole lot when we rode through that narrow pass, still thinking that would be a right handy spot for an ambush, but we cleared the walls, and the sun was blazing, and we just kept trotting along.

"Easy pace." I instructed Jingfei the same as I'd told Peach Fuzz how to drive. "These are the only horses we got."

An hour or two later, I made Jingfei stop to give the two grays a breather, and, once they'd cooled down, made Peach Fuzz fill his hat with some water for the horses.

"Why don't you use your own hat?" he snapped.

"Because mine's full of holes," I reminded him.

As the Percherons drunk their fill, I unbuckled my rig with the Spiller & Burr and tossed it into the backseat, and settled back down on the comfortable but rather dusty leather.

"What's your plan?" Jingfei asked.

I took off my hat to wipe my brow, but I wasn't sweating because I was afraid of Jingfei. I mean, the temperature had to be approaching a hundred degrees.

"Well . . ." Even Peach Fuzz looked over the horses, waiting to hear my plan. "Need to see how they've set up their camp. How many sentries they got posted. Where the horses are picketed. Lay of the land. Where the girls are. Things like that."

Peach Fuzz moved to the other horse. Jingfei stepped out of the carriage and studied our back trail. Which was fine with me, as I now had to figure out just what in the hell we was going to do once we caught up with Candy Crutchfield—other than get ourselves killed. Jingfei's joining our pursuit did give us an extra gun. Two revolvers—one of them an old cap-and-ball that was hard to cock and prone to misfires—a new Colt and a Winchester. Up against twenty, thirty, forty men.

"What if they just keep riding?" Peach Fuzz put his waterlogged hat on his head, and moved around the team, back toward the carriage. "I mean what if they just ride all the way to Calico?"

"Can't," I said. "It's still too far." Jingfei climbed aboard. "Especially hot as it is, dry as it is."

"What's this?" Peach Fuzz asked as he crawled into his seat.

I told him it was a .36-caliber Spiller & Burr and I was loaning it to him until all this was over.

He said, "This thing's apt to blow my hand off. Can't I have the Colt?"

Jingfei's whipping of the horses choked down my cussing.

Thirty minutes later, Jingfei was yanking hard on the lines, and as soon as the team stopped, she and I and Peach Fuzz was jumping to the dirt, and looking back.

"Sounded like gunfire," Peach Fuzz said, and he decided that now might not be a time to be too particular about what weapons he'd been loaned, so he buckled on my belt that I'd loaned him.

"Because it was gunfire," Jingfei said. She pushed her hair over her shoulder.

Another cannonade reached us, muffled, pretty far back I'd reckon, but close enough so that we could hear. That didn't please me none. I bit my bottom lip again, loosened my bandanna and used it to mop the sweat off my face, then I took off my hat, tossed it onto the seat, and combed my hair with my fingers.

"We'd better go," I said.

Jingfei looked at me. "Who cut your hair?"

I blinked. "Ma'am?"

"You're wearing new clothes, too. And that's a new—well, it was a new—hat."

"Yes'm," I said. "I bought new duds when I was in Calico."

We got back into the buggy, and the Percherons continued taking us down the trail.

"You looked awful when Maud found you that night." She set the whip back in its holder, kept the two grays at the right pace, though they was starting to tire.

I said, "Maud?" I'd always figured it was Whip Watson who'd found me.

"Yes." Her voice was curt, sad, and she brought up two of those long, wonderful fingers and dabbed at the tear rolling down her perfect face.

That's when I recollected poor Maud Fenstermacher, she of the broken neck who'd gotten pitched out of the overturning Conestoga on account of that lying rapscallion Jürgen Baader who claimed to be a lawman drawing three hundred dollars a month in Calico. I ground my teeth, clenched my right fist.

Maud, Jingfei told me, had gone out to answer nature's call at night when she found my body lying against some rocks. She called out to the guards, but they figured me dead, and went through my pockets to see if I had anything of value. Then she started screaming at the two men, one of whom was the late Conrad and the other who, Jingfei announced, had gotten mortal shot through both lungs during Candy Crutchfield's attack. Maud had called her guards vermin and fiends and ghouls, which they was. Those shouts had drawed Juan Pedro and Whip Watson out to the rocks. It had also drawed Jingfei.

Thing like that causes a fellow to stop and

ponder. My life had been saved because a gal had to go relieve herself.

Then I asked, "They sent guards when you had to pee or—"

She cut me off. "Always."

The way things worked, Jingfei said, was that the women in the train were allowed to do their business only one at a time. With one or two guards. For their own protection, Whip Watson said, but Jingfei knew better. It was so they couldn't escape. That's where Jingfei had been and what she'd been doing when I'd first seen her and she come and finished cooking our supper that night at Whip's camp.

Sudden-like, it struck me that I hadn't seen Jingfei wash her hands or nothing like that before she went to them pots.

My stomach churned about, but that food was long gone, and I hadn't gotten sick, so I said, "Do you think Whip was expecting Crutchfield to attack?"

"No," she answered. "He was making sure we didn't run off."

"But you've got a contract," I said. "You're betrothed to Lucky Ben Wong."

She turned, her eyes hard, boring right through me, and I realized I'd done blown any bluff I might have been able to try. "How did you know that?" she demanded.

I took off my hat, pointed to my hair.

She grinned. Honest to goodness, she grinned, and shook her head, and slowed the horses down a mite because she knowed something about horses herself, and those Percherons needed another breather. A couple minutes later, we found a shady spot, protected by some peaks of red spires, and she reined in, set the brake. She wanted to rest the horses.

And talk.

"Is he a good man?" she asked.

Hell, I'd only knowed him for a few hours. I know in a lot of towns, the barber knows everyone and everybody knows him, but that was my first visit to Calico and my first meeting with Lucky Ben Wong.

"Seems like," I said, and I meant it, too. I wondered if Jingfei partook of opium.

Then I realized that I had actually met Lucky Ben Wong in the flesh. He had cut my hair. Fixed my bath. Jingfei hadn't even met the guy in person, and she was gonna wed him.

I nodded. Made up my mind. Some folks, you know almost instantly. "Yeah," I said softly. "Lucky Ben Wong's a good man. A real good man."

"Tell me," she said, "about Rogers Canfield."

Who wasn't good at all. A dark, black-hearted son of a bitch, but all I told Jingfei was, "He's dead."

"Yes," she said. "You said that already. Killed by Whip Watson."

After my head nodded again, I told her everything I knowed.

"Canfield hired Candy Crutchfield," I said, and felt Peach Fuzz lean forward and rest his arms on the backs of our seats so he could hear better. "She's bringing in twenty-four brides herself. She and Canfield worked out some deal where Canfield was supposed to make sure Whip and me and Guttersnipe Gary—"

"Where is Guttersnipe Gary?" Peach Fuzz interrupted. "Y'all leave him back in Calico?"

"Yeah," I answered. "Dead."

"Guttersnipe Gary?" Peach Fuzz's head shook. "I can't believe he could get kilt."

"Shut up," Jingfei said, and, damn right, she was Quiet Not. Peach Fuzz got quiet. Jingfei told me to keep on talking.

So I told her what had happened. How two men had tried to gun me down in her betrothed's bath house, but that I had outshot both of them, and saved Lucky Ben Wong's life. I didn't tell her that Lucky Ben Wong lived in a house made of empty cans of coal oil, and found it hard to picture a goddess like Jingfei living in such filth. Then I told her, and Peach Fuzz, how Guttersnipe Gary had sent one of his two killers to the bad place, and how I had avenged Guttersnipe Gary's death with a pistol shot at seventy-seven yards. I told her how Whip Watson had dispatched his two killers, and then how we'd caught up with Rogers Canfield. I mentioned how Whip had gotten Canfield to confess his arrangement with Candy Crutchfield, and then how Whip Watson had shot him dead.

Then we was all silent. Peach Fuzz passed one of Whip's canteens. We each taken a drink, then that canteen was dry. I handed it back to Peach Fuzz. "How we doing on water?"

He picked up Whip's other canteen. "This one's 'bout empty, too," he said. "That pot's empty. Got the bladder, though, and a gourd." He steered us back to our original conversation. "But I don't get all this. If Candy Crutchfield was a-bringin' in her own brides, they'd have their own menfolk. Ain't like that Lucky Ben fellow wants to marry some other girl, and it ain't that that peckerwood of a drummer. . . ." He stopped talking.

I pulled my now ruined six-dollar hat back on my

head. "I ain't figured everything out yet myself," I said, and looked back at Jingfei. "But you know something."

She stared. Quiet Not got suddenly quiet.

"Back outside that canyon passage," I reminded her, "you said, 'This isn't what we agreed to.'" She'd make a savvy card player herself, because her porcelain face remained stone. Didn't even blink. "My guess is that you realized Rogers Canfield and Whip Watson wasn't exactly honest about your arrangements."

"We have signed contracts," she said.

"I warrant so do the girls Candy Crutchfield's hauling to Calico."

"*If* she has mail-order brides," Jingfei said. "She could be lying."

She wasn't. I knowed that because Candy Crutchfield stepped from behind a one of them tall red rocks, armed with a new Marlin repeater, and she said, "Oh, I ain't lyin', girl. And I reckon I gots me one other wench to bring to Calico."

CHAPTER FOURTEEN

She appeared to be on the short side, maybe five-foot tall, and that's in them big stovepipe boots with two-inch heels that she wore. Certainly, she didn't dress like Jingfei, and I'd hate to picture her in a gold-trimmed *changyi*. What she wore was patched Army-issue blue trousers that was too big, and she wasn't exactly on the skinny side, neither, held up by the dirty canvas suspenders and the gun belt around her waist that holstered an ivory-handled Schofield. A six-button bib-front shirt, red and black checked, one nasty-looking bandanna, and a linen duster that blowed behind her because the wind had started blowing. Her black slouch hat looked worser than the one I'd left behind in Calico.

At first, I thought she had some giant boil or cyst on her cheek, but then she turned her head a mite and spit, and the wind blowed brown tobacco juice all over the tan vest of the fellow who stood behind her. He didn't complain none, and I couldn't blame him.

I'd knowed some whores who dipped snuff, but

never a lady who chawed Starr Navy tobacco by the crate-load. Not that I'd ever mistook Candy Crutchfield for a lady.

That's 'cause Candy Crutchfield was one mean-looking woman. Her dark eyes was too close to-gether, her face scarred and dirty, her nose swole up and crooked from having been punched too many times. She had greasy brown hair, streaked with gray, that touched her dirty bandanna.

"So you're the Celestial queen Canfield spoke 'bout so much." Candy Crutchfield stopped to chew her tobacco some more. Tan Vest moved to the other side of her. "Reckon I see why. You's real purty. Be a fine addition to The Palace of Calico."

While she was admiring Jingfei's beauty, I counted the men who stood behind her. Seven of them, a hard lot of hard rocks. Heard some laugh-ter behind me that I knowed wasn't coming from Peach Fuzz, and I figured there'd be two or four men back of us, too. Too many for me to take, so I kept my hands so Candy Crutchfield would see that I wasn't planning on trying nothing. Trying nothing but staying alive.

"Real purty rig you got there, too." Crutchfield spit tobacco juice that didn't hit nobody. She trained them beady eyes of hers on me. "Last I saw, we had commanded two of Whip's wagons. One didn't make it up the hill."

I guessed she was asking me what had happened. I said, "It wrecked."

"And Mal?"

My expression must have told her I was trying to say, *Who the hell is Mal?*

"One of my boys. Bragged how he could ride an

ox and get that prairie schooner movin' like the Pony Express."

Last I'd seen of Mal he'd been rolling down that hill.

"He lied," I said.

She nodded matter-of-factly. "Figured. The girls in that prairie schooner all right?"

"They're all dead," Jingfei answered. "Thanks to you."

Crutchfield's eyes left me and sized up Jingfei. "Whip Watson's a wonder with a whip," Crutchfield said, "but I skin with somethin' better." She braced the Marlin's stock against her belly, kept the barrel in our general direction, and moved her left hand toward the blowing tails of the duster, so I could see that big, bone-handled knife sticking out of a sheath that I hadn't seen before. If the blade was anywhere near the size of the handle, I'd hate to get cut by it.

"I skint buffalo. Skint bloatin' cow carcasses. Skunks. Beavers. Coyot's. Wolves. Fish. Dogs. Cats. An' I skint men and women, black, white, red, brown. Skinnin' an uppity yellow-skinned bitch with a big mouth wouldn't bother me at all."

Brave man that I am, I turned Candy Crutchfield's attention back to me. Hooked my thumb back toward the south and said, "Whip Watson'll be coming this way right soon."

She laughed. Spit. Brought her left hand back to the Marlin. "Nah," she said. "He can't. He's dead."

Reckon me and Peach Fuzz and Jingfei all blinked at the same time. Which got Candy Crutchfield cackling so hard she liked to have swallowed her tobacco, which would have made her sicker than the dirty dog she was. But she didn't, just turned her head the other way and spit more brown juice that this time landed on Tan Vest's right pants leg. Some of the boys sniggered at Tan Vest's luck, and I might have too had I any saliva in my mouth to do any sniggering.

Jingfei whispered, "The gunshots we heard."

"That's right." Candy Crutchfield had a good set of ears. I'd barely heard Jingfei myself, and Crutchfield stood about ten yards in front of us. "I left a dozen of the boys back at that pass."

The pass! The one I'd warned Jingfei and Peach Fuzz about. "I told you!" I exclaimed. "Said that was a perfect place to set up an ambush."

"And you was right, iffen it's the same place I'm talkin' 'bout."

Had to be. I was about to describe the canyon, but Peach Fuzz said, "But how come we got through?"

With a snort, Crutchfield turned around, and Tan Vest backed up and over quite a ways, but this time the woman didn't spit. Started to, but stopped, and wiped her mouth with the back of her left hand, keeping her right on that big rifle. "I ain't no fool," she said. Had to stop, to spit, but the juice just went down in front of her own boots on account that the wind had died down. "And my boys ain't idiots, neither." She turned, looked at some of her boys, reconsidered her thought as she spotted Tan Vest, and added, a bit softer and with less boast. "Most of 'em, anyhow. Nah, the boys had orders to kill Whip Watson and his men. Not a China princess and her two servants on a little picnic ride. They let y'all pass. Good thing, too. I'da shot 'em all dead iffen they was to harm a hair on her precious head. So Whip and his lot is feedin' buzzards. Verne should be bringin' word to me shortly. Told the rest of the boys to head out to Calico, get things ready for us. No idiots ride with me. I ain't like the late Whip Watson."

The wind picked up again. Crutchfield stepped back. She motioned at me and Peach Fuzz.

"Speaking of idiots, step down off that buggy."

"What for?" Peach Fuzz said.

I whispered to Peach Fuzz, "Idiot."

Candy said, "So I can kill you."

Peach Fuzz gasped and sank back into his chair. My stomach did some teetering and some tottering. Jingfei just stared real hard, her porcelain face granite, her hands still on that Winchester in her lap, which, to my reckoning, Candy and her idiot boys hadn't spotted yet.

"I don't wants to get blood and brains on 'em leather seats," Crutchfield said. "Step off. Act like men."

Peach Fuzz was about to stutter, or, since I couldn't see him, was about to pull that Spiller & Burr and likely get hisself and Jingfei and me killed. So I leaned forward, smiling my best, warmest smile, and said, "You don't want to kill us. You have need of men like me." Even jerked my thumb toward Peach Fuzz. "And him."

"I don't need no fools," she said. "That's why I let Mal try that damned fool stunt."

"How many men do you have?" I asked.

"Enough."

"You lost more than Mal back at Whip Watson's camp."

"Good. Don't have to pay 'em nothin'."

"I wouldn't be surprised," I said, "if you lost some more at that pass."

She spit. "Balderdash."

"What," I asked, "if your boys didn't hold off Whip and his men? You thought about that?"

"Don't need to."

"Don't you?" Now Jingfei was staring at me, with that *do-you-know-what-the-hell-you're-doing?* kind of look.

I didn't, but I told Crutchfield, gesturing again toward Peach Fuzz, "Me and him, we deserted Whip. Woman-napped the Chinese princess here." Now Jingfei was really giving me an evil eye.

She snorted—Crutchfield, not Jingfei, who was too ladylike to snort or fart or chew tobacco or anything like that except to answer nature's call with two armed guards—and spit out more juice. "You're borin' me, and I want to get back to camp, have me some whiskey, and do some celebratin'.."

"You think Whip Watson would just let us go on a . . . picnic?"

She brought the Marlin up, braced the stock tighter against her shoulder, and said, "Try not to bleed all over 'em leather seats."

My voice rose an octave or two, and I doubt if I sounded much like that thespian who'd played Captain Bang in *Our Island Home,* as I sang out, "You'll have need of every gun you can muster if Whip Watson ain't dead, and I'm real good."

By grab, I had killed that guy with the bandolier back during the fight at camp just a few hours earlier. And the fellow in Rogers Canfield's office over in Calico—blowed his sorry hide right out a second-story window. Not to mention Pink Shirt in China-town. Sure, I hadn't popped a cap on him, but I had been the last person down the ladder and that ladder did cause Pink Shirt's death. And I'd shot down a real ass named Sean Fenn in New Mexico

Territory. And also had killed that drover in Missouri and the idiot in the Indian Nations whose faces still gave me fits every now and then when I was trying to sleep. And I figured that I might have to kill another, perhaps two, maybe just one of those Percherons by accident, if I had to dive out of this Columbus carriage and pull the Colt and start blasting until I was blasted to Purgatory.

But I didn't have to shoot nobody. Yet. Because Candy Crutchfield was lowering the rifle, piddles of tobacco juice dripping over her thin lips, laughing, and shaking her head till tears flowed, cutting paths through the dirt on her face.

"You say you're good with a gun?" she finally managed.

"There are six dead assassins in Calico," I said. Which was true, even if I'd only killed one, two if you counted Pink Shirt.

Peach Fuzz picked the wrong time to speak up. "And I'm better than he is!" he shouted.

I don't believe she believed me or Peach Fuzz, but she turned and tossed the Marlin to Tan Vest. Then pointed a finger at me, or maybe it was Peach Fuzz.

"Then I tell you what, Mister . . . ?"

Nope, she was looking at me.

"Bishop," I said. "Micah Bishop. Wanted in New Mexico and Missouri and Texas and in the Western District of Arkansas Which Includes The Indian Territories."

"All right," she said, and she didn't bother asking Peach Fuzz his name. "I ain't had much fun lately, so here's the deal I'll make y'all whilst I'm waitin' on Verne. If one of y'all can kill Buster, just shoot him dead, then I'll let y'all live. Let y'all ride for me. Since Mal's dead."

"Promise?" Peach Fuzz asked from behind me.

"Candy Crutchfield's a man of her word," she said. "Which one of y'all wants the chance to shoot down Buster?" None of us moved, even when she added, "State of Nevada's put up a seventy-five dollar reward on him."

"You go," Peach Fuzz said, and give my shoulder a push. "You've got the newer revolver."

Course, I just sat there, till I seen Jingfei's finger slipping into the trigger guard on that Winchester and her thumb pressing on the rifle's hammer. Then I was out of that buggy, and taking off my hat, and dropping my right hand near—but not too close to—the butt of the new Colt I'd bought in Calico. I was praying that Buster was Tan Vest because he didn't appear to have no luck this day.

Tan Vest's name wasn't Buster.

Buster stepped from behind the horses that were being held by a fellow still wearing the remnants of what he had been issued in prison.

Buster looked to be about the size of the Percherons put together. Didn't wear no shirt, but it was a hot day, only a vest, and I seen bulging muscles I'd never seen on no man or no draft horse. He also had only one eye.

Problem was, he didn't have a patch over the other eye, the one that wasn't there no more. So I just found myself looking into that hole, and trying not to cringe, and not to be rude, and finally made myself look at the rest of him—so I wouldn't be staring at that eye that wasn't there no more.

He wore Levi's and fancy boots with big Mexican spurs with bigger Mexican rowels, and a porkpie hat. His long black hair blowed in the wind, and he was reaching down toward his waist, and I spied a brace of Colts, butt forward on both of his hips. And my hand was about to try for my own Colt, but hell, he wasn't reaching for his guns, he was tugging on the belt and buckle, and next thing I knowed those guns had dropped into the dirt, and Buster, still grinning, was making his way right for me.

My left hand pointed. "Put those guns on," I demanded.

"I won't waste a bullet on you, pig," he said.

Candy Crutchfield laughed, spit, and give me some advice. "Iffen I was you, Micah Bishop, I'd shoot Buster down right now."

Till that moment, I'd never know this about me. I'm a swindler and a cheat and a thief. I've killed men. I've broken a dozen or so Commandments. But I ain't never shot no unarmed man, especially an unarmed man with only one good eye. Even if that unarmed, one-eyed man had arms the size of telegraph poles and stood about a foot taller than me. Nope, I just stood there, watching Buster come, me still pointing at that gun belt he had dropped, and telling him, begging him to go arm hisself, and then he was right atop me, putting a ham of a hand on my left shoulder, practically pinning me to where I stood, and his right fist, more like a cannonball, slammed right into my belly.

Air whooshed out of my lungs, which begun trying to suck in some life out of the desert air, and I knowed I was vomiting, and gagging, and practically dying, and I felt Buster's big right fist drop to my holster. Something other than vomit fell by my feet. Buster was saying something—later Jingfei told me what he said was, "We'll settle this like men, with our fists," after he dropped my Colt—and then pushing me to the dirt.

Hitting the ground, I somehow managed to roll over, and was trying to get back to my feet. Well, my knees was on the ground, and so was my palms, even though my lungs still wasn't quite working the way they should.

That's when one-eyed Buster kicked me in the ribs, and I flew another ten feet.

Somebody yelled something, but all I heard was harps. Later, Jingfei said it was Peach Fuzz who was yelling something and what he was yelling was, "That ain't fair, Crutchfield. He's 'posed to kill 'im with his guns."

My lip, the one I'd busted when Lucky tossed me over his neck, started bleeding again. My arm, the one that was purple and black from my wrist to my elbow after that same wreck, throbbed. My ribs ached. My head rang. I couldn't see nothing. Then I knowed I was jerked to my feet, and that Buster had me in a bear hug, and maybe I was screaming, but I couldn't hear nothing, not even harps no more, just Candy Crutchfield muttering something.

Later, Tan Vest told me what Crutchfield said was, "Told you, Micah Bishop, you shoulda shot Buster dead whilst you had your chance."

I thought Buster might have given me a hernia, and that's no fun at all. Felt myself flying up in the air, then fell on some rocks and sand and cactus, and I just lay there. My eyes cleared at last, and I knowed I was about to die because my life was flashing right before my eyes like it's supposed to.

Only that flashing was stuck on just a few days ago, back in that canyon that separates Calico proper from East Calico's Chinatown. I was staring up at Paul With The Winchester, who was pointing his rifle at me, and I was focused on his one open eye.

Only, it wasn't Paul With The Winchester. It was Buster, who had picked up his Colt—no, it was my Colt—and had thumbed back the hammer, and was aiming and saying something.

Later, Candy Crutchfield told me what Buster was saying was, "I play by the rules. If I have to kill you with a gun, I'll do it. But it'll be your bullet. Not mine. Do you know how much a pack of ca'tridges cost in Calico?"

Only it wasn't Buster, yet it had to be, 'cause it wasn't Paul With The Winchester. I was staring up at his one eye that was open. Not because the other eye was closed so that Paul With The Winchester could sight down on me better. It was because Buster only had one eye.

I must be crazy, I thought, then corrected myself. *No, I must be dead.*

I was right. It wasn't Paul With The Winchester. It was Buster With My Colt, but it was happening just like it had happened with Paul With The Winchester. Because I was staring at that eye, Buster's gray eye (not the empty socket), and, just like it had happened with Paul With The Winchester, that eye just plain flat-out disappeared.

CHAPTER FIFTEEN

Back when I was just a button and getting my knuckles slapped on a frequent and regular basis by the Sisters of Charity, that old blind crone, Rocío, kept telling me all about dreams. She'd say how dreams was God's way of letting you know about things, why they happened, even what was going to happen. Back then, I wondered how Sister Rocío could even dream since she couldn't even see me squirming on that pew a foot from her face. After she practically broke my knuckles—on account of how I'd spoke to her, disrespectful and unrepentant—she told me that John Milton dreamed when he was blind, and that she wasn't always blind and could recall how things looked when she was a younger nun, and that God, Jesus, Mary, Saint Lucy, and even Saint Simeon could do wonderful things.

I rarely dream. Oh, I'll have them here and there—like that really terrific one about Jingfei that I had on the trail back from Calico. But that sure wasn't God communicating with me and I was damned sure what I dreamed about with Jingfei wasn't going to happen no time in the future. But dreams with real meanings? Never happened. It's 'cause God and Jesus and Mary don't really care much to communicate with a fool like me. Can't blame them none.

But that day, after getting my arse whupped by Buster . . . I dreamed. It went something like this:

First, I'm standing in a desert of dunes, the wind blowing sand like grapeshot. No trees. Nothing but sand and dunes and the cloudless sky and the torrid sun. Behind me, I hear Jingfei's voice, only sounding a different kind of foreign:

> *"When I consider how my light is spent,*
> *Ere half my days, in this dark world and wide,*
> *And that one talent which is death to hide,*
> *Lodged with me useless, though my soul*
>   *more bent . . ."*

I turn, and there stands not Jingfei but some guy who is dressed in duds like them actors wore when me and Big Tim Pruett snuck into that opera house to watch some play—San Antonio, I think it was. Hell's fire, I couldn't make heads or tails out of nothing in *Henry IV, Part I,* though I must admit that I would have enjoyed drinking ale with that Falstaff fellow, even if he dressed in bed sheets and sandals. Big Tim Pruett liked that play real fine, even spoke some of the words before the actors themselves did. Me? I'd rather sing along with Captain Bang in *Our Island Home.*

"Mister Milton," I tell the guy, because I know he's John Milton despite the fact that I've never met the odd little poet that Sister Rocío admired so much, "what is going on here, sir?"

John Milton smiles and stares at me. I can't see his eyes, because he's wearing these oval-shaped spectacles with smoked glass over his blind eyes. "Pray tell, Micah," he says at last, "is this not that which you signed on to do?"

I tell him, "I didn't sign nothing with Whip Watson."

"But your word . . ." he says.

I say, "I've broken many, many times."

"Not this time." Them words didn't sound like John Milton at all. Or Jingfei. Sound just like the Word of God.

So I turn back because I hear that whip snapping in the air.

Ain't in the sand dunes no more. I'm standing on the main street in Calico, across from the Globe Chop House and Lucky Ben Wong's bathhouse of coal oil cans. The geography ain't quite right, but I don't say nothing. I'm just staring at Whip Watson.

He's standing maybe fifty yards down the street, slinging two blacksnake whips in each of his hands. And that's what they are, too, black snakes. I can see their fangs glistening in the sun, venom dropping off them, as they pop in the air. He don't say a word, just grins. I notice that he's wearing smoked oval spectacles, too.

So is Candy Crutchfield. She's right beside him, tossing her giant bone-handled knife up in the air, catching it easily, laughing.

Behind them isn't the mines or Miller's store or the carpenters working on that fancy building. Only thing I can see, and it's blocking out those brown hills, is a castle. I mean, one of them real storybook castles with spires and bell towers and round tables and knights and damsels from one of those foreign countries like Spain or Nova Scotia. A veritable palace. There's even a moat around the castle, which must be where the Calico Water Works Incorporated fills its water wagons. The drawbridge is down.

The palace is all aflame. Smoke blackens the sky. Mr. Milton is talking again:

> *"A Dungeon horrible, on all sides round*
> *As one great Furnace flam'd, yet from those flames*
> *No light, but rather darkness visible*
> *Serv'd only to discover sights of woe,*
> *Regions of sorrow, doleful shades, where peace*
> *And rest can never dwell, hope never comes*
> *That comes to all; but torture without end . . ."*

And I want to tell Mr. Milton to shut the hell up, but I can't take my eyes off this scene: a castle burning like Hell itself, Whip Watson whipping his twin snakes, Candy Crutchfield tossing that knife. Then here come the girls.

Maud Fenstermacher . . . Darlene Gould . . . Annie Mercer . . . Chris McGover . . . Molly Reid . . . Aibreann Halloran . . . Bonnie Little . . . and lots of girls I ain't ever met, old and young, fat and slim, pretty and plain, even a couple of red-haired twins. They're just walking down the street, every last one of them wearing a *changyi*. The snakes whip over their heads, but they don't even blink. Just walk between Whip Watson and Candy Crutchfield, and I start to step toward them, but can't move no more.

I look across the street, over the heads of Molly Reid and Bonnie Little, and I yell at Mr. Slater, and

Mr. McCoy, and Mr. Applewhite, and a bunch of other guys dressed in brown suits. I yell at them, "Don't just stand there. Help them poor, poor girls."

But they don't move, don't speak, don't lift a hand to help. Probably because they're all blind—even Peach Fuzz and Lucky Ben Wong, who are sitting on a hitching post in front of the rammed-earth adobe building of Mr. Slater's brother, the undertaker, who's licking his lips and rubbing his greedy palms together. I reckon the undertaker can see. I know everyone else, though, must be blind because all of them are wearing black wire spectacles with dark oval lenses.

I'm looking down the street again. Watching the girls cross the moat. Their embroidered silk robes commence to smoking even before they go through the palace gate, where they just erupt in flames, scream, and vanish into dust.

Maud Fenstermacher.

Darlene Gould.

Annie Mercer.

A fat, plain-looking, gray-haired grandma.

Chris McGover.

Molly Reid.

The redheaded twins.

Aibreann Halloran.

Bonnie Little.

I turn back to Whip Watson, and yell, "Whip! Stop them! Stop them!"

Whip's snarling, fanged whips snap in my face, and I fear they'll bite me, but they don't, because Whip has jerked back the black snakes, and I recollect how he can snap a horsefly off an ox's ear without touching the ear.

I hear Whip's voice:

> *"To reign is worth ambition though in Hell:*
> *Better to reign in Hell, than serve in Heav'n."*

I yell again, and then I see her, reach for her, but she just walks past me, 'cause she can't see me—as she's wearing those same spectacles—and can't hear me because, try as hard as I can, I can't say nothing, do nothing.

Jingfei is last in the line. Other girls are smoking on the bridge over the moat, turning into flames and dust at the gate.

Finally, my voice works, and I hear myself screaming, "Noooooooo!"

Jingfei is between Whip Watson and Candy Crutchfield, and Candy laughs, turns to me, and says, "You want this girl, do you, Micah?"

Suddenly, Candy's giant knife slashes forward, and I choke and gag and moan and cry as the knife slices through poor Jingfei's neck. Her body drops into flames and dust. Down the street, the castle explodes. Lucky Ben Wong's house and the chop house and Miller's store and everything else in Calico burst into flames. Even the rammed-earth adobe houses are burning.

Candy Crutchfield holds Jingfei's head by the hair. Blood pours out the bottom.

"Here she comes, Micah!" Candy yells, and she starts slinging poor Jingfei's head, holding it by the black hair, whipping it around like Whip Watson's blacksnake snakes. She rears back and sends Jingfei's dead head right toward me.

All I can do is watch as Jingfei's dead eyes open, and her mouth opens, and she has turned into a Mojave rattlesnake, with fangs that drip venom, heading right toward my face.

* * *

Which is when I woke up.

What I mean is that I jerked straight up, sitting, only I almost doubled over immediately because of the pain that went rifling through my entire body. Lungs burned, and I knew I was screaming, then falling to my side on something soft.

My six-dollar hat.

"Tsk, tsk, that was a fantastic dream you must have been having, my good man," a voice said.

Dream? Hell, that was a son-of-a-bitching nightmare. I preferred the kind of dream, rare that it is, the one I'd had with Jingfei a few nights back camping in the Mojave.

My eyes was shut tight, trying to seal off the pain, and while slowly the smarting lessened, it did not go away entirely. A rough hand lighted on my shoulder, and that man's voice said, "Roll over, kind sir, and permit me to examine your ribs," and I guess I obeyed.

I cringed at the touch.

"No," the voice said, "I stand by my earlier assessment. No ribs broken. Bruised, yes, and quite severely. But you shall live, Micah Bishop."

Eyes still shut, I groaned. "What about my hernia?"

The man chuckled. "No hernia, either." I heard a Lucifer spark, and moments later smelled that sweet scent of a pipe being smoked.

Still wasn't sure I could open my eyes, so I asked, "And my arm?"

The arm got lifted, and fingers pressed down on the inside of my forearm, and I groaned, damn near cried, before the arm dropped onto a bedroll.

"The arm?" the voice said. "Yes. That is one fat hematoma."

"Buster gave you a fair thrashing," the voice said. "But he was not his old self, God rest his soul. I thought you might have sustained some internal injuries, but you pissed in your pants, and I detected no blood."

I groaned and sniffed over my new $3.79 woolen britches, brown with the navy stripes and most of the duck blood and feathers cleaned off.

"You shall recover is my prognosis." The voice stopped to suck on his pipe stem. "Unless Candy kills you."

Which is when I remembered the nightmare, the fight with Buster, his one eye disappearing the way Paul With The Winchester's had, and I recognized the voice that was speaking to me.

Sounded deep, soothing, and real fine like he was talking Shakespeare but speaking English.

My eyes opened. It was dark. I was blind. That's what the dream was telling me. No, it was night. I saw the pipe, one of them fancy, yellow-ivory bowls with a whale engraved on it. Reminded me of Moby-Dick. There was a fire going right beside me. The voice leaned over, so I could get a better look at him.

He was the spitting image of John Milton. At least, the John Milton from my dreams, only he didn't wear bedsheets and sandals.

The hair was dark gray, with a few strands of black, the mustache and beard well groomed. He wore spectacles, but those lenses wasn't smoked. In fact, one didn't have no glass at all, just an empty hole. His eyes were the most beautiful blue I'd ever seen on a man. Like the oceans I'd always heard about, dreamed about.

Black suspenders over a real fine, real white—no dirt or dust or blood anywhere—shirt with a pleated front, pearl buttons, and a paper collar, from which hung a black silk string tie that needed tying.

Couldn't see nothing else about him.

One hand held the pipe, and the right one disappeared, come up with something, and then he moved closer to me again, and held out a little pill. Well, it wasn't little.

"Take this," he said.

"What is it?" I asked.

"It is a Tabloid, for the pain." Which was all he had to say. I fingered the pill.

"I need something to help me swallow it," I said.

His hand disappeared and he sat up a bit so he could pull something out of the back pocket on his pants. That something was a nickel-plated flask. "Will London gin work?" he asked.

It did.

When I woke up next time, it was still dark, and the fire was still going, and I heard some people beyond John Milton, who had shunned his sweet-smelling pipe for more gin.

I had figured that had been another dream, but, nope, he was still there, and I was still hurting, though not as bad. And not as dead.

"I ain't dead," I said, which got him to notice that I wasn't dead but was awake.

"Not yet," he said, and capped the flask, which went right back into his pants pocket.

"What happened?" I asked.

"What is the last thing you remember?" he asked.

First thing I thought of was Jingfei's snakehead coming right at my face, but that wasn't it. That had been God trying to tell me something. I said, "Buster's eye."

He tapped one of his own blue beauties. "Yes, it was a very fine shot indeed."

"Second fellow I knowed to get shot right through the eye," I said, trying to make myself remember to thank Peach Fuzz for saving my sorry hide.

John Milton shook his head. "No, that is not what happened, dear Micah," he said. "The bullet struck Buster here." He tapped the left side of his head. "From my vast experience, I would say the leaden bullet passed through the brain, causing massive cerebral hemorrhage, before exiting here." He poked the other side of his head. "Yet as said leaden bullet tore through the late Buster's skull it built up enough pressure to blow Buster's remaining eye right out of the socket." He pointed at his pretty blue eye.

"Oh."

I didn't want to think about even a cutthroat like Buster getting his eye blowed out like that. Something else seemed more pressing to me.

"How come I ain't dead?"

He tried to explain. "The deal Miss Crutchfield made was that if one of you shot Buster dead, all of you could live. Candy Crutchfield is a man of her word."

My head nodded a bit as though I understood.

"What about the palace or castle or whatever it was that was . . . ?"

Now he started to give me a look that suggested that I belonged in a house for the insane, but I shook my head a mite, and said, "No, that was a nightmare I was having. Where are we?"

"Cornfield Spring," he said, and hooked a thumb. "Other side of Providence."

"Rhode Island?" I asked, and have no idea where or when I'd ever heard of Providence, Rhode Island, because I've never been east of Sedalia, Missouri. Then again, I couldn't recollect ever reading John Milton except for that poem that Sister Rocío had recited all them years ago back in Santa Fe. Now, I will have you know that the lady from the fancy society has read some from *Paradise Lost,* and I recognized a lot of them words from my dream, but Folsom prison come later. Time I'm telling about, I was in the Mojave Desert. So God was speaking to me, I guess, in that dream. And John Milton was here, only not blind, and talking to me in a camp at Cornfield Spring.

He laughed. "The Providence Mountains." He handed me a gourd. "The mountains are not much, and the spring is not much, but it is water and it is wet, and I am fresh out of gin."

He was lying about the liquor, but not about the water. I drunk some.

When I handed the gourd back to him, I saw some folks approaching our fire. Just shadows at first. John Milton taken a swallow from the gourd, and set it on the dirt. "With your permission, kind sir, I will take your leave so that I might interview our chef and try to persuade him into allowing you to sample his extraordinary soup."

"Thank you, Mister Milton," I said.

He give me a real curious look. "The name is not Milton," he said. "It is Kent. Franklin Kent, M.D."

Then he was gone, heading toward another fire,

and the shadows appeared, and one of the shadows was Peach Fuzz.

"Thanks for shooting Buster for me," I told him.

Peach Fuzz's expression must have been a lot like the one Doc Kent had just give me. "I didn't kill that giant," Peach Fuzz said, and nodded to his left. "She did."

CHAPTER SIXTEEN

Her *changyi* was gone, replaced by a real fancy outfit, a silky copper-colored blouse—*moiré,* was what the cloth was called, which ain't Chinese but French (Doc Milton would inform me about all that the next morning over breakfast)—and black buttons down the front, puffed sleeves that tapered down to the wrist, the waist tied in the back to show off her slim waist, which then accented her small, firm breasts, which I recalled so fondly from my dream (not the one when she got her head chopped off, but the other one, the good one).

The skirt matched, too, and she wore black boots that must have taken hours to button.

I didn't see Whip's Winchester. Looked back to Peach Fuzz and didn't see his—*my*—Spiller & Burr .36, belt, holster, and pouches, neither.

Back to Jingfei, she must have washed her hair. Well, we were at Cornfield Spring, so there was water to be wasted on such luxuries, and her face looked clean and shiny. Her eyes, however, remained hard, even as she tried to smile at me.

"How do you feel?" she asked.

"Fine," I said, which was a lie as my ribs ached and my arm hurt. "Thanks to you."

She looked down.

"You find the rest of the girls?" I asked.

Her head lifted, and she nodded slightly. "They are well. Bonnie Little." Which got a sheepish grin from Peach Fuzz. "Adina Freberg. Donna Shaw. Betsan Priddy. And the twins, Caireann and Caoilainn Lannon."

With a groan, I managed to sit up, but kept my eyes shut tight because it still hurt to move. "Let me guess," I said. "The twins have red hair."

My eyes opened to find Peach Fuzz giving me the damnedest look.

"How the hell did you know that?" he sang out. "You ain't never laid eyes on them gals afore. Come all the way from Savannah, Georgia, they did. Boy-howdy!"

Jingfei wasn't there. I didn't see her standing beside Peach Fuzz no more. Then I smelled yucca and jerked my head to see her kneeling right beside me. Her face seemed to be full of fear, and she was reaching toward me before I jerked my head around. That startled her, and she retreated a mite.

"You were in pain," she said, and the hand reached for me again. I didn't make no sudden motions. She found my bruised right arm, then tugged up my shirt, and looked at those ribs, those bruises.

"I'm all right." Jutted my head toward where the doc had disappeared. "John Milton yonder says I just have fat hematomas. Nothing busted, inside or out." But I still ached.

Peach Fuzz looked behind me at the main campfire. "I thought his name was Franklin Kent," he said.

I didn't respond. Because Jingfei had put those

slim fingers under my chin, and brought my head up so she could stare, real mesmerizing, into my eyes. I didn't hurt so much. Her hair smelled of yucca.

"You are a brave man," she whispered. "I was wrong about you." The fingers moved up to my cheek, then slid across that stubble I had, and pushed a lock of sweaty, dirty hair out of my head. The hand fell to her side, and she stared at me.

"My Ben Wong does fine work as a barber, is it not so?"

My heart sank, but I managed not to sigh. "Does right well," I said, running my own fingers through my locks, even though it hurt just moving. "You should see where he lives and works."

She smiled, but her face—especially those eyes—hardened again, and her voice dropped to an urgent whisper. "We have escaped Whip Watson, but Candy Crutchfield is no better."

I puffed up my chest some, and ground my teeth so I wouldn't cry out in all the pain that act of buffoonery or bravery caused. "Well," I said when I thought I could speak, "we'll just have to escape here, too."

"You were right," she said.

Which ain't something I hear often.

"There are twenty-four other girls with this Crutchfield crone."

I liked how she said *crone*. Made me beam. The smile didn't last long, however, because I started doing some ciphering. "Did the fellows who ambushed Whip come in?"

Her head shook.

Peach Fuzz got bored trying to eavesdrop on all

we was discussing, so he come over and sat right beside me.

"Damn," he said, "that's one nasty looking bruise on your arm."

I pulled down my sleeve. "It's a big fat hematoma," I told him. "That's Doc Milton's verdict." Back to Jingfei. "Nobody come?"

Her head shook. "No bandits. And none of the other girls."

Done some remembering then. The boys Candy Crutchfield had sent to wipe out Whip and his crew was supposed to head on to Calico. Get things ready for Crutchfield. Least, that's what I thought she'd told us. I reckoned how that could mean that Candy's boys was supposed to haul the girls to Calico with them. But someone was supposed to bring word of their success to Candy Crutchfield.

"So Verne hasn't showed up yet?"

Both Jingfei and Peach Fuzz shaken their heads.

"How long was I out?"

"Not long," Jingfei said. "After I shot that evil ruffian through his head, they took our guns. They threw you into the back of the wagon—"

"Let me drive!" Peach Fuzz chimed in.

"And," Jingfei continued, "brought us across the desert, through a pass in the Providence Mountains, to this place."

Cornfield Spring. Though I doubted, come morning, if I'd find any fields of corn, this being the Mojave and not Missouri.

"The doctor . . ."

"John Milton." It was my turn to interrupt.

"I swear he told us his name was Franklin Kent," Peach Fuzz said.

Professional card player that I am, I read

Jingfei's face, which told me she was tired of getting interrupted by what she considered worthless bandying of words.

"Go on," I told her. Then ordered Peach Fuzz: "Let Jingfei talk."

"The doctor treated you," she said. "They let me help. In Manchuria, we have learned many ways to treat injuries such as those you sustained."

"Thank you." Didn't let on that I still hurt like hell, but she must have knowed that from all the groans and gasps I'd let out when I sat up.

She looked at the sky, and I lifted my head. God Almighty, the stars. They was brilliant. Not a cloud in the sky, just stars lighting up the desert evening. Almost as beautiful as Jingfei herself.

"We arrived at this camp shortly after nightfall. It is now two in the morning."

She could tell time from the stars and blow out a one-eyed man's eyeball by shooting him through his temples. Yes, Jingfei was a hell of a woman.

"Crutchfield show any concern?" I asked. "With no Verne? No word from her bushwhackers?"

"She cares not," Jingfei answered. "At least, that is how she tries to act. But our girls, and her girls, are not guarded. Not to the extent that Whip Watson guarded us. She has several men posted as sentries. Only Candy Crutchfield, Doctor Milton or Franklin, and six others remain in camp."

"How many guards then?" I asked. Because I think I'd have to count them as being in camp, too.

"Seventeen."

Which seemed to be real good counting.

"All right," I said, which didn't mean nothing.

Then Jingfei touched my shoulder, which didn't hurt at all, and stared deeply into my eyes. Her eyes weren't hard, her face wasn't concerned, she just spoke easily, like she trusted me. The only problem was what she said reminded me of what I'd told her, and what I'd told her had allowed me and Peach Fuzz to climb into that Columbus carriage and get ourselves into our current situation.

"So," Jingfei asked, "what is your plan?"

I tried not to give her the dumb look.

"How do we get out of here? With Bonnie and the twins and the others? And with the women who Candy Crutchfield wants to turn into slaves?"

I got saved by Candy Crutchfield. Saved from having to tell Jingfei the truth—that there wasn't no way anybody, even Whip Watson or the late Big Tim Pruett, who could get thirty (thirty-one if you counted Jingfei herself) girls out of a camp guarded by seventeen men who'd likely be situated all in them rocks around Cornfield Spring and in the Providence Mountains. Especially since I didn't know where we'd go if, by some miracle, we managed to get out. The Mojave's a real big desert, and the only town I knowed of was Calico.

Candy come real quiet for a bawdy woman who cussed and burped a lot. Sent tobacco juice into the fire, which sizzled, and knelt beside me and Jingfei, her joints cracking like the log Peach Fuzz had tossed into the flames.

"Mad Dog told me you was awake." She hooked her thumb toward the sawbones who might have been knowed as Franklin Kent but was the spitting image of John Milton from my dreams. He held a tin mug of soup in his hands.

Pushing the brim of her hat up, Candy Crutchfield inched closer to the fire.

"How you like them purty duds I got for you, honey?" She wasn't talking to me.

"They are nice," Jingfei said, but I could tell she didn't think too much of that real nice-looking outfit.

"Good." She cackled, rocking on her heels. "Can't have my Celestial Queen dressed in a robe all the time. You got to be fancy, look real fine, when we bring all y'all to Calico."

She stopped rocking long enough to move the tobacco to her other cheek, spit, and nodded toward the main camp. "You two get back yonder. So Zeke can keep an eye on y'all."

Peach Fuzz shot up, helped Jingfei to her feet. Both of them looked at me.

"Go on," I told them, like I was bossing things here.

They left. Doc Milton just stood like an oaf, holding that mug of my soup.

When they was out of earshot, I looked at Candy Crutchfield, who appeared even dirtier now. The log Peach Fuzz had added to our fire was burning good, and I could see the specks of tobacco between her brown, crooked teeth. "So . . ." I tried to make some polite conversation. "You got a Zeke riding with you, too."

"What the hell are you yackin' 'bout?"

"Zeke," I said, but she didn't give me no chance to explain.

"I'm a man of my word," she says, which was something everyone said about that woman. "Said if one of y'all kilt ol' Buster, I'd let y'all live." She snorted, the spit into the fire. "Course, I hadn't counted on my Celestial Princess killin' ol' Buster, but hell, that's the way the bullets blow folks' brains out. So you and that young whippersnapper with an eye for one of my gals deserted Whip Watson. Eh?"

"That's right." It was truthful. Sort of.

"You'll notice that I run things a mite different than Whip Watson." She tilted her head toward the main camp. "Whip, now he's what you might call a tyrant or a martinet. I'm more easygoin'. And I don't want my gals to feel no pressure. Puts stress on 'em. And if they's stressful, they don't look so fine. Causes warts it will, anxiety will. Which is why we've been campin' here. Letting them get washed and curried and feel all fine. Put some good clothes on their backs. I'll keep 'em out of the sun, much as possible in this pit of Hades where we're at. Take it easy. No anxiety. Pret' soon, we'll be ridin' down the streets of Calico."

I stared.

"Verne ain't back yet." She spit. "Which might mean somethin'. Might mean nothin'. I'm kina hopin' what it means is that he got kilt, and the rest of the boys I sent with 'im ain't got old coffee grounds for brains, so maybe after they'd kilt Whip and all his boys, they just done like I tol' 'em to do, make for Calico, but don't go to the town yet. Wait in one of 'em canyons outside of the digs. Till I gets there."

I said, for no good reason, "You think that's what happened?"

She shrugged.

I said, for no good reason, "You think you could keep your boys in a canyon when there's plenty of whiskey to be had in Calico?"

She answered with a pretty good reason. "If

they've got Whip Watson's eighteen survivin' brides
to entertain 'em, yep, I surely do."

Which made me sick.

"Seventeen," I corrected, just to be a smart aleck.
"Jingfei's with us."

"Lucky her," Candy said.

Which made me even sicker thinking about
those poor girls I'd never met, never even seen.

"I trust you, Micah Bishop," she said, and before
I could thank her for the sentiment and ask her
about my Colt or even my Spiller & Burr, which I'd
loaned Peach Fuzz, she added: "'bout as far as I
could throw you."

She knelt forward to spit into the fire. Wiped her
lips, straightened, said as if she'd read my mind, "I'll
let you have your shootin' irons when I knows for
sure. That I can really trust you." She turned, staring at the main campfire. "You like that China doll,
don't you?"

I shrugged. "She's all right. She ain't Geneviève."

"Who's that?"

Another shrug. "A girl I knowed." Didn't like the
smirk she was giving me, so I added, truthfully, "A
nun."

"Yeah, I bet she was a slice of heaven. Same as
that Chinese gal's gonna be."

It was my turn to point down to the wagons and
the folks around the campfire. "Whip Watson was
bringing in twenty-four mail-order brides," I said.

"So am I." She grinned her ugly teeth at me.
"Only I got thirty now. No, thirty-one."

My head started hurting worser than my arm
with the big fat hematoma and the ribs what was
bruised considerable but not busted and the back
that didn't have no hernia. I pinched the bridge of

my nose, shook my head, tried to shake off them aches, which was now throbbing like a bunch of kicking, wild, rank mustangs inside my skull.

"You had a contract with that *shadchan,* too, didn't you?"

"Who?"

"Ronen Kanievsky," I said, then shook my hurting head. "I mean Rogers Canfield."

"I guess you could say that. We shook hands and all, and ask anybody in California, and they'll let you know, plain and pure as gospel, that Candy Crutchfield's a man of her word."

"I don't get this," I said. "I don't understand nothing. You were bringing in mail-order brides and so was Whip. You ain't bringing them to the same grooms. I mean, last I heard, bigamy ain't allowed. This ain't Utah."

She slapped her knee. Dust flew off her britches. "That's real funny. I'm startin' to like you. Not trust you. Not yet no how. But like you. Utah. Damn, you're funny."

Didn't feel funny. Felt like hell. And sicker than a dog.

"Canfield's dead," I said. "Whip killed him."

She nodded again. "Saved me a lot of trouble. And sweat. Aimed to skin him alive and cut off his balls, the sorry cur. Then draw and quarter him, for old time's sake."

"Well . . ." Stopped. Thought. Rubbed my temples this time, but that didn't do no good. Then I said, "The contracts . . ."

"Was with," she finished, "the late Mister Canfield to provide a new home—husband, I reckon—for the girls once they lighted in Calico."

"Yes, but it ain't like the contracts died with him."

She smiled, only this time she wasn't finding nothing funny, and that smile sent a shiver up and down my backbone that hurt worser than a hernia.

"Oh, yeah," she said. "They did."

Still didn't have a clue as to what was going on, so I said, "So all that money . . ."

"Is about to double. For me. And my pard in Calico. And"—she gestured back to camp, and thirty-one mail-order brides—"my girls. Ever' last one of 'em."

Which is when I knew exactly what that dream meant, and that Sister Rocío had been right all along. God did speak to folks in dreams, even a heathen like me.

I whispered: "The Palace of Calico."

CHAPTER SEVENTEEN

I had grown sick of her wretched cackling, not to mention all that knee-slapping and tobacco-spitting.

"You ain't as stupid as I thought you was," she said. "Whip mentioned my Palace to you, I warrant."

My headache got real stressful by this point. Figured I might start sprouting warts. I could barely nod. "In passing," I said.

"It's gonna be the finest business in Calico," she said. "And make me richer than God."

I said, "A whorehouse."

She shook her head. "Nah, I prefer to call it a House of Pleasure. But The Palace of Calico does sound a lot fancier, and more pleasurable than Candy's Hog Ranch, which is the last brothel I owned. Actually, I called it Candy's Bagnio, but ever'body 'long Orinoco Creek called it Candy's Hog Ranch, and most of my whores and most of my clients was hogs, so it fit."

Another slap on her knee. "Hell, I sold out for three times what I'd started the damned bordello for. So they could call it anythin' in the book. Hell, they did."

More crowing.

Somehow, I managed to lift my head. I met her hard eyes. Tried not to sound like some sky pilot or temperance lecturer or no hard-shell Baptist when I said, "But these are good girls. How can you . . . a woman . . . how . . . ?"

She wagged a fat, grimy finger at me like she was scolding a schoolboy.

"How many whorehouses have you frequented, Micah Bishop?"

"Well . . ." I stuttered and stammered. "Maybe . . . a couple." Quickly adding, "Long time ago."

Don't think she thought I was being totally truthful, but she didn't argue none. Instead, she asked, "How many of 'em was run by a man?"

Which stopped me.

"Like I figgered," she said. "Men ain't got a monopoly on the market of marketin' a girl's goodies. But don't you worry none. We'll treat our gals mighty fine at The Palace of Calico. Charge customers Calico prices, and the girls'll get half of that, lessen expenses, naturally. Room and board. Doctorin' bills. Wardrobes and all."

She gestured toward the soup-holding John Milton, still standing there silently like a wooden Indian.

"Even brung along Franklin Kent, M.D. The 'M.D.' stands for 'Mad Dog' on account he intentionally kilt someone in Bodie, but I reckon she deserved it, her being a wealthy widow who'd put the doc in her will and all. But he's a fine doc, speaks like a real English dude, and he'll treat our gals, make sure they don't pass on no ailments to our customers."

She paused just long enough to spit. "And I ain't

gonna call 'em whores. At The Palace of Calico, they'll be courtesans. And I'm a-bettin' that the most popular, who'll command a right high price, will be The Celestial Queen, your Jingfei."

I was too sick to leap up and stove in her head. All I could do was shake my head, and that hurt.

"You can't," I said softly. "These are good girls." 'Course, the only one I'd met, or even seen, other than the six dead ones, was Jingfei, though I'd heard enough from Peach Fuzz about Bonnie Little, and I had dreamt of the Irish redheaded twins. "You can't turn them into soiled doves."

"Can't I?" She done more of that coyote-sounding cackling. "You don't think ever' girl workin' the tenderloin wasn't once a 'good girl'?" Which caused some more guffawing. "Hell, Micah Bishop, these girls I'm bringin', like as not they've spent their last dime just to come out to California to get hitched. So instead of wedded, they'll get bedded. They won't have much of a choice."

My head stopped pounding and I had a moment of clarity. I sang out, "But they signed contracts!"

"With the late Rogers Canfield, but there's some real fine print in 'em contracts. One important part states that should Rogers Canfield meet an unfortunate demise before completion of the contract, the rights would go to the heirs, and since he had no heirs, the dirty dog, ownership would go to the late Rogers Canfield's business partners. Which includes whoever could bring twenty-four courtesans to The Palace of Calico."

My head started drubbing again. That sounded a lot like slavery to me. I could see Honest Abe Lincoln giving one of his stern looks out of his tomb in . . . I forget where he's buried.

"What about the husbands?" I managed to say. "They signed contracts, too."

"But they only paid a down payment, and the final bill can rise accordin' to expenses and such, which is also in 'em contracts, or, in case of the death of one of the signers of the contract—in this case, the death belonging to Canfield, the contract is void. Besides, men can be bought off, 'specially when we got more womenfolk they might marry. Hell, Micah Bishop, we only got rooms—or will have rooms—for twenty-four courtesans in The Palace of Calico. Twenty-five, now that I've seen the Irish twins. We can still make some of 'em ol' boys happy, and the girls, too. And make us a tidy profit, still."

"So . . ." I began. "Jingfei . . . she might still marry Lucky Ben Wong."

"Hell, no. A girl like that? You think I'd just turn her loose? Miners, hell, men in general, they want somethin' exotic. And she's not only exotic, she's a Celestial Queen, the Mistress from Manchuria. She'll bring triple what the other girls will bring, includin' 'em red-haired twins who I aim to . . . well . . . never you mind 'bout that."

My eyes shut tight. Heard more sizzling and figured Candy Crutchfield had spit into the fire again.

"You like to gamble some, I figure. Seein' how slick your hands is. So I'll guess that you can count, at least to fifty-two. Well, try out these numbers. Twenty-five courtesans. The prettiest between Denver City and San Francisco. Twelve hundred people in Calico, out of which maybe twenty is women, and only two or three of 'em whores. Now, go out to Wall Street Canyon, Mule Canyon, Mammoth Stope, and the borax mines. Way we got that figured out, there's probably thirty-five hundred folks that Calico serves. And we'll serve. Serve 'em the finest courtesans to be found. Feather mattresses. Beds with springs. And real lovely 'Fair but Frails.'

"That's why Whip bought 'em fancy buggies like the one y'all brung me. Whip aimed to bring his gals right up Main Street, so ever' man in Calico could see what was comin' to The Palace of Calico. A driver duded out in evenin' duds, escorting a gal with a fine dress and parasol in the backseat. That'd be a parade better'n anythin' you ever saw on Independence Day."

More hooting. "Whip had a good plan. Thought haulin' all those other sundries with him would fool anybody else bound for Calico. Or fool me. But Whip was the fool. He thought he could reach Calico first, get a jump on things, win the race to bring the whores to town. But he didn't count on Candy Crutchfield. Which is a good thing you deserted him when you done so. But he done me a favor, Whip Watson. He killed Canfield for me. I'll say a few words in remembrance when we open the Palace. After I show the girls the contracts they signed. And this." She patted her bone-handled knife.

Once again, the mustangs quit trying to build up pressure inside my skull to blow my eyeballs out of both sockets long enough so that I could tell her: "There's no damned way Jingfei would ever have signed a contract like that," I said. "And no way Rogers Canfield would have, neither."

"Sure they did. And it's bona fide. Locked up in the office of Rogers Canfield's pard. They signed it. All the girls. And Canfield, the dumb oaf, hisself." She winked. "They just didn't know they was signin' it."

My head shook. I was aching and now confused.

My mouth started to ask *How*, when I heard John Milton's voice again. He said:

"Pray tell, Micah, have you ever heard of invisible ink?"

That doctor from Bodie who looked like John Milton but was named Franklin Kent and was a Mad Dog M.D. who had murdered a widow woman for the inheritance sucked on his sweet-smelling pipe, which now made me sicker than a mad dog, and knelt across the fire. And handed me my soup, which was cold, and he hadn't brung no spoon.

Candy Crutchfield patted my leg, and rose, her knees popping again. She shot a glance to the doc.

"No sign of Verne?"

The doc shook his head.

"Well, like as not, he'll show up tomorrow."

He nodded, but I don't reckon either one of them believed that.

"Y'all don't stay up too late, Doc," she said. "Busy day tomorrow."

She was gone, leaving me with a dying fire, cold soup, throbbing head, aches all over the rest of my body, and a murderer smoking a sweet-smelling pipe that was souring my stomach.

"If it's invisible," I said, "how do you know what it says?"

Laughing, he withdrew his pipe and tapped the bowl on his boot. "The technique dates at least to the thirteen hundreds," he said, "but I believe you can trace it—trace, no pun intended, but, bully, that is a bloody good pun—to the first century. An officer in the army of Rome used milk from the tithymalus plant as invisible ink. Pliny the Elder was that officer."

Saying the name like Pliny was as great as Ulysses S. Grant or George Washington.

"Can't see it," I said, "can't read it."

"That is precisely why you use it," he said. "In your damned Revolution, spies from your side as well as mine used invisible ink with great effect. It proved valuable in the Indian Mutiny back in fifty-seven, and now is quite common thanks to Henry Solomon Wellcome. That Tabloid I gave you for your headache. That was one of Wellcome's inventions. By thunder, that certainly is better than drinking something dreadful or dissolving a powder in your gin. Quite so, quite so."

I give him a look that Big Tim Pruett tried for years to teach me to give, but Big Tim was bigger and meaner and stronger than I'd ever be, but I tried to convey, without no words, to Doc John Milton that I didn't give a damn what some dude named Wellcome done. Then I drunk all my cold soup, and pitched the mug into the dirt behind me.

This time, my look worked.

"There are different methods of invisible ink, but most are quite common," he said. "Vinegar, saliva, urine. Even sperm." I crossed my legs at that remark. "But seeing how I do not know what the bloody hell a tithymalus plant looks like, I used lemon juice. It is likely the most common method used, and rather good. Quite so, quite so. No trace of it on the paper—until!" He snapped his fingers. "You apply heat." He held out his hands over the coals of the fire.

"The lemon juice becomes visible." He shrugged. "Thusly, the contracts become legal."

"In a pig's eye," I said.

"You have been to Calico, Micah," John Milton

said. "It is a pig's eye. And Rogers Canfield, now
deceased, paid a lawyer a great sum of money to
record those documents as legal. Even the parts
written in lemon juice, which now, thanks to a great
hand"—he was staring at his own right hand like it
was some great painting—"with remarkable skill
with scalpel for surgery and quill for forgery has
been rendered and traced so that no one can tell
Rogers Canfield's handwriting from . . . say . . .
Jingfei's."

"You're a peckerwood," I told him.

He emptied his pipe, shrugged, and returned
the pipe to a pocket. "My mother being a soiled
dove in Liverpool, I had no control over my
birthright."

"You're still a peckerwood."

Another shrug.

I looked past him. My heart broke. There was
Jingfei, and Bonnie, and I could make out Peach
Fuzz. I heard music. Well, not real music, not like
that real fine band that played in Dodge City on that
New Year's Eve in eighty-one, but there ain't much
one can do with a jaw's harp and a banjo missing
one string. Jingfei, I pictured 'cause I couldn't see
her face, was holding hands with Bonnie, who was
holding hands with some other girl, who was holding and holding and holding. And they was all
looking at two girls, whose hair appeared to be red,
and was dancing a jig and laughing, and it was a
fine good time over by that other fire. Though I
knowed Jingfei was smiling and pretending to be
happy because she had to put on that brave face
and act strong and not let the other girls know that
they was in for a terrible experience.

I pointed over toward the dancing twins, who

had to be Caireann and Caoilainn Lannon, who didn't know what they was in for, neither.

"Never knew a slave runner," I told John Milton. "How do you live with yourself?"

Funny. I guess you never get too old to learn something new about your own mortal soul. I was pretty much a heathen, even a whoremonger. I cheated at cards. I stole horses. Had broken the eighth and ninth commandments a whole bunch of times, even the sixth a few times, maybe the seventh once—no, twice—and most of all them others. One judge once said, and made sure the stenographer and newspaper reporter got it down just right, that I was so low-down, I'd have to look up to see a rattlesnake's belly.

"There's some things," I told John Milton, "that even I won't do."

"That is a luxury, my poor friend," he said, "that could get you killed."

Didn't say nothing. Just looked at those dancing, laughing girls, and, honest to God, felt tears welling in my eyes.

"Come now." John Milton was speaking like that judge had when he was pronouncing a three-month sentence on me. "How can you stop Miss Crutchfield? You cannot, my good man. To do so would be suicide. Do you think I want to be here? Do you think I enjoy this company of ruffians?"

I give him a Big Tim Pruett stare.

"Doc Milton," I told him, "you killed a woman, an old widow-woman, 'cause she writ you down in her last will and testament."

Which caused him to sag, like I'd broke his heart or give him a punch in the kidneys, and he brought both hands to his face like the pressure of a bullet going through his skull had blowed them both eyeballs of their sockets. He groaned, shook his head, and said, "Yes, yes, yes, damn your vindictive soul, I killed Joan Lamore."

When the hands lowered, and I could see he still had both eyes, but both of them was filled with tears, he sniffed, and said, "But she asked me to do it. She was suffering so horribly from the carcinoma. Do you know what that kind of bloody anguish is like, Micah? Even laudanum does not ease the torture. So I killed her. Out of mercy. Hell, I did not even know I was in her damned will until afterward. By then it was too late. They wanted to hang me in Bodie. They still want to hang me."

He looked up at those thousands of stars, and began speaking pure poetry:

"Her face was veiled; yet to my fancied sight
Love, sweetness, goodness, in her person shined
So clear as in no face with more delight.
But, oh! as to embrace me she inclined,
I waked, she fled, and day brought back my night."

He spoke pretty good. Like that thespian who'd played Falstaff in San Antonio.

When he lowered his head, our eyes locked across the coals. I figured him to be an ally, like Peach Fuzz and Jingfei. That made us three. Against seventeen hidden out in the rocks and six down yonder. Plus Candy Crutchfield, wherever she'd gotten to. Then I looked down at the girls, all jolly and young and pure and good. And a crazy notion run through my head:

If we could arm all those women . . .

Only that thought died because of something Doctor John "Mad Dog" Milton just said.

What he said was, "As far as those others were concerned . . ."

I studied him again. "What others?" I asked.

He waved off my question. "What does it matter? I am bound for the cord just as my mother's midwife preordained when she pressed me into my precious mother's arms. Bound for the cord. Doomed to the gallows. The others . . . to hell with their wretched souls! A wife-beater. A rapist. A drunkard who had kicked a puppy. A debtor who owed me thirty-seven dollars and ninety-one cents and bragged how he would never pay. A cheater of cards. A leper. Death was their true desserts, and death was my prescription, my cure."

About halfway through that soliloquy was when I started thinking that maybe I'd just better count on me and Jingfei and Peach Fuzz.

He leaned forward, lowering his voice, saying harshly, "But Micah. Those men I cured by killing them, but I killed them with scalpel twice but usually with narcotic analgesics." He smiled. "They never knew. Never suffered. Merely died and woke up in Hell."

The voice got even lower, only this time it didn't sound like John Milton or a Shakespearean actor down in Texas. It sounded like . . . the Voice of God.

"But she . . ." And by *she* I knowed he meant Candy Crutchfield. "She lives to inflict unendurable agony."

CHAPTER EIGHTEEN

The last thing Mad Doc Milton told me that night before both of us turned in was that I needed to get plenty of rest. "Tomorrow," he announced grimly, "we enter the Devil's Playground."

Next morning, after breakfast—with still no sign of or word from Verne or Crutchfield's boys—we got a lecture that we'd be entering some rough country, to go slow, keep a lookout, not tax our horses or mules. Get through this next stretch, Crutchfield said, and it was smooth sailing all the way to Calico and a new life for the girls who'd traveled so far.

New life. Hearing that lie made me spit out my coffee.

That morn, I got a good look at how Candy Crutchfield run an operation of running mail-order brides. No Conestogas. No farm wagons. And only the one Columbus carriage that Peach Fuzz had procured. What Candy Crutchfield put her girls in was omnibuses, and I ain't talking about the normal conveyances that you might see hauling folks from train depots to their hotels. No, sir, these

was two-deckers, pulled by fine, mighty big draft
mules. Two benches along the sides of the bottom
where our ladies could sit and face each other and
talk about the lives they expected to live once they
got to Calico. The top deck had seats going the
other way, shorter, and more benches, but I didn't
think anybody would be riding outside that day.

Not in the Devil's Playground.

And I was right. Sorta. Although six fellows
climbed atop each of them three mule-pulled
buses. The driver sat next to a guy riding shotgun
but armed with two Marlin repeaters, but what
caught my attention was the four gents on the next-
to-last backseat. Affixed atop the very backseat was
something covered in a canvas tarp, and I stared,
perplexed, watching as two of the boys on the backseat worked on the knots on the ropes that held
that cover in place. Eventually, the knots got undid
and the canvas come off, and I gasped. Mean to tell
you I actually sucked in air hard and loud, which
hurt my ribs and my back fierce. Gasping ain't
something I ever do, even when that tinhorn up in
Leadville had turned over a straight flush whilst I
thought I was sitting pretty holding kings over aces.
What was secured onto the very backseat was something I'd never seen on no bus before. Hell, I'd
never seen it on any wagon, only in woodcuts in
magazines and once at a fort where I was being
incarcerated in a stockade back during my brief
tenure as an Army courier.

I spotted a couple of boxes beside the gent sitting
closest to the edge near me.

"That can't be," I said.

"Aye, but it is, lad, it most surely is," John Milton
laughed, then he slapped my shoulder and hurried

to one of the buses, where I watched him climb into the bottom floor of the wagon. He picked the same bus that was carrying the redheaded twins from Savannah . . . and Bonnie Little . . . and even my Jingfei.

Thinking of that crazy mad-dog doctor riding in the same coach as sweet Jingfei, I liked to have stepped on a barrel cactus, did a little jig to get away and managed not to fall on my face, and moved— still at a gingerly pace—to my wagon.

Peach Fuzz had already hitched the team, and when I climbed into the seat beside him, he leaned over, give his head this secretive nod toward the first omnibus, and he says in one of those conspiratorial voices: "If we could clumb atop one of 'em horse- buses, we could shoot down all of Crutchfield's boys, don't you reckon?"

He straightened up, staring at the gray horses' tails, waiting for me to answer but not cause any- body to suspicion what we was thinking.

"No," I said. "They look good, but Gatling guns are prone to jamming. All show. That's all they're good for."

Course, I was also thinking that Jingfei might also be thinking about getting to the Gatlings. Didn't like no thoughts of how a fool stunt like that would turn out for my China doll.

"A citizen can't own a Gatling gun," Peach Fuzz said. "Can she? I mean, I thought they was for the Army only."

"I'm sure the Secret Service would like to talk to Candy Crutchfield about those," I said.

"Do you know how to shoot one?" he asked.

"No," I snapped. "But here's something I do

know. They got two boxes of ammunition along with those guns. On each wagon."

I told him a few other facts. They was .45-70 cartridges, and those were fairly new fast-shooting guns, could fire four hundred rounds a minute—a lot more in theory, but theories don't always count—and had two rows of bullets. While one row was being shot, the other could be reloaded. Which meant one gun could do a ton of shooting.

Yes, sir, you sure do learn things like that playing poker with boys from Fort Mojave in card games at Beal's Crossing.

"Forget the Gatlings," I told Peach Fuzz. "You try for those guns, you'll get shot to pieces."

"Thought you said they jammed all the time," he told me.

I told him to shut the hell up.

Next, I done some figuring. Six men on each omnibus. That made eighteen. Plus John Milton in the last coach, the one carrying Jingfei. Nineteen. Up ahead, talking to the driver of the lead wagon was Candy Crutchfield and Candy's—not Whip's—boy Zeke. Twenty-one.

There was two other fellows wearing big sugarloaf sombreros on real fine horses. Arabians. Chestnuts that had to stand almost fifteen hands high, with those beautiful sloping shoulders and arching their tails real high, real proud, 'cause they knowed they was Arabians and likely the finest horses between Sacramento and Prescott. Real good. Let Peach Fuzz try to get to one of them Gatling guns. I'd rather steal one of them Arabs.

Twenty-three.

Which meant, if my ciphering was right, that there was two guys missing. Unless Jingfei had miscounted the boys last night, and I didn't think Jingfei would make a mistake like that. I stared into one of the omnibuses, one of the two that John Milton hadn't climbed into. Maybe they was inside the coaches, which made sense. But I couldn't see nothing but dresses of the finest *moiré* in a rainbow of grand colors.

Scouting ahead? That was possible. I stared out into the empty desert where we was going. Where else could them two boys be? I looked at the creosote and the couple of Joshua trees growing near where we'd camped. Covering our back trail? That was possible, too.

Two missing men. Hell, it took only one to kill you.

"Let's ride, boys!" Candy Crutchfield was mounting her horse. "Get ready for a fun excursion, ladies."

Folks say that the Devil's Playground is where the Mojave River gets swallowed by sand. Which is all I saw. Sand. Oh, there was the occasional tree, a sturdy and stupid honey mesquite. Every now and then we'd come to patches of grass or some damned fool shrub trying to climb out of the sand, to blow in the wind. Around us, I spotted the faraway purple shapes of distant mountain ranges, beacons I reckon. Mostly, though, for miles and miles on end, all I saw was sand.

We were trapped in an ocean. Lost at sea.

Here's something I learned about sand. It's hard on horses, and especially big-ass omnibuses loaded with women, at least six men, Gatling guns, and boxes of .45-70 cartridges.

Four times or forty—that number I disremember—we had to stop, dismount, push or dig or somehow

get the wagon rolling after either one of the big rear
wheels or smaller front wheels, or, criminy, sometimes
two of the wheels sank deep into that sand.

It was during one of those pushing and digging
exercises—the one where I slipped when the mules
stopped being ornery and got to pulling and the
omnibus (one without Bonnie or Jingfei or Doctor
John Milton) lurched forward, and I fell facedown
in the sand—when the nightmare come right back
into my head.

*Standing in a desert of dunes . . . the wind blowing
sand like grapeshot . . . No trees . . . Only sand forever,
a sky without clouds, the sun baking down on us.*

"You all right?"

I spit out sand, rolled over, wiped my face with my
bandanna.

"Yeah," I told Peach Fuzz. My ribs hurt from the
fall, but I managed to get up on my own accord, and
then Candy Crutchfield rode up, laughing like the
coyote dog she was.

"You think that's somethin', wait till what we gots
next." Another howl, then she reined around her
horse, and pointed ahead of us.

It was a wave, one of those tsunamis I read about
in a *Harper's Weekly* some years back. A giant wall
heading right for us. Only it wasn't moving. Yet it
was. And after a while I understand that what was
moving was the sand, blowing like snow in a blizzard
in that horrible dream I'd had.

Most of the country we'd traveled across, excepting the wash we'd crossed maybe four miles from
our camp at Cornfield Spring, had been flat. Ahead
of us waited hell.

The wave was a dune of sand, only more like a
mountain of sand.

"Six hundred feet or thereabouts, I'd wager," Crutchfield called out. She must have been talking to the driver of the first omnibus. "But make it up that hill, and the others, and it's all downhill till we climb up to Calico."

"There must be a better trail to get to that mining camp!" the driver shot back.

"Course there is! Iffen you think Verne an' 'em fools I sent to run a man's errand did their job, and just didn't come back to us because they's all ignorant. If you want to risk things. If you think Whip Watson is burnin' in Hell. If you know for a fact that that slick sharp Rogers Canfield didn't have other pardners in his nefarious scheme. Sure, we'll just take the Mojave Road and the Calico Trail all the way into that there burg. That what you want to do, fool?"

That told me something. Candy Crutchfield didn't think Whip Watson was dead. I didn't think so, neither. But where the hell was he? It sure didn't stand to reason that he had run back to Wickenburg or Prescott to try to round up twenty-four other mail-order brides and win the race to bring whores to Calico.

No, he was out yonder waiting. Like a Mojave rattler—planning to strike.

We nooned before we got to the first dunes. Grained and watered the horses and mules, chewed on jerky and hardtack ourselves. Candy let her boys mingle with the brides—now, she stood over us like a chaperone, perched atop one of the omnibuses, sitting on a crate of .45-70s and spitting tobacco juice.

"Y'all can talk all you likes," she said. "But no touchin'. Don't want to make 'em husbands waitin' in Calico to get all jealous." Which she followed by more spitting and then that dreadful howling.

Brave soul that I am, I moseyed over to Jingfei, knelt beside her without asking, then taken the parasol she held to keep the blistering sun off her porcelain face, and held it for her. That's the kind of gentleman I am.

"Have you seen the Gatling guns?" she asked.

I twirled the parasol like a regular lady.

"Yes," I whispered. "I've seen all three of them. I get one. Two others get me. And fill me full of holes that'll likely blow both of my eyeballs out of their sockets."

I was looking around, watching the men, watching the two chestnut Arabians, watching for a chance. I knowed one thing. Omnibuses full of petticoats and Gatling guns don't move fast. Not up a sand dune. But an Arabian. Me and Jingfei would stand a chance on them two beauts. Maybe not much of a chance, like making a straight when you need a king and three of them is already showing. But it's been done before. Hell, I'd pulled that off two or three times.

"There are three of us," Jingfei allowed. "You and me and him."

I sighed, and turned to see Peach Fuzz, only Jingfei wasn't nodding at Peach Fuzz, who was busy conversing real quiet-like with Bonnie over in the shade of one of the omnibuses. Her smooth jaw indicated John Milton.

"Him?" I asked.

"Yes. Franklin Kent."

Murderer of widow women—I don't give a damn about his reason—and killer of kicker of puppy dogs. The parasol stopped spinning.

"What the hell did you two talk about all morning in that coach?" Sounded, I reckon, like a jealous husband.

Her head shook, and she sighed. "Lawrence Barrett," she said. "Do you know that Doctor Kent played on stage with that legendary thespian?"

"Really?" Like I give a damn. "Who'd John Milton play, Falstaff?"

That did make Jingfei look up and reconsider me, and I had to thank, silently, Big Tim Pruett for dragging me to *Henry IV, Part I.*

"No," she said after a moment. "Doctor Kent was a one of the Plebians, but to be on stage, watching the great Barrett play Julius Caesar."

I said, "Et tu, Bruté?" which prompted another reconsidering look from Jingfei and caused yet another thank-you to the late Big Tim Pruett for spouting off Shakespeare in all those cabins and caves and jails we hid out in during our many sojourns before his untimely demise.

While Jingfei was giving me that second look, I found myself looking at the Gatling guns. Then I glanced over at Peach Fuzz and Bonnie. Next I was wetting my lips, dry as they was, and I realized that the only person near one of them Gatlings was Candy Crutchfield. And she wasn't looking out at us no more, but kept her eyes pealed toward the dunes. Most, if not all, of her boys was talking to our mail-order brides. So I handed the parasol back to Jingfei, and took a tentative step toward one of the other omnibuses.

I felt a hand on my leg, above my new black boots with the fine stitching and the seventeen-inch tops.

Looked down and saw that beautiful face staring up at me with eyes that wasn't reconsidering or hard.

"Don't," she said. "You'll be killed."

Which was a right good prediction. Before I could do something stupid like tell her "I must" or merely fell to my face because my knees had begun to buckle, Candy Crutchfield was standing atop her perch and barking, "We're burnin' daylight. 'Em there dunes ain't goin' nowhere, so let's get at 'em, boys!"

Later, it struck me that Candy Crutchfield's impatience had probably saved me from getting killed.

The first hill proved dreadful. Our mules and horses were well fed and well watered, which made them lazy and cantankerous and heavier. I can't say the humans in our group was well fed, but we was cantankerous, certain-sure. Then Candy Crutchfield, the damned idiot, came up with the brilliant idea that if we got the brides out of the coaches, the coaches wouldn't weigh near as much.

A damned lot of them gals moaned—six of them throwed veritable hissy fits—about having to walk up the first dune. But it made me right proud that Jingfei didn't say nothing at all, just made a bee-line up that shifting sand. Hard to do. Hard for everyone. Bonnie didn't complain none, either, but hell, she had Peach Fuzz helping her along the way.

After I got the Columbus carriage to the crest, I walked down and helped the redheaded twins up. They were real polite, and thanked me kindly. You ever heard an Irish brogue with a Georgia twang? It's something. Let me tell you, it sure is something to hear.

Not long after that, all I heard was grunting and farting and cussing. We had to hitch long ropes to

the double trees and practically pull them buses
up that tall dune of shifting sand. Others got behind
the wagons and pushed. I happened to be on
rope-pulling duty, which caused me to cuss myself
for not having the foresight to spend $1.19 on
thirty-five-cent thick work gloves at J. M. Miller's
store in Calico.

After an eternity of backbreaking work, we got all
three horse-buses up that dune. Then let the ladies
ride down. Then told them to haul their asses out,
and we went to work getting them wagons up the
next hill.

Which is how our the rest of our day went.

And . . . pretty much . . . how the next day went,
too. See, after that first night in the dunes, I was too
damned beat to try to get to no Gatling gun. Ate
some soup, drunk some coffee, and lay down on my
battered new hat, and fell fast sleep.

Naturally, the next day the wind kicked up, so
sand begun blowing in our faces all that morning as
we pulled and cajoled and cussed our mules, our
women, ourselves, the heavy Gatling guns, cussed
everyone but Candy Crutchfield because she had
that big knife. Noon come and went. We was too
tired to eat. My hands was scarred and blistered,
and I wondered if Candy Crutchfield would consider me a slick-handed card sharp now.

Jingfei, bless her, come by and rubbed some kind
of salve on my hands. Did the same with Candy's boy
Zeke. Even Mad Dog John Milton's. She didn't say
nothing, just rubbed the medicine, which did soothe
a bit after it burned like hell. Course, she didn't put
salve on Peach Fuzz's hands. She let Bonnie do that.

After our noon rest without much rest, and no
grub, we attacked the next dune. By two or three

in the afternoon, I figured I might as well just drop down and die. But Candy was saying that we had made it to the last dune, and I blinked, and coughed up sand, and shielded my eyes because the wind was really howling by that time, and I could hardly see nothing. Just made out Candy Crutchfield on her old nag, waving her hat atop the last hill we had to climb, probably spitting juice.

"We've . . . made . . . it . . . boys. . . . No . . . more . . . damned . . . hills of sand!"

Didn't feel like celebrating. And then I seen something, something I couldn't quite make out off in the distance. Atop the same dune Candy Crutchfield was on, but off to the east. It was a rider. No, two riders. And I thought to myself, *At last, I've found Candy Crutchfield's two missing men.*

Quick-like, I knowed I was wrong. Because one of them riders shot Candy's horse out from underneath her.

CHAPTER NINETEEN

Let's see if I can describe this right. All that sand blowing, me wishing I had a pair of black-rimmed spectacles with smoked oval lenses, but only my bandanna pulled up over mouth and nose and hat brim pulled down low kept me from getting drowned by or blinded from sand.

Candy Crutchfield cleared her boots from the stirrups, hit the hillside, her horse rolling downhill, her tumbling right after it. Shots barked, but not all of them was aimed at our leader. Most of us remained below, having just gotten down the next-to-last dune, however, Peach Fuzz kept whipping those Percherons, driving the Columbus carriage up the hill. With all that howling wind and blinding sand, I don't know if he could see what was happening or not. And a moment later, I couldn't even spot him or that buggy. The sandstorm had swallowed them.

To make matters worser, the sky begun darkening like a monsoon was about to blow in.

I yelled out that we was being ambushed, but the wind carried my warning away. A few boys stood next to me beside the omnibus, and one of them, giggling like a schoolgirl, pointed at the somersaulting Candy Crutchfield and her tumbling horse. Reckon he thought that Crutchfield's horse had lost its footing and had thrown the boss lady. Then bullets rained down on us, slamming into the ground, horses, men, even the omnibuses. Through breaks in the blowing sand, I could see what looked to be an entire army topping the ridge now.

"It's Whip Watson!" yelled Crutchfield's Zeke.

Then he doubled over, gripping his stomach, groaning, sinking to his knees. Still, game as he was, he kept trying to draw his revolver till another bullet caught him plumb-center, then he wasn't trying to do nothing because he was dead.

I had been standing beside an omnibus, hoping to get some more salve rubbed on my palms by Jingfei. Realizing what was happening, I reached for my Colt or my Spiller & Burr, only to remember that I was unarmed. A bullet tore splinters out of the omnibus and sent a few of those splinters into my cheek above the bandanna.

So I yelped, and wiped my face, knocked clear the slivers of wood, felt the blood, and heard the women inside the coach screaming. I jerked open the door.

"Get out!" I yelled.

First girl out wasn't a girl. It was John Milton, doctor, killer, coward.

"What the hell—" I had to duck as another bullet slammed off the iron-rimmed wheel. Candy Crutchfield's orders had said only girls was to ride in the buses, and even then they could only ride downhill.

The doctor didn't hear, but he found his backbone, and turned around to help the first mail-order bride out of the bus. Turned out to be Bonnie, who took off running up the hill, ignoring my shouts that she should crawl underneath the bus.

Next out was one of the red-haired twins, but I couldn't tell them apart. Didn't matter because the next girl was the other of those sweet-talking girls, and I helped both of them get under the wagon.

"Lie flat. Keep your hands over your head. Don't move."

While I was helping them get all situated, I saw one of the sombrero-wearing boys riding his chestnut Arabian up the far hill. Running. Damned coward. But a bullet caught him in the back, and he dropped from the saddle, and rolled back down, and that Arab just kept right on running, up the hill, over the ridge, out of sight.

One of the mules caught a bullet, and fell dead in its traces. I was backing out from under the coach when a girl stepped on my back. I flattened, groaning, and she fell. Quickly, I rolled over and gripped her hand, practically dragged her beside the two redheads. Didn't bother to give her no orders. Once more, I backed from under the rig, getting to my feet before I got stepped on again.

The Gatling guns opened up. I turned to look, first at the top of the hill, but all I could see was the occasional muzzle flash of bandits shooting down at us. Something wet slapped my neck. I hoped it was rain maybe, and not blood. Back to the chore at hand, I jerked a real chubby blond-haired woman out from the bus. She kept screaming and clutching her cross, and I told her to calm down, but she just yelled at me in some harsh language that I didn't understand at all. When I pointed, though, she got the general idea. Whilst she was crawling underneath the bus, *the Gatling kept spitting out fire and smoke and lead and death.*

Those words I've underlined aren't words I thought up. I'm borrowing them from this Beadle and Adams five-cent novel, *Massacre in the Mojave; Or, Whip Watson's Duel With Death,* a novel in which I appear, though this Colonel Wilson J. M. Drury changed my name to Michael and made Whip Watson a hero rather than a son of a bitch, and there's not a whole lot of truth in the writing, but the boys here at Folsom find it entertaining, though I'd rather hear the lady read from *Moby-Dick.*

Flames, smoke, and more deafening racket came from the other two horse-buses, and I tried to tell the drivers to get moving, get them girls out of this death trap, but John Milton pointed out that was impossible. At least two mules lay dead in each of the harnesses. I looked at the omnibus I was unloading. Those lead mules was dead, too.

A body toppled over the side of our coach. A bullet smashed into the door.

Turning, I shouted up at that hill, "Don't shoot the wagons! There's women inside!"

Course, nobody up that hill could hear me, not with three Gatling guns barking—nope, only two now. The one off to my left must have jammed—the wind howling, women screaming, men screaming, horses snorting, mules braying, and rifles and re-volvers cutting loose from Candy Crutchfield's gang. It was pure bedlam.

I grabbed John Milton's shoulder and slung him forward to the nearest omnibus. "Help those women!"

He turned around, staring.

"Get them out of that bus!" I yelled. "Get them on the ground, under the wagon!"

A bullet tore off his hat. That prompted him to move, and, to my surprise, he done just what I'd told him to do.

I went back to helping another woman out, hoping it was Jingfei, but it was some skinny woman with spectacles. I pointed her in the right direction, then helped the next lady.

Another body dropped right beside us. One of the boys working the Gatling, the top of his head blowed off.

The woman saw that, and her eyes rolled back in her head, and she fainted dead away into my arms. As she was not a slim woman, but another one of them plump ones, I fell backward, and my ribs groaned, and my back hurt like hell, and I hit hard and farted, which, thankfully, none of the ladies heard. Had to dig myself out from underneath her, and wanted to drag her, but another woman was leaping out through the door, and she was about to bolt right up that hill—which, even money, would get her killed—so I tripped her, and she screamed, rolled over, and kicked me in the nose.

Not much I could do, but hold the bandanna over my nose. Tan Vest come by, though, and he took the woman, yelled something, pushed her to her knees, and practically shoved past me and underneath the bus. Then a bullet slammed through his back, came out through the front, and he fell hard to the sand.

I saw a revolver holstered on the late Tan Vest's hip, and I started for the gun, but a figure exploded out of the blowing sand, and I saw him cocking a Winchester. I spun, dived, slammed into a brunette, driving her back into the omnibus. Climbed off her, yelled, "Stay down! Everybody, on the floor!" Rolled over, looked through that open door.

The rider reined up, dropped the reins over his horse's neck, stood in the stirrups, and shot that Winchester as fast as anybody I'd ever seen, wounding or killing the men who had been shooting that Gatling atop our bus. Then he jacked another round into that rifle and aimed that long gun—my Winchester—at my head.

"Zeke!" I yelled. "Don't shoot. It's me!"

Whip Watson's Zeke shot anyway, but the hammer snapped empty 'cause he had fired the last of his ammunition at the boys with our Gatling, and as he cursed, the Gatling—the last one that wasn't jammed or had just got its gunmen all shot dead—opened up, and sand was spitting all around Zeke and his horse, and I wished the sand was blowing harder down here, because I seen and heard Zeke and the horse he was riding screaming as .45-70 slugs tore into their bodies, and I sure didn't want to see that, so I shut my eyes and held back the bile rising in my throat, and rolled over, and covered my head.

Till the sound died.

"No!" yelled the brunette I'd knocked back into the coach. "Jingfei! Stop!"

That got my attention. I pushed myself up, having to breathe now through my mouth since my bandanna was soaked with blood over my nose and now caked with sand. Got only a glimpse of two boots with many buttons and a copper skirt outside the window on the far side.

"Damn it!" I reached, but the boots and legs disappeared.

Jingfei had climbed out the window and onto

the upper deck. She was going for that damned Gatling gun.

Got to my knees, saw a few more ladies in addition to the brunette huddling on the floor. A bullet tore through the wood a few feet to my right, blowed out a chunk of wood, and slammed into the other wall.

"Just don't move!" I told the ladies. Seemed a lot safer to keep them lying on the floor than getting out, which was what I was doing.

Only I was going after Jingfei.

Once through the window, hands gripping the railing along the roof, I started pulling myself up.

A bullet tore through my left arm while I was hanging there, and I cried out in pain, but didn't let go. Blood rolled down my arm, soaked the sleeve, and I already knowed from experience just how hard it is to clean blood from a blue cotton shirt. Another sixty-five-cent shirt, which had cost me $2.50, ruined.

My boots got their footing on the bottom of the window, and I hauled my aching, bleeding, sand-battered body onto the top of the wagon. Come to my feet, crouched, sucked in another mouthful of air, started one way, tripped over one of the damned benches.

Realized I was going the wrong way, toward the coach. Behind me, the Gatling gun cranked out round and round. I came up, holding my bleeding arm, then tried to wipe some of the sand and blood off the bandanna. By this time, the sand had hit the valley harder. Something else hit me, too, and this time I knowed it wasn't blood. But rain. Just a few drops for the moment. By this time, it was pretty dark.

Then I just made out the dead man in the driver's box. One of the guards. What's more, I caught a glimpse of one of his Marlin repeaters, so I hurried over, pried the rifle from his dead grip.

Holding the Marlin, I ran back toward the last row, careful to step over another dead body—Whip Watson's Zeke had shot down the entire gun crew— and I dropped to my knees beside Jingfei.

She turned the crank, and the six barrels spit out lead so fast the heat felt just like I squatted next to a potbelly stove. Jingfei's face tightened, the hair loosened and blowing in the wind. She tilted the gun up, cranked, and fired.

"Who in hell are you shooting at?" I yelled.

"Them!" she snapped.

Which I guess meant Whip Watson and his boys.

Only the guys at the other Gatling gun opened fire at us.

"Hey!" I was about to yell that we was their friends, which wasn't the truth, since I didn't count none of Candy Crutchfield's boys as even acquaintances, but then I understood. Whip Watson's boys had taken over that Gatling—the one that hadn't jammed but had all its crew shot dead.

Bullets chewed up the seat in front of us, and sent splinters into Jingfei's left leg.

She grimaced, slipped to her knees, but turned the gun toward them.

"No!" I yelled. "There's girls in that rig, too!"

I don't know if she heard me or not, because from all that shooting, I was practically deaf, and didn't even hear my own shouts. Maybe she understood that she might kill some brides accidental at the same time I yelled. Whatever, she didn't pull

the trigger, but turned away the gun, and glanced
at me.

I figured hers would be the last face I ever saw,
and that wasn't such a bad way to go, because their
Gatling kept *spitting out fire and smoke and lead and
death,* and I knowed we was dead.

She reached for me, Jingfei did, and here's
where things begun moving real slow, I mean so
slow that I could almost count all the grains of sand
as they flew past us, mixed in with raindrops, and
.45-70 bullets from a Gatling. She taken my hand,
and I dropped the Marlin, and we was both leaping
over the edge as bullets and sand and rain zipped
past us, and we fell, dropped past the omnibus, hit
the ground, landing flat and hard.

Bullets stung as they slapped into my body,
only . . . they wasn't bullets. Taken a spell before I
realized it was water. Rain. Icy, cold, bitter, stinging
raindrops pelted me without mercy. My bandanna
had fallen across my throat. I spit water out of my
mouth, had to reach up to push up the brim of my
hat—yes, even after all that, it was still on my head—
so I could see better.

I reached for the Marlin, but it wasn't there.
Reached for Jingfei, who, thankfully, was there. Wet,
but alive. She was sitting up, drenched by the soak-
ing, numbing rain. Thunder boomed. Lightning
flashed. I held my bleeding arm, but realized that
my nose wasn't bleeding no more. Realized something else.

No longer did I hear the Gatling roaring. In fact,
I didn't hear no gunfire at all, just pounding rain.

I got a handful of *moiré,* and pulled her into
my arms.

"Are . . . you . . . all . . . right?" Had to space out

my words so she could hear, the rain was falling so hard and heavy.

She answered in Manchu. I pulled her close, and saw a hand reaching out from underneath the omnibus. A girl's hand. Then a girl's head. It was one of the Irish twins from Georgia.

"Get . . . under . . . here!" she yelled.

Which sounded like good advice. I let Jingfei go, and pointed with my chin toward the wet ground.

She sighed, give up, whispered, "All right." Couldn't hear her, but I read those lips. Then that wet porcelain face of hers hardened once more, and she jumped on me, knocked me to my back, damned near broke those ribs that had previously only been bruised considerable, and was on top of me, and it was still raining, and I was cold, and my face was suddenly just inches away, and there was her lips.

After blinking rainwater out of my eyes, I turned my head away from those beautiful lips. Didn't kiss her, damn it. Because even with the guns quiet, I knowed this was no time for romance. Through that wall of water I saw dead men, dead horses—one of those, damn it, was the other Arabian, its rider underneath him, also dead. As the rain slackened, I made out a figure running up the hill, and I guessed that it was Candy Crutchfield. She topped the rise. Then vanished.

Lightning flashed. Thunder rolled. The rain moved on, and the buckets of water turned into a sprinkle, then nothing at all. The wind seemed to be dying down, and suddenly I knowed something else.

I saw boots all around us. And the legs of a dun horse. The battle, ambush, set-to, fight, whatever you wanted to call it, was over. For the most part.

"You two," a voice said. "Get up."

Jingfei pushed herself off me, and leaned against the large real wheel of the omnibus. I tried to sit, but couldn't, so Jingfei and one of the Irish girls who had crawled from beneath the bus, eased me up. My eyes closed, and my head swam, and I thought I might just pass out, but the dizziness passed like the big thunderclap and sandstorm.

When my eyes opened, I hoped I'd be staring into Jingfei's eyes, but, nope, what I saw was the entrance to a deep cave that I knowed was the barrel of a Colt revolver.

CHAPTER TWENTY

Whip Watson lowered that big pistol, and swung down from a dun horse. The .45 disappeared into his sash, and, grinning, he handed the reins to one of the dudes in two of the boots I'd first seen, then knelt beside me and Jingfei. His whip was looped around his saddle horn.

"You owe me one." He grinned. "Almost shot you dead." His black hat, tilted so that water poured off the brim and onto my trousers, lifted so that I didn't get no wetter, and he smiled at Jingfei. "Good thinking. Getting her away from that Gatling gun. Thought I'd have to shoot her myself."

Somehow, I managed to sit, and grabbed my left arm, slung it over into my lap.

"Why were you shooting at us?" Whip asked. "We come to rescue you."

After an unladylike snort, she said, "Kill you first. Then Crutchfield's assassins."

Which got Whip laughing almost as hard as Candy Crutchfield, but his laugh didn't sound like hyenas or coyotes. Sounded more like old Satan

himself. He turned around to bark an order at
Mr. Clark.

"Find Crutchfield. If she's dead, shoot her again.
If she ain't, kill her, then bring her body to me."

I didn't give him no indication as to which way
I'd seen, or thought I'd seen, Candy Crutchfield
run. Whip barked more orders about making sure
the dead was dead, getting the brides together,
seeing how many mules were fit to haul some of the
wagons. I saw two Whip Watsons, then four, then
eight, and was about to fall back when I realized
that I was now in Jingfei's arms, and she was holding my arm.

Cloth ripped, and somehow I knowed she was
wrapping that bullet wound with the silk fabric of
her copper blouse.

"You hit?" Whip had just noticed that I was bleeding like a stuck pig.

"If you please," a deep baritone intoned, "allow
me," and I saw Doc John Milton sitting on the other
side of me. His hands reached for my arm, and I was
too weak to scream, because I could just see that
Mad Dog ending my life with a scalpel or one of
those Tabloids he'd make me swallow.

"Aren't you Franklin Kent?" Whip Watson asked.

The doctor was too busy tending my arm, with
Jingfei his nurse.

"'What's in a name?'" he said, not even looking
at Whip. "'That which we call a rose by any other
name would smell as sweet.'"

If they had asked me, I would have told that Mad
Dog doctor to go work on somebody else, and let
Jingfei nurse me, but I hurt too much to talk,
nobody asked me, and somebody was helping
Jingfei up, away from me, leaving me in the care of

John Milton, to whom I whispered: "I ain't never kicked no puppy, Doc."

His expression didn't change, but my arm suddenly hurt like hell, and I cried out.

Juan Pedro rode up, and he and Whip Watson palavered while the doctor asked one of Whip's other boys to fetch a black bag from the omnibus. He lifted a bloody hand to push the spectacles up on his nose. Only now, both of his lenses was missing from them glasses.

"Do not fret," he told me, and he smiled. "Sepsis is usually the danger of a wound such as this one, but the bullet passed completely through while striking neither bone nor artery. I should be able to remove the thread and cloth and have enough gin left to stop any infection."

I thought I'd rather drink the gin, but my stomach was dancing and my head was getting foggy, and I wasn't sure I could say nothing.

Whip's boy returned, and his face was ashen. He dropped the bag down by John Milton and shook his head. "God," he said, "what a mess."

By that time, Whip was done talking to Juan Pedro, who spurred his horse and rode off to bark his own orders in Spanish, and Whip knelt beside us. Then I jumped because Jingfei jumped and John Milton jumped, and I was real thankful that Milton at that moment wasn't trying to pull some thread and cloth from the hole in my arm with them real sinister-looking tweezers he was gripping.

Another pop sounded, and I jerked again.

"Ah," Whip said, and he smiled the ugliest smile I'd ever seen. "The coup de grâce."

His boys was finishing off the wounded, and from the way Whip had spoke and that light in his eyes, I understood that he wasn't talking about putting wounded mules out of their misery. I rolled over and vomited. Right in Jingfei's lap. She didn't even seem offended. That's the kind of woman she was.

"You rest," Whip told me. Then he told me everything that had been going on since Candy Crutchfield had attacked his train.

After the wagonload of women got taken by Candy Crutchfield's crew, Whip returned to camp to see how bad things was. All in all, he surmised, it wasn't that bad of a loss. Oh, sure, six of his brides had been woman-napped by Crutchfield, and six more was lying dead, along with several oxen, a few mules, and a healthy number of his gunmen. But he said he still had twelve women to get to Calico.

"Eleven," one of his men pointed out. "The Chinese bitch stole your horse."

Whip drawed his Colt and shot that fellow dead, Whip Watson never being the type of killer who tolerated being corrected, especially after just getting caught with his britches down, so to speak, and being whupped by a woman bandit.

"Canfield said Crutchfield was bringing in her own whores to Calico," Whip told his surviving boys. "If she's bringing twenty-four, that'll give us forty when we take them back."

This time, nobody, not even Juan Pedro, corrected Whip's math.

When Mr. Clark come back with some of the horses that had run off during the fracas, they cut the oxen loose, and decided to transport the dozen brides in one of the farm wagons. Whip needed to make good time, so he sent a few of his men with the remaining women to Calico. He also sent the remaining Columbus carriages, as he still refused to give up on his idea of parading the brides straight down Main Street in fancy wagons all the way to The Palace of Calico.

They were ordered to wait in one of the canyons in the Painted Hills near Calico, since Whip Watson and Candy Crutchfield obviously often thought a lot alike.

The best of Whip's gunmen, of course, come with him, riding after Candy Crutchfield on mules and horses that had been pulling farm wagons. Crutchfield's tracks was easy to follow. Whip saw the Conestoga wagon that we'd seen, saw how Crutchfield's boys had transferred the contents of that Conestoga onto fast horses, and had lit a shuck into the Mojave. Whip saw how we was following them in Peach Fuzz's Columbus carriage. He saw the canyon and the pass they'd have to go through. He saw how it was the perfect place for an ambush.

They didn't go through that pass. They dismounted, using the old Army tactic of having one man hold four horses, and the others go to battle. Sneaked into the rocks, found the culprits, and opened fire.

Which was the sound of gunfire we'd heard. Candy had thought—at least she'd said she thought— that was the sound of her boys murdering Whip Watson and his boys. Turned out, 'twas the other way around.

Candy Crutchfield was jo-fired to get us through the Devil's Playground and over those dunes, but Whip Watson knowed who he was after. He knowed she wouldn't take one of the easy trails to Calico, knowed she couldn't.

He had found Crutchfield, and had set up the ambush.

Course, it had cost him. Zeke was lying dead on the other side of our omnibus, shot to pieces by the Gatling gun. I noticed how Juan Pedro held a bloody right arm, and spied that Bug Beard's left ear had gotten shot off. Saw a lot of dead horses, too, and few mounts with empty saddles. I wouldn't call this fight something to brag about, but Whip Watson looked like he was amused by everything.

He even smiled when Juan Pedro rode up, slid from the saddle, and whispered something. The only words I caught was *patrón* and *puta,* but I knowed what the Mexican was talking about. Whip sighed, then shrugged.

"She has no horse," he said. "No water. In these dunes, she'll be dead in two or three days. Forget her."

So Candy Crutchfield had made it away. To what? Stuck afoot in the Devil's Playground, it might have been better for her had those first bullets of battle killed her, and not her horse.

"All right," Whip ordered, "let's see what we have left, what wagons will work, how we can get our brides"—he grinned at the girls, those who had been woman-napped from him, and those he was woman-napping from the soon-to-be late Candy Crutchfield —"see how we can get these poor brides to their awaiting husbands in Calico."

I looked behind me. The girls, those who had crawled from underneath the omnibus, and those who had moved from the other horse-buses, stared right back at Whip Watson with cold, deadly eyes.

I think now, after all they'd been through, after all they'd seen and endured, they all knowed that this wasn't what they had bargained for. And they understood that they wouldn't find some nice prince and a real preacher awaiting them in Calico.

Even the redheaded twins, Caireann and Caoilainn Lannon, looked mighty tetchy.

Jingfei helped me up, though I was so weak, I had to lean on her. Well, maybe I didn't, but it felt good.

Caireann, or perhaps it was Caoilainn, had been leaning against the omnibus. She turned, opened the door, started inside, then jerked back like she'd been snapped at by a Mojave rattler. "Oh . . ." She clutched her bosom, and sank to her knees, Caoilainn—or perhaps it was Caireann—hurrying over to assist her twin.

Jingfei left me, and hurried to that open door. She peered inside, turned away real fast, squeezing her eyes shut but for a moment, bringing a tiny hand to her delicate mouth, then leaping into the coach. Some of the girls started for that door, but one of the twins managed to block their stampede. "No," she said. "Don't . . . look."

I had stumbled over to the bus, behind the redhead, almost fell against the horse-bus, and looked through a window.

What I saw, I won't write down. Ain't fit to describe, because it wasn't fit to see. Inside, even Jingfei sobbed. Whip Watson came to the door, peeked inside, then said, "There's nothing you can do for them, my China doll. Come on. Come on out."

I didn't know which ones they were, if they'd been among them woman-napped by Crutchfield or were some of the brides Crutchfield was bringing to Calico. Lucky, we had gotten most of them out, and even some I'd told to lie on the floor had managed to get out. The brunette, for one, she was standing beside me, crying real loud.

All I knowed was those few girls still inside that coach, which had been shot to pieces with a Gatling, had come a long way with high hopes of finding true love, only to find death in the Devil's Playground.

Whip fetched his whip and walked away, the Irish twins from Savannah now hugging each other, crying on their shoulders, and other brides-to-be cried to one another. It was real sad. Worser even than when Jingfei and me had hauled out those dead brides from the wrecked Conestoga.

When I helped Jingfei out, she didn't say nothing, and her face had turned to stone again, eyes full of hate. We went around the mules still in their traces, waiting patiently, walked around the two dead ones, and I heard Whip cussing. He was running up the hill.

"NO!" Jingfei pulled away from me, and chased after Whip.

I saw it, too, and if those dead girls in that omnibus had broken my heart, the ugly scene on that hillside sure done the job. I couldn't run so fast, not with my arm patched with Jingfei's *moiré* sleeve and some of John Milton's bandaging and gin purification. I stumbled a few times, but kept climbing up that dune of wet sand.

Whip circled the carriage, breaking the Commandment about not taking the Lord God's name in vain.

Jingfei knelt over a body. I'd heard her gasp, and cuss, and even sob, but never had I heard her wail. Yet that's what she done, crying like her heart was broken. Both of our hearts had busted wide apart on that dune.

I staggered past her, though, and looked at the Columbus carriage. Two dead Percherons still in their harness, the canopy ripped the shreds, bullets from the Gatling gun having torn through the leather seats.

"This coach—this carriage!" In his own way, Whip Watson's heart had broke, too. "Three hundred dollars it cost me in Prescott. And it's ruined. Jesus Christ in heaven, it's ruined." Some more broken commandments, then he started popping that whip, like he was blaming it on God.

No, this wasn't the hand of God. Couldn't even blame Candy Crutchfield. It was all Whip Watson's fault.

Holding my throbbing left arm, I knelt beside Peach Fuzz.

Let go of my arm long enough to brush sand off his cold face, thinking: *I told him Gatling guns was prone to jam. And likely it had. Only not till after it had killed him.*

Felt something run down my bearded cheeks.

Some things you just can't figure. I didn't even know if Crutchfield's boys had shot the carriage. Maybe they thought Peach Fuzz was racing up that hill to join Whip Watson. Perhaps Whip's boys, after they'd taken over the Gatling, they had opened fire. Maybe . . . maybe . . . It's one of those questions we'll never know the answer to.

What I knowed was this. Peach Fuzz lay dead, chest blowed apart. I guess he'd stumbled out of the carriage and was trying to reach Bonnie when he'd died.

Though tears blinded me, I turned toward Jingfei, who kept wailing. And I saw poor Bonnie, who was reaching out, trying to be touching Peach Fuzz when she'd died.

They'd killed her, too.

"Three hundred dollars!" Whip railed. "Three hundred dollars that I'll never see again!"

That's when I went berserk. Completely mad.

I forgot all about the bruised ribs, the back, the bullet through my left arm. I stumbled to my feet, and went up that still-wet sand, and Whip stopped and stared at me and I'll never forget that look on his face when my right fist connected to his jaw and down he went.

"You son of a bitch!" I roared. "Those two lovers are dead and all you care about is that damned carriage."

He was getting to his feet when I decked him again.

But that was all I had in me. My left arm commenced to spasming and I twisted and groaned and fell to my knees. I saw Jingfei, her porcelain face streaked with tears. She wasn't bawling no more. She was looking at me with either bewilderment or praise. Then I saw fear in those lovely eyes, and I saw her mouth open, but never heard her warning.

That's when Whip Watson's blacksnake whip tore through my waterlogged and already ruined blue shirt.

With a yelp, I fell facedown in the Devil's Playground. The whip sliced again. I tried to get up, but something burned across my back, and my mind kept telling me, *Stay down, stay down, he can't castrate you if you're lying facedown.*

But I was so riled, so mule-headed, and now Jingfei started screaming, so I kept trying to get up, and my back was burning and bleeding, and my shirt, wet now from blood and the downpour, already in tatters. Suddenly, just like that, it stopped.

Jingfei wasn't screaming. Whip wasn't cussing. His blacksnake wasn't slashing. Even I wasn't saying nothing, but I stopped trying to get up, and just lay there in the sand, staring at Jingfei and the bloody body of the late Bonnie Little. Doc John Milton had run over, and he had both hands on Jingfei's shoulders, maybe to keep her from charging into Whip's whip to protect me. Juan Pedro and Mr. Clark and three or four of Whip's men stood on that hill, too. Not speaking. Staring. Fear shone in their eyes, too.

"No." That was Whip's voice. "It ain't right." Heard footsteps in the sand, and seen Whip's black boots and black trousers. He had moved between me and Jingfei and John Milton. "You don't kill a man whose life you've saved. It ain't right. Mister Clark."

Mr. Clark, I figured, could kill me since he hadn't saved my life. I pushed myself to my knees. If I was going to die, it wasn't going to be lying down in this sand.

"Hand me your Spencer."

Mr. Clark tossed him that big carbine.

"Doctor Kent."

John Milton left Jingfei in a hurry. Whip threw the big gun to him.

"Kill him."

"Sir?"

"Kill Micah Bishop. Shoot him down like a dog. Or I'll flay the hide off you."

Jingfei started to stand, but I shot out, "No." To my surprise, she stopped, and even a bigger shock to me, I managed to climb to my feet.

Whip looked back at me. Give me some satisfaction that his lip was bleeding.

John Milton cocked the Spencer. He shrugged. "Truly, I am sorry to have to do this, my good man, but you see how things are."

I walked a bit downhill. To get closer.

"I tell you what, old chap," John Milton said. "To make things sporting, you run up that hill." He pointed to the other hill, meaning I'd have to run down the one I was halfway up, then climb the other one, the one that probably rose two hundred feet. "I shall let you reach the top."

"Kent," Whip Watson said, "if he lives, you die."

"Fear not, my new friend," John Milton told Whip. "I have had much practice at these kind of things." He was already wetting the front sight with his thumb. "Shooting uphill makes things sporting, but during the late war, I gave many Transvaal Boers the same chance I'm giving you, Mister Bishop." The peckerwood even winked at me. "You had better hurry," he said softly.

So I ran. Well, running ain't the best way to describe it. More like weaved and staggered. Even tripped a couple of times. You'd run, too, especially if you knowed what a .56-.50 round will do to a human body at close range.

The Irish twins from Savannah shouted, "Run, Micah, run!"

Breath heaving, heart pounding, me sweating, my left arm was bleeding again, back burning and also bleeding from Whip's blacksnake, I did my best to make the top of the hill. Funny thing is that briefly, for just an instant, I thought that I might even have a chance.

Reached the top.

Then John Milton shot me dead.

CHAPTER TWENTY-ONE

Dear reader, I reckon it won't shock you to learn that I wasn't dead. But, by jacks, how I died! Once again, I have to thank the spirit of Big Tim Pruett for saving my hide. You see, having seen *Henry IV, Part I*, I knowed plenty about how actors died on stage, and, now that I think on things, having seen as many people shot to death as I've seen, that also played a bit into how I died so fine.

Anyhow, as soon as I heard that Spencer roar, I arched my back real good, leaped off my feet, but not too far, and let out a groan, put some rattle of death in my breathing, fell hard to the ground, and rolled down the hill, not all the way down, because rolling that far might have made me sick, and then I'd be on my knees and vomiting when Whip or John Milton or some of Whip's boys rode up top to make sure I had gone under.

Rolling down the dune, I also bit my bottom lip. Likely, that helped persuade whoever would ride up that hill—I heard the horse blowing real hard—because blood had poured down my chin from my mouth, so it must have looked like I'd been lung shot. I held my breath, tried not to shake, move my eyes, do nothing that might give me away.

"Looks deader than dirt to me!" Mr. Clark called out.

"Make damned sure," came Whip Watson's voice from the other side of the dune.

Which is when I figured how I was about to be real dead, because the horse's snorting growed louder, and I heard that the sand sliding underneath the weight and pressure, the horse snorting, the rider saying, "Easy, boy, easy," and then I figured if I opened my eyes, I would see Mr. Clark's pistol, and then I'd see nothing else at all.

"Open your eyes," Mr. Clark whispered.

That's when I wished I had watched more actors die on stage.

I tasted blood in my mouth, figured I'd soon taste more. My eyes opened. Yep, there was Mr. Clark's pistol.

Flame shot from the barrel, and I smelled brimstone, and felt sand kick into the side of my face that had already been stung from those splinters from the horse-bus. My ears rang. I sucked in a deep breath. The gun roared again, and I felt sand sting my cheek that hadn't been stung by splinters.

Over the ringing in my ears, my eyes now closed, I heard Mr. Clark say, "You owe me one."

His horse lunged back up the hill, and I realized that I had pissed in my pants—but since I'd done that already after the late Buster had beat the hell out of me, it wasn't that bad. Like my ruined blue shirt, those striped pants was already ruined.

Yet . . . I was alive. Thanks to John Milton, who was either as good a liar and as bad a shot as I was, or had intentionally saved my life. And thanks to Mr. Clark, who had definitely saved my hide.

For the time being. If I run off, and Whip Watson or Bug Beard or somebody else come up to check my corpse, and didn't find me, then Mr. Clark and John Milton would feel Whip's whip, and, most likely, a few of Whip's .45-caliber bullets. The way my back and arm felt, I didn't wish that on nobody, excepting Whip Watson and Candy Crutchfield and that miserable cur Corbin who had almost got me hung in New Mexico and those sore losers from Fort Mojave who I held responsible for getting me in this fix. Besides, where was there to run to? Back across the dunes? Try to find Candy Crutchfield so we wouldn't die of thirst alone in the Devil's Playground? No, what I needed to do was stay put, for the time being.

So, closing my eyes, I lay still, and tried not to breathe too much just in case somebody else come up that hill to make sure I was indeed dead. I could hear that commotion on the far side of the dune, some cussing from Whip, sobs of girls, mules being harnessed. I tried to think of what Mr. Clark had done, tried to put some reason into it.

It couldn't be that he liked me. I don't think we'd said more than five-six words to each other in the short spell I'd knowed him. We hadn't played cards together, because then there would be no damned way he would have wasted two shots on my account. Maybe he'd liked Peach Fuzz, who was a good kid. Maybe, like Peach Fuzz, he had started to fancy one of the women Whip was woman-napping.

Some bad men, I decided, ain't all bad. I'd like to think people think the same of me. Maybe Mr. Clark had seen too much of Whip Watson, what he was doing to people. Bringing women who thought they was gonna get hitched only to learn at some point that they was to be forced into the tenderloin. That rankles . . . even the hardest soul.

Then another thought come to me, and that one was that maybe I didn't owe Mr. Clark nothing, maybe he was as wicked as Whip Watson. I thought he might have left me alive in the Mojave so that the Devil's Playground could torture and torment and eventually deal me a right hard death.

That's what I was thinking when I passed out.

'Twas practically dusk when I woke up, my arm throbbing, but not bleeding, my back burning like somebody had poured coal oil on my hide. Strange sounds come from the other side of the dune, but it sure didn't sound like teams being hitched and women crying and Whip Watson cussing.

No, even in my poor, wretched condition, I knew that Whip and his boys—and Jingfei and all those other poor girls—was long gone, bound for the Painted Hills and Calico, California. I got to my knees, head bent down, waiting to throw up, but nothing come up. Moved a bit on my knees, then tried to stand.

Fell the first time. Second. Even third. Fourth try, though, saw me make a few yards up that dune, which didn't even look like it had ever been rained on. That's something about this Mojave country. It can come up the biggest turd float a body ever seen, and a few hours later, the place had turned back to its original condition, which was drier than an old buffalo bone.

I forced myself to stand back up, and head up the

dune, my boots digging and slipping and sliding in the sand. Up I went, then flat on my face I fell. After two more falls, I just kept low on the ground, and climbed.

Climb up, slide down.

Climb up.

Slide down.

Climb up.

Slide down.

Every three feet I'd make it up that dune, I'd lose a foot, sometimes even two. Yet you ask any of the nuns who remember me from the Sisters of Charity orphanage in Santa Fe, New Mexico Territory, and they'll swear in front of the Mother Superior and the archbishop from Lamy that Micah Bishop has the head of a mule.

As the moon rose, I reached the top of the dune, and looked down.

Went out of my head again. I started screaming, waving my arms over my head, yelling, cussing, then I was falling and rolling down the hill—all the way down, not stopping myself, and certain-sure not playacting no more.

I got up, everything around me still spinning, and tried to throw up, but there wasn't nothing in my belly but air. And when you get those dry heaves, it sure plays havoc on bruised ribs, a flayed back, and a hole in your left forearm. Only thing to come up came out of my nose, and that was snot. But here's how crazy I was. I still stood up, and kept waving my hands, and kept yelling, dizzy as I was, and somehow I managed to scare off all those critters.

Wolves or coyotes, I couldn't tell. Ravens? Turkey buzzards. Things that lived off the dead, and there was plenty of dead things between those two dunes.

* * *

Can't rightly recollect how much time passed.
The moon and stars lighted the scene. All I knew
was that the animals had all gone. Oh, I doubted if
they'd gone far. Probably just sitting atop one of the
dunes, watching, waiting for me to leave them to
their supper.

Two of the omnibuses was missing. From the
tracks I made out, I figured Whip had loaded the
girls into them, rode off with all the mules and
horses not killed. Left the dead where they'd fallen,
including the three dead brides-to-be in the back of
the horse-bus that had been riddled with bullets.

Sometimes, you find strength somewhere deep
inside you that you never knowed you had. I could
barely walk, yet I went up that next dune to the already bloating carcasses of two magnificent Percherons. I didn't drag Bonnie Little. I scooped her into
my arms, and carried her down the slope. Didn't
fall. Don't even think I stumbled. I brung her to the
remaining bus, and got her inside, putting her
hands across her chest, folded, trying to make her
look as peaceful as possible.

Turned away, then looked at her again. At her
dress. I reached, pulled my hand back, cussed
myself, reached again, but I just couldn't do it.
Peach Fuzz had told me she had a money belt underneath her corset. A five-hundred-dollar dowry.
But I couldn't rob the dead. Not her, at least.

That was something else I learned about me that
night.

A few minutes later, I was back beside that
ripped-up Columbus carriage, catching my breath,
trying to find more of that strength. Which come.

Just like that, it come, and I hadn't prayed or begged or found some Manhattan rye whiskey to drink. Next, I was bringing poor Peach Fuzz back down the hill.

Him, I laid right beside precious Bonnie Little.

Folded his hands over his chest, then thought better of it. I brung his right arm down to his side. Taken Bonnie's left arm, and let it drop. And clasped their hands together.

Never knowed how sentimental I was, neither, till that dreadful evening.

After that, it was sort of hit and miss. Tan Vest was easy, since he had gotten killed right beside the wagon. The two Zekes, Candy Crutchfield's and Whip Watson's, I wasn't so careful with, but got them into the bus, too, though I cussed both of their corpses for all the blood they got on my already ruined clothes. The Mexican pinned under the dead Arabian I couldn't do nothing with. Horse was too heavy, and so was the dead rider, and the sand around them had hardened like adobe bricks.

"Hell," I remember saying, "coyotes got to eat, too."

So I moved to one of Candy's vermin who'd gotten his head blowed off.

One guy I was dragging to the bus when I dropped his corpse, eased down to my knees, and bent over to look at him closer.

"You son of a bitch," I told him. "That's my gun."

So I unbuckled the rig holding Spiller & Burr that I'd won in a game of chance at Beal's Crossing and then had loaned to Peach Fuzz. Strapped the belt across my waist, put the holster in a comfortable position, and left that guy where I'd dropped him. Hell, the vultures had already picked out . . .

oh, never mind. Still makes me sick just thinking about it.

Kept at it, calling myself Micah Bishop, Under-taker of The Devil's Playground. Just . . . well, I wasn't thinking clearly, till I'd discovered another dead body by another dead horse. What I also found was a canteen.

Whip Watson hadn't been too careful hisself, but you can't blame him. He was in a valley in the Devil's Playground between two sand dunes, and all around him was dead men, dead women, dead ani-mals. Quick as he could, he left. I stayed. With the moon up. And coyotes and wolves and ravens crying out their impatience. I stayed. Done my duty. That's something else I learned about Micah Bishop.

When I had loaded the last body into the om-nibus, I taken a swallow from the flask I found in the inside vest pocket of Tan Vest, toasted the dead, and poured the rest of the forty-rod on the floor.

Other things I'd discovered was Doctor John Milton's black bag, some cash and coin, a Hamilton pocket watch, a deck of cards that was so badly marked it wouldn't have even fooled Sister Rocío. Several canteens, though most of them was empty.

Tan Vest has also had some Lucifers in another one of his pockets, so I struck the end on the iron rim of the wheel, stepped back, and tossed the match into the coach.

The rotgut whiskey caught, and flames began lap-ping across the floor. The bus wasn't as finely waxed as the Columbus carriages Whip Watson had bought in Prescott, but they'd been out in the desert sun a long time. Went up like a tinderbox. That's all I needed to see, all I could stomach, and I started staggering away, fast as I could make myself go, up the hill, hearing the coyotes or wolves yipping at the building fire.

"Shut up!" I yelled. Those animals still had plenty of dead horses and mules, and three or four bodies I just didn't have the strength to move.

The animals didn't listen. I kept walking, though now all my muscles began to ache, and I had to use the Marlin rifle as a crutch to make it up that final dune.

Odd. The night was beautiful, all the clouds having moved on, and the desert sky is always so majestic after a thunderstorm. Stars lighted a path across the midnight sky. Looked like a painting you might find in a storybook.

Behind me, down below, however, was no storybook.

Stopping at the summit, I turned. Made myself look down at the coach, now engulfed in a roaring waves of orange.

I didn't worry about nobody seeing the fire, or even smoke. By this point, I was too tired to care about anything.

Flames lit up the valley of sand. I didn't smell anything—likely a real good thing—and I watched for several minutes.

A Spiller & Burr was strapped to my hip. I had a Marlin repeating rifle with I don't know how many bullets remaining. I had one canteen full of water, another one half-full, and a flask containing maybe three or four shots of Mad Dog John Milton's gin. I knowed where I was going, but had no idea how I'd ever fine Calico.

Had to be forty or fifty miles from where I stood.

Odds was, I'd never make it.

Even from the top of the ridge, I could feel the warmth of the flames below.

Here's where things get real strange. I was speaking, sounding like I was in *Henry IV, Part I*. Sounding like I was reading a book of poetry to Sister Rocío back at the Sisters of Charity orphanage. Maybe that's where I'd first heard it. Maybe that blind nun had recited the poem to me. Maybe I was being touched by the hand of God.

Staring at the fire, I said:

> *"Thus, in short,*
> *into eternity the most just sequence of all things*
> *shall proceed,*
> *until the final flame shall devastate the world, far*
> *and wide*
> *encompassing the poles and the summits of the*
> *deserted sky;*
> *and the frame of the universe shall burn up in a*
> *vast funeral pyre."*

Then I turned and walked down the last dune.

After that, the country flattened, more or less. Well, there wasn't no more shifting sand dunes I had to climb. I dropped down into a wash, following it along a southerly basis. Came to one fork, and taken one, but when it turned north and west, I went back. The next fork also proved to be a dead end.

Eventually, the wash ended, and I climbed out. Kept walking, hardly even stopping to slake my thirst. Crossed an alkali playa, moved into rougher country of creosote and yucca. Kept walking.

At some point, with the graying sky behind me

telling me that dawn was nigh, I come to a water hole, and I stopped, dropped to my knees, and thought about drinking. Now, I had one canteen full of water, and I had another which still held enough to get me through maybe one more day. Yet here was water, smelled fresh from that big thunder-clap we'd had. I dipped my fingers in it, felt the coolness, wondered if I should drink, if I should fill my second canteen.

Wondered, also, if this was an alkali hole, or pure poison and would kill me dead.

That's a tough thing to endure, and my body, by now in complete torment from all I'd been through, just couldn't take no more. I scooped up a handful of that water, and drunk it down. My empty belly roiled, and I fell onto the ground, staring up at the stars, seeing Jingfei's face in the night.

"Bless me, Father," I said, "for I have sinned," but didn't get around to telling the stars all of the sin-ning that I had done. I closed my eyes, and for the second time that day, I, Micah Bishop, died.

CHAPTER TWENTY-TWO

The sun blazed high overhead when I woke up, the muscles in my arms screaming from all the heavy lifting I'd done back in the dunes. Usually, the only lifting I do is cards and beer steins and whiskey bottles, and the occasional saddle when I'm too broke to tip the kid at the livery stable to do it for me. Shielding my eyes from the sun, I slid up against the rocks by the pool of water. Found the hat I'd slept on, put it on my head, and said, my voice raw, "Water wasn't poison. I ain't dead."

"You will be soon," a voice said, and I turned to see some wretched creature with an evil grin on its monstrous face. It spit venom between my legs, and I reached for my Spiller & Burr, but it wasn't there. The creature held it. Cocked it. Pointed it at my private area.

"You burned my bus, Micah Bishop. That rig cost me a bunch of horses I'd stole in Utah."

The monster moved around, till its big head blocked the sun. I could see clearly now, and my mind hadn't been playing tricks on me. I wasn't suffering sunstroke. Indeed, it was a monster.

"Crutchfield," I whispered.

The sun had burned Candy Crutchfield's face to the point it looked blistered. She'd lost her hat, and you sure needed something on your head in this furnace. The .36 trembled in her right hand, she could barely keep it aimed at me, and a Spiller & Burr ain't no heavy Walker or Dragoon. She hadn't yet even cocked the hammer, and, betting man that I am, I'd give good odds that she didn't have the strength to do it.

"That horse-bus was ruined," I told her, "thanks to Whip Watson."

The revolver lowered, and she snarled and cussed and practically foamed up in her mouth like a hydrophoby dog. "I'll kill that peckerwood," she said. "Kill him dead."

"That's the best way to kill a person." I watched her try to steady the pistol with which she seemed intent to kill me dead.

"You followed me," I said.

Her head tilted a bit in affirmation, but she didn't lower her—*my*—gun.

"I had to burn the wagon," I said.

"Cremation." She nodded.

"Couldn't leave them to the buzzards and coyot's," I told her.

"You left Emilio."

I give her a look of bewilderment.

"Emilio," she snapped. "Emilio Aldana y Narváez. You left him under Yago."

Yago would be the dead Arabian. I shrugged. "He was stuck."

"Wolves managed to dig him out," she said. "Others, too."

The water in my belly got churned to butter.

"Well, you could have come help me," I told her. "Instead of stayed atop those dunes watching me."

She didn't have nothing to say to that. I'd guessed right. She had come back, waited on the dunes, then followed me. Which meant the sun had clearly touched her bad because no sane person would have followed me.

Tiring of this conversation, I decided to do something else to torment her. I drank. Just reached over, cupped my hands, filled it with some water, brought it to my lips.

Now, the way I figured it, she had likely drunk some water when she reached this spot. I don't think she just taken my .36. She had likely filled her belly, but she'd still been out in that sun all of yesterday, and without water since Whip Watson's ambush. The sun was already fairly high up in the sky, and it had turned hot, dry, and miserable.

I drunk some more.

Just drunk my breakfast as she watched, eyes darting this way and that, then cooled off my neck and face with the water. It didn't taste as cool or as fine as it had right before dawn, but the sun was fairly high by now. Bathed my left arm, and untied my bandanna, dipped it in the water, then gingerly placed that rag on the welts on my back.

That caused me to gasp.

But sight of all that water, my luxury bath, it cracked poor Candy Crutchfield, and she dropped the pistol she'd taken from me whilst I slept, and fell to her knees, and plunged headfirst into the small hole.

Drunk like a hog. I mean, even as hurt and weary and miserable as I felt, listening to her slurp up that water sickened my stomach. While she lay on her

belly, drinking and making dreadful noises, however, I moved and picked up my Spiller & Burr.
Then I went around so that when she finally drunk
her fill, and sat up, she'd be facing the sun, and I
wasn't going to be her parasol.

Finally, just before my stomach was about to roll
over, she stopped snorting and cavorting, put her
hands in the pool, pushed herself up. I aimed the
.36 at her broad back, thumbed back the hammer,
and waited. For a moment, she was still, then she
sucked in a deep breath, gasped, and fell facedown
into the water, her greasy hair floating. Bubbles
come up. But she didn't move.

Well, I cussed, lowered the hammer and shoved
the revolver into my holster. Walking on my knees,
as I was too damned tired to stand up, I made it over
to the pool, reached over, and taken her by the
collar.

The human body and the human spirit can act
real strange. Last night, I'd been able to carry or
drag the dead all across that sand, somehow lift
them, or push and pull them, even toss them, into
that battered omnibus. Did it without complaint,
and some of them bodies weighed more than
Moby-Dick.

That had been last night. This was late morning.

I heaved, damn near give myself the hernia
Buster hadn't give me. Got her head out of the
water, then my fingers lost the grip, and she
splashed back into the water. She was muddying up
that hole real bad, and I thought I could see the oil
coming off her greasy hair, polluting my source of
water even more.

Cussing her, I reached down, and taken a better
hold, and pulled, leaning sidewise, groaning, but

making progress. She cleared the water, and the mud, and I dropped her in the dirt. Once I'd managed to catch my breath, I moved around her, got my hands under that stone-hard belly, and, cussing some vile words, rolled her over.

As soon as I'd beached that whale, I saw her mouth open, watched her suck in a deep breath of air, and then I knowed I'd done a real foolish thing, and that I should have let her drown. In the corner of my eye, I seen that bone handle of her big knife come at me.

It caught me just shy of my temple, and down I went, not losing consciousness but definitely losing the grip on the Spiller & Burr.

I had underestimated Candy Crutchfield. While I was trying to push myself up, her boot caught me in my lower ribs, the ribs that hadn't been busted during my fracas with the late Buster. Either that water had revived her like the Fountain of Youth, or she was a fair hand at running a bluff. Up I flew, only to land hard on my back. Groaning, I forced my eyes open, and spit out blood from the lip I'd bit while I'd been rolling down the dune the day before trying to fake my demise.

Candy Crutchfield hovered over me, and I got a look at that knife.

"That's it?" I said. "That's your knife?"

She stepped back, glanced at the blade, then come a bit forward, glaring. "It does the job," she said.

"The handle is five times bigger than the blade," I told her, and slid myself up against more rocks.

"So?"

"That handle's huge. But the blade . . ." I sniggered.

"I'll peel the hide off you, Micah Bishop," she said, "and show you just how good this knife works."

"Knife that small, it'll take you a week."

"Will not."

"Will, too."

"Not."

"Too."

Flustered, she sheathed the knife. I ain't fooling. That bone handle was a foot long, thick as the palm of my right hand at the bottom. The blade though wasn't more than four inches long. Looked more like a dagger than a skinning knife.

"The hell with it," she said. "I'll just shoot you dead."

She reached down to pluck the revolver I'd dropped. I was too tired to move, so I sat there and watched her squeeze the trigger. The cap popped, but that's the only thing that worked. She thumbed back the hammer, tried again. Not even the cap sparked this time. Again. Nothing.

"It rained yesterday," I told her. "Remember? Hard rain. Fouled the powder."

She cussed the gun I'd won at Beal's Crossing and shoved it into her waistband. "If I hadn't lost my own guns after gettin' my hoss shot out from under me, you'd be dead now."

I nodded my agreement.

"But you's already dead." She drew her knife, just to keep me at a safe distance. "Don't try nothin'. This blade may be small, but it'll find your throat or heart."

Figured she was right about that, so I just stayed there, and watched as she walked around. She taken the Marlin repeating rifle, and the two canteens, though she didn't have sense enough to fill the one that wasn't full with water. She also didn't have the brains to shoot me dead with the Marlin, which I was fairly certain would still fire, brass casings generally protecting the powder from water and all.

"Give me your hat," she ordered, and since she now seemed to be of mind to take only what I had but leave me alive, I tossed the hat to her. She caught it, cradled the Marlin under her armpit, and jammed it on her head. Tried again. Cussed, and pulled.

I also had sense enough not to laugh at that hog head of hers.

Finally, she threw my fine hat into the pool of water. I picked it up, shaken the water off, and put it on my head.

"Bet your head ain't the only part of your body that's so damned puny."

Uneducated insults seemed better than getting my head blowed off with a .40-60-caliber bullet.

"How 'bout that kerchief."

I flung the wet bandanna to her, and watched as she tied it on her head like it was a schoolmarm's bonnet. She looked damned ridiculous, but again I held my tongue.

By this time, she had all she needed from me. She pointed the Marlin's barrel off toward the east, and laughed. "How long you reckon it'll be till that water hole dries up?" she asked.

Already, my throat started to feel parched.

"Don't rain often in this country," she said. "And, as you reminded me, it rained yesterday. I'll be leavin' you here, Micah Bishop. My bet is that come a day or two, you'll be wishin' I had kilt you with my knife."

I watched her walk away, heard her singing "Blow the Man Down."

Didn't move until I couldn't see or hear her no

more, then I made myself drink some more of that
muddy, greasy water, drunk long and hard, then
soaked my hat. Then I done a foolish thing. I
walked after her.

Having lived in desert country, I knowed what I
should do, what you had to do. Hell, just a year ago,
I'd been stuck in *Jornado del Muerto* in southern New
Mexico Territory, without horses, without water,
without no chance. But I'd survived.

Because I knew, for one thing, you don't go walking across the country in the heat of the day. You
wait.

I didn't wait. I walked.

The sun dried out my hat pretty quick. I couldn't
see Candy Crutchfield, and this ground was so hard,
there weren't no tracks to follow. I stopped to listen,
but the only voice I heard was my own.

"Way, hey, blow the man down."

"Stop singing!" I yelled at myself.

Staggered along, holding my left arm, my back
burning once again. The country looked the same,
flat but rugged, rocks, yucca, creosote. That's all you
could see for miles, that land, and the endless sky.
No clouds. Just a sun that was directly overhead.
Still, I walked. Wasn't much in the way of shade
anyhow.

Walked on and on.

The sun was in front of me, and I had to pull
down my hat. My lips had already cracked, and my
throat was dry. Yet on I walked. Let's see, what did I

have to do? Go fifty, maybe sixty miles to Calico?
Without water?

Kept on walking, though. Singing "Blow the Man
Down" and not stopping myself.

Till I come to a quick realization. I stopped
singing to myself and begun conversing with myself.

"Calico is to the west. I was walking west. The sun
was on my back. Then it was over my head. Then it
was in my face. Yes, yes. That would be right. Walking
west. The sun sinks in the west. That's right. That's
how it should be. Right. But . . . this doesn't make
sense. The sun is on my back. It's low. Getting cold.
How long has the sun been on my back? What's it
doing sinking there? I've walked all day. I've . . ."

I smelled the water. I staggered to it. Wasn't
muddy. Wasn't greasy. Wasn't as deep, but it was
there. I saw the marks left by boots. Of a scuffling. I
saw the rocks. I turned and looked west and saw the
sun dipping below the horizon.

"You damned fool," I told myself. "You've walked
all day in one damned circle. You're exactly back
where you started from."

Nodding in agreement with myself, I laughed.
"But hell, you've got water."

So what I done was exactly what Candy Crutchfield had done. I dropped to my belly, and I lapped
up that precious, cool, sweet-tasting water like a
dog, or a rattlesnake. I drunk my fill, wet my face,
my back, my hair, my hat. Then I crawled over to the
rocks, satisfied, content. I closed my eyes, and sang
myself to sleep singing "Blow the Man Down," and
dreamed of sailors and ships and whales and Captain Ahab. Dreamed of water. Water. Water.

* * *

"Damn you, Crutchfield," I heard myself saying drowsily, "stop snorting up that water."

Crutchfield didn't listen, but kept right on making a racket as she drunk.

That's when my eyes shot open. It was dusk, and I was back at the water hole, and somebody else was drinking, but it couldn't have been Candy Crutchfield. Not unless she'd gotten as lost as I had.

It wasn't.

I held my breath.

"Hey," I said softly after realizing that this was no mirage.

The chestnut Arabian horse stopped drinking, lifted its head, stared down at me.

I came up slowly. The horse stepped back.

"No," I cooed. "It's all right." The ears flattened against his head. Not a good sign. I tried to be stiller than I'd been when I'd been playing dead. The horse studied me, but I knowed it might take off at a gallop at any second.

First I smiled. Then I wet my lips. "Hey, Yago," I tried. Stopped myself. Yago was the Arabian horse who'd been killed. Yet the name caused this horse's ears to perk up as if he was interested.

"Yago," I said again, softer, cooing, and the horse stepped toward me. I smiled, wishing I had a cube of sugar. The horse snorted. I caught a rein. Breathing much easier, I got to my feet. Took the other rein. Let out a sigh of relief, and come to the horse, rubbing my hand on his neck.

The cinch was loose, but the saddle was still there. So were the bags behind the cantle. And there was a Winchester in the scabbard. Even better, there was a canteen wrapped around the horn.

"I don't know what your name is, boy," I told the Arabian, "but it's Yago from now on."

I let the horse drink more, then I filled the canteen, checked the bags, which had some clothes that wouldn't fit. But smelling my own duds, and seeing the hobbles in the other bag, I decided everything has a purpose. I hobbled Yago close to the pool, and replaced my bloody and ripped shirt with a fancy one of red silk, and exchanged my pissed-on, and bloodied, and dirtied striped trousers with a pair of *vaquero* pants of deerskin the color of a palomino. They were too long, and too big, but they slid into the tops of my boots, and the gun belt would keep them from falling down.

Of course, I was still something out of my head, because after I'd put the hobbles back in the saddlebags, and swung into the saddle, I was yelling, giving Yago plenty of rein, letting him find his own lope.

The sun was down, but I rode that night. I rode, cussing Candy Crutchfield and Whip Watson. I rode west, and this time I wasn't gonna go in circles. I'd find Calico.

I yelled to the sky:

"'And I looked, and behold a pale horse'—I mean a chestnut. 'And his name that sat on him was Death!'

"You hear me Crutchfield? You hear me Watson?

"'And Hell followed with him!'"

CHAPTER TWENTY-THREE

Some folks at Folsom argue this point, but shortly after I left the sand dunes, my madness ended. I slowed Yago down, then reined him to a stop. Climbed out of the saddle, loosened the cinch, and waited till the moon rose. Then, after letting the Arabian hurriedly drink from my shot-up hat, I tightened the girth and got back in the saddle. I kept the pace at a walk, moving into a trot every now and then when the country—and my ribs, back, and buttocks—could handle it.

When dawn neared, we found us a spot that would be shady. That's where we stayed, waiting till the sun was going down, and the weather had cooled. Then we'd ride till it got dark, rest and wait for the moon to rise, and hit the road again.

That, my friends, is how we made it out of that furnace alive.

Oh, it wasn't easy. Taken us three and a half days, and the last day was without water, my canteen by that time dry. I was leading Yago down the trail late in the day, the sun sinking behind some big clouds, following a well-traveled trail that I remembered as the Calico Road. Ahead of me, I spied dust, so I taken the Winchester from the scabbard, pulled back the hammer, and approached slowly.

Slow, that is, till I topped a rise and saw what was making that dust. Then I pulled myself into the saddle, kicked Yago into a lope, and hurried down the hill toward the wagon, rode right past it, before I wheeled the horse around, blocking the road, and give the driver and his companion a polite nod.

"Howdy," I said.

They just stared. Slowly, both men raised their hands.

"You robbin' *us*?" one of them asked.

I blinked.

The fellow who had asked that damned fool question looked to be older than Methuselah, bald underneath the most miserable excuse for a hat I'd ever seen. You might have mistook his duck trousers and muslin shirt as leather. That's how dirty, greasy, and awful they was. I doubted if they'd been washed since the last rain. His face was the color, and texture, of leather, thanks to who knows how many years in the desert and not a razor handy for a week or so. He had real beady green eyes.

The other guy was maybe a hundred or two hundred years older, but he had hair, white as Moby-Dick. Hair he had, but no teeth, and his face had more wrinkles than Rip Van Winkle. He did have second helpings of muscles. Old man like that, but he seemed sturdy, solid, and tough. Well, maybe not that tough. I mean he had lifted his hands way higher than his pard's.

I said, "Nice dog."

The dog, a bony mutt of black ears and patches of black here and there where the mange hadn't taken off the hair, looked to be trying to hold its front legs up in the air, too. The dog, I figured, was older than the two desert rats combined.

Yet that dog wagged its tail. The two men stretched their hands higher.

"Don't shoot us, mister," the man with the big arms pleaded.

That's when I remembered the Winchester in my hands. Quickly, I eased down the hammer, and slipped the rifle into the scabbard.

"Boys," I said, "I'm no highwayman."

Well, I had robbed a cattle buyer in Denison City, Texas, some years back, but only because I'd been cleaned out by some crooked faro dealer and needed a stake and the cattle buyer had money to spare.

Only the dog seemed to lower its paws.

"You look like one," the big one said. "Don't he, Cicero?"

"Shut up, Kermit," the driver said.

"Listen." I pointed back toward the east and north. "I've been in that hellhole for more days that I'd care to remember. Haven't had water in a day. I'd be obliged."

The old codgers glanced at one another, then even looked at the dog, and finally turned behind them as if they didn't know what they was hauling into Calico. After the longest while, they both turned back toward me.

The big cuss scratched his chin with dirty fingers.

The driver patted the dog's head, then sighed and said, "But this wagon belongs to the Calico Water Works . . . Incorporated."

"It's a water wagon," I said, "and I'm dry."

Again, they looked at each other, without speaking, turned to the dog for advice, who wagged his tail, and looked again at me.

"It'll cost you," the driver said.

The big coward sang out, "Not because us, no sir. Iffen it was up to us, you see, we'd let you even take a bath. But, well, we work for the Calico Water Works . . . Incorporated."

"Three dollars." That driver's beady green eyes had brightened and gotten bigger with greed. "To fill your canteen."

My shoulders slumped. I pushed my hat up. I stared at the big coward, then the dog whose head had dropped onto the edge of the pillow that was sticking out of the driver's butt. At last, my eyes locked on the driver.

"It only costs two dollars," I reminded him, "in town."

The sorry excuse for a man grinned. His teeth was white and shiny and straight. Well, the three he had was, anyhow. "Yeah, mister, but we ain't in Calico . . . yet."

Hell's fire, the only thing I could do I done. The Winchester came out, and I eared back the hammer, and I pointed it straight at the driver's dirty buttons on his shirt.

"You get out. You come here. You get my canteen. You fill it. Or I fill that water barrel behind you with holes. Then you can explain this accident to the Calico Water Works . . . Incorporated."

Both of them started off the wagon, but I turned the rifle barrel and pointed it at the big cuss. "Not you, mister. You stay and scratch the dog's ears."

That's what he started to do.

"And you give me information."

He nodded. The driver was already at my horse.

Keeping the rifle on the big one, I used my other hand to unloop the canvas strap so the skinny one could take my canteen to the back of the water wagon.

"Is Whip Watson in town?" I asked.

"Who?" the big one asked back.

"You'd know if he was." Which meant he wasn't. Waiting then, because even with those buses loaded down with petticoats, parasols, and Gatling guns, he should have reached Calico by now.

I didn't expect Candy Crutchfield to be in town yet, not walking. Hell, she was probably dead in the desert. But I asked anyway.

"Who?" both men answered. The skinny driver was hurrying back with my canteen.

"Any women in town?" I asked.

"What kind?" the big one answered.

"Not boardinghouse operators," I told them.

They blinked.

"Soiled doves!" I snapped.

They blinked again. "Well," the skinny driver said as he inched back toward the mule-drawn wagon. "You mean . . . Betty?"

"No. Not her." While the driver climbed back into the box, I took the canteen he had draped over my horn, pulled out the stopper, and let that tepid, awful, iron-tasting water go down my dried-up tongue and throat and into my empty stomach. Not too much, though. Didn't want to get sick.

I spit out some, because I knowed I wasn't going to die of thirst, or pay for water, and told the driver, "You'd charge a man three dollars for this?"

He shrugged.

The big guy wore a bowler. I told him to fill his hat with water so my horse could drink. It taken him a lot longer to climb out of the wagon, and he had to ask the driver for instructions on how to get the water out of the back.

"Same way we get it in," the driver yelled back, "only in reverse."

I could have ridden to the Colorado River and back by the time Yago got to drink, but I kept my interview going during that eternity.

"How's The Palace of Calico?" I called out to either the skinny one, the big idiot, or hell, even the dog.

"The what?" the dog answered.

I'm funning you. It was the skinny driver who said that.

"Big building. Wood frame. Going up at the end of town. Next to Miller's store."

"It's gonna be a palace?" the driver asked.

The big one from the back of the water wagon said, "With princesses and knights and fairies?"

I sighed. Holding up water wagons ain't what it used to be.

"Is it finished?" I demanded.

"Fancy windows went in the other day," the big one called. Then he yelled. "Hey, Cicero, how do I stop the water from coming out?"

Cicero's head shook, and he rubbed his temples with his thick, disgusting fingers. "Stick your finger in the dike," he said.

"What?"

"Just turn the knob the other way."

"Oh."

Moments later. "Hey . . . that worked."

The dog whimpered. So did I. Hell, I think Yago rolled his eyes.

"Listen," I said, trying to show some patience. "Is there any strangers in town?"

"Are there?" Kermit was coming around, water slopping over the edges of his brown bowler. He slid to a stop in front of Yago and held out the water for the Arabian to drink.

"What?" I said.

"He used to teach school," Cicero said. "But got kicked in the head by a mule."

Yago drunk. I yelled, "Is there any strangers in town?"

"Are there?" Kermit said, his face smiling. "*Are* there any strangers in town? Not, *Is* there. That's just ignorant."

"Some new miners," Cicero called out. He looked worried. Might have thought I was about to kill his pard, which, I must admit, had just crossed my mind. "Even some more damned Chinamen."

I lowered the gun. What I thought was a pretty good notion had struck me.

"No gunmen, though?" I said. "Just miners?"

"Gunmen?" Kermit stepped back, but that was all right because I didn't want Yago to drink too much water. Especially the water that was to be stole, or even bought, from the Calico Water Works Incorporated in that wagon.

"Not since the last shooting," Cicero said. "That was some affray."

Affray? He must have gotten that from Kermit during one of his lucid spells.

"Do you know that Colonel Wilson J. M. Drury, the famous writer, is in town?" Kermit said, lucid for a spell. "He's writing a novel about what happened a week or so ago."

"Thirty men killed," called out Cicero, who wasn't lucid.

"He's staying at the Hyena House," Kermit said. "Waiting on remuneration from his publisher for his last work for Beadle and Adams Five Cent Library."

The Winchester returned to the scabbard, and I nodded at the dog. "Thanks for your help, gentlemen," I told Cicero and Kermit. "Don't tell anybody that you saw me."

I let Yago lope up the hill, into the canyon, even pushed him into a gallop. Had to get away from Cicero and Kermit, or risk becoming stupid and ignorant. Well, I quickly decided that I was being harsh on those two boys. They had a nice dog. Didn't mean no harm. And they had even give me an idea.

Whip Watson wasn't in town. Not yet. The Palace of Calico wasn't finished. Maybe Whip was waiting for its completion, but that might take awhile. At some point, though, he would ride into town. Only he'd think I was dead. He'd think he could ride in, and start charging Calico prices for . . . well . . . you know.

Yet if my plan worked, he'd be riding right into an ambush. I could get Calico's vigilance committee behind me, but I needed someone who knowed who was who and what was what and how Calico run things. Someone who was trusted by everyone in town. Someone who trusted me. And I needed not to be seen by one of Whip's boys, because even if Whip and the girls wasn't in Calico, I had to think he'd have some spies lurking on that main street.

That took me right to the Calico cemetery.

As boneyards go, it's more than fair. Big rock wall

all around it. White cross on top of the wall with a nice, big gate. I reined in Yago, slid from the saddle, pushed open the gate, and let the horse inside.

Then I closed the gate, looped the reins over the arm of the nearest crooked cross, found myself a shady spot, and sat down with the canteen of tepid water.

Lots of towns I've been in, they have all sorts of cemeteries. There's one for the Catholics and another for the Israelites. You'll find another for the Negroes, and usually a real big one for all the paupers, the tinhorns, the cowboys, the gunmen. Calico only had one cemetery. Now, it was divided into sections. I saw the six-pointed star off in one corner, and figured that was for the Israelites. And the one without no markers, nothing, that had to be where the Chinese got planted. And way off yonder in the back, the biggest section of all, must have been Calico's potter's field. That's where I saw the mounds of fresh dirt. Eight of them. Would have been backbreaking, sweaty work to dig all those holes, then shovel dirt and rocks back over the coffin, or tarp, or nothing but the dead men's clothes. Just sticks in the ground for tombstones, with six of them already washed away or blown down. Made me wonder which of them mounds was Guttersnipe Gary's final resting place, and if Rogers Canfield knowed he'd be spending eternity with gunmen and not alongside regular, law-abiding folks like "Here Lies Joe Turning, Killed in Cave-In, 1883" or "Whit Stacey, Struck by Lightning" or "John R. Robinson, Hanged By Mistake." Calico's finest.

Wasn't long till I heard the squeaking wheel of

the Calico Water Works Incorporated wagon. Then I heard nothing. The sun sank, the wind began to moan, and I waited in the graveyard. Which would unnerve quite a few people, I reckon, but I'd dragged dead bodies into a shot-to-hell omnibus in the middle of the night with angry coyotes and wolves and ravens and buzzards giving me their evilest eyes. I'd survived the Devil's Playground, the worst sand dunes I'd ever seen except in *Frank Leslie's Illustrated Weekly,* and the cruel Mojave Desert. I'd been whipped by Whip Watson and lived to tell about it.

I wasn't frightened by no ghosts.

When the moon rose, I led Yago out of the cemetery, climbed into the saddle, and rode around the long rock wall. Rode into the canyon, which widened, then narrowed, then deepened.

Soon, I saw lights and smelled food cooking, heard dogs yapping, finally growling and barking at me. I rode past the dismal huts, past the chickens and ducks. I came to the ladder that had fallen and taken Pink Shirt to his demise. Well, it wasn't that ladder. Was a new one, sturdier, but still not built for the likes of me.

I tethered Yago to a clump of creosote, put the hobbles on his front legs, taken the Winchester, and went up the ladder to the ledge, then up the steps in the rocks, and found myself in East Calico.

Course, I had to feel my way around. It's one thing when you're walking through Chinatown at night. Things look different than when you're in broad daylight and running from building to building, shack to shack, trying not to get killed by two hired assassins.

Eventually, I found a place I knowed all too well. For a second, I stood there amazed. I mean, Lucky Ben Wong had fixed up his bathhouse, which I'd damned near destroyed. Maybe that's why he used empty coal oil cans.

As I come up to the entrance, the makeshift door of India rubber tarp swung open, and I stepped aside, pulling my hat down low. Didn't want no one to recognize me, even East Calico.

"Look fine, look fine, best-looking gentleman in Calico." Lucky Ben Wong was right behind this tall, stout gent in what appeared to be a brown sack suit. Lucky Ben Wong was dusting off Brown Sack Suit's shoulders with a fine linen handkerchief.

"Yes, yes, yes, look fine, fine, come."

Brown Sack Suit grunted and hurried away from the house that smelled of dirty bathwater and kerosene. If he seen me, he give no indication.

Lucky Ben Wong kept bowing after the guy's back, till he rounded the corner, then Lucky Ben Wong straightened, started to go inside, but caught my shadow. He leaped back, and I stepped forward.

"Don't worry," I whispered. "It's me."

"Haircut?" he asked. "You look awful. Awful. Me fix. Me fix. Ask anybody. Haircut. Bath. What need you?"

"It's me, Lucky Ben," I said.

He still didn't recognize me.

"Opium?" He grinned. "Best in California. No find good stuff even on Barbary Coast. Good stuff. Make you crazy."

"Lucky Ben . . ."

"Stake? Miner? Want money? Come back in morning. No money business this time dark."

By that time, I'd stepped into the light coming out of the cracks between the coal oil cans. That stopped him and his silly damned accent.

"Jesus Christ," he said. "Micah Bishop, what in hell happened to you?"

CHAPTER TWENTY-FOUR

Since I was already there, it seemed like a pretty good idea, so I had me a hot bath, and Lucky Ben Wong brewed up some real fine tea, rang a little bell outside what passed for that front door, and this Chinese girl appeared quick as a genie would in a storybook, and Lucky Ben Wong handed her all my clothes and told her to run to her ma's laundry and get my duds as clean as possible and return them immediately. I didn't tell them that the clothes wasn't mine to begin with, and I'd never heard of leather pants being sent to a laundry, mainly because I was pretty relaxed by this time. The water and soap burned at first, but before long the welts on my back, and the bullet hole through my arm, and the rope burns on my palms didn't hurt so bad. Felt rather content, or as content as I could feel with all that was going on—and all that would be happening soon.

No, I didn't smoke no opium.

Sitting, relaxing in the tub, sipping tea, I told Lucky Ben Wong all that had happened. But I kept that Winchester rifle leaning against the tub, cocked, ready . . . just in case I had been spotted. I mean, the last time I'd been at Lucky Ben Wong's place, I'd damned near gotten myself killed, and things like that I don't often forget.

Lucky Ben Wong had to pull up a stool, and sit down, head bowed, shaking his head as I dealt him my story. He didn't interrupt me once, the Chinese being real polite. When I was finished he stared at me and asked:

"You were alone with my Jingfei . . . at night?"

"No." Almost spilt tea into the soapy, dirty water. "Never alone." Hell, I had Peach Fuzz for a chaperone. And Candy Crutchfield.

"But she is all right?"

All I could do was shrug, and kind of hedge my bet, so to speak. "Well, she was. I mean she was alive."

He nodded, and pushed back the little cap on his head.

"How many were killed?"

"Well," I said, "that would take some tallying." I hadn't kept track of all the bodies I'd loaded and cremated in that omnibus. "There was Peach Fuzz . . . the two Zekes—"

This time, Lucky Ben Wong lost his patience. "The girls." I detected an edge in his voice. "How many girls were killed?"

"Six when the Conestoga rolled," I told him. "Bonnie Little. Three others in the back of the horse-bus." Didn't like thinking about those poor girls, but now I had to. "Couple others might have gotten scratched up or winged, but nothing that looked mortal."

"And Jingfei . . . she was . . . unscathed?"

Well, now, I couldn't exactly say that anybody, male or female, had come out of that ruction unscathed. Granted, I didn't think none of them had been as mauled and mutilated as I'd been. Jingfei had caught some splinters in her leg, probably had a few more cuts and bruises, but as I done some studying and remembering, I was also looking into Lucky Ben Wong's eyes, and they'd had turned as hard as Jingfei's was prone to do. So I told him:

"She's finer than frog's hair cut eight ways."

His look didn't change.

"She wasn't hurt," I said. Not saying, but thinking, *Too badly*.

"That is good." He bowed. "That is good. I thank you, Micah Bishop. My Jingfei thanks you."

I finished the tea and reluctantly climbed out of the tub. Lucky Ben Wong fetched me a real soft towel and one of them nice silk robes. I dried myself off and put on the robe, waited for that girl to come back so I could get dressed in clothes fit for a man to wear.

Then I sat down on the bench, and pushed away the opium pipes, keeping that Winchester on my lap. When Lucky Ben Wong returned, handing me a cup of tea, he couldn't take his eyes off my rifle.

"You are nervous?" He nodded at the long gun.

"Careful," I told him.

He fired up a cigar and plopped down on the stool again.

"So there are thirty-eight brides? Between these girls being transported by this Watson man and this Crutchfield woman?"

"That sounds about right."

His head shook. "And this Palace of Calico . . . it was to be . . . a . . . a . . . a . . . ?"

"That's right."

"But you cannot make anyone do what one does not wish to do? This is America, is it not?"

"It's California," I told him.

"My Jingfei would never do what they wish her to do."

I smiled. He read "Quiet Not" the same way I did.

"She'd rather die," Lucky Ben Wong said. "She would die first."

Which killed my smile. I set the China cup on some drool left by the last person to partake of Lucky Ben Wong's opium.

"Well, Watson thinks I'm dead. So I've been trying to come up with a plan—so that Jingfei don't have to do nothing drastic and dramatic and all."

He leaned forward. "You are good at planning?"

I shrugged, then nodded, then had to shake my head. "Not really . . . but there are the vigilance committee."

"Is," he said.

I said, "How's that?"

He said, "There is the vigilance committee. Not are. *Are* is plural. *Is* is singular."

"I see," I said. What I saw was me beating the hell out of Lucky Ben Wong and Kermit Of The Calico Water Works . . . Incorporated During A Lucid Moment.

"That's why I'm here," I went on. "I don't know Calico. I don't know this country. Watson said he had sent his girls, the ones he had left, to hole up in some canyon around these parts. Then he was bringing in Crutchfield's gals and the six Crutchfield had woman-napped, and, of course, your Jingfei. They'd meet up in that canyon."

He sighed. Puffed on the cigar. Shook his head.

"There are many canyons in these mountains." Holding up his right hand, he started with the thumb and progressed to his fingers. "Wall Street Canyon . . . Mule Canyon . . . Odessa Canyon." Me? When counting on my hands, I always started with my pointer finger as my Number One, and I'd knowed some who'd use their thumb as Number One, but I'd always used my thumb for Number Five, but Lucky Ben Wong started with his pinky finger as Number One, which was just real strange.

I stopped him. "He has thirty-eight girls with him," I reminded him. "He'll want to parade them into town. That's why he had those Columbus Carriages—cost three hundred dollars for one in Prescott."

"Some of the canyons are big enough to hide not only thirty-eight women, but wagons and horses and mules—"

"And gunmen and Gatling guns," I reminded him.

"Those, too." His head bobbed.

"But if he's gonna parade them women down Main Street, get the men folk all excited . . ."

Lucky Ben Wong got my meaning. "He'd want them fresh. Clean." That's why Lucky Ben Wong run a bathhouse.

"That's right." I smiled.

"He'd need water."

"Which ain't common here."

"Five miles from here." He waved his hand in what I took was the general direction of where this town got its water.

"But I saw a water wagon from the Calico Water Works Incorporated coming into town late this afternoon. Watson wouldn't want Cicero and Kermit, or even their old dog, to see those women."

"But he could hide them in a nearby canyon."

"That's a good place to start looking," I said. "We've narrowed down the most likely spot he'll be hiding out. Now here's the second thing I was thinking. Do you know who runs the vigilance committee?"

His head bobbed again. He flicked ash onto the dirt floor. "The owners of one of the mercantiles, Slater and McCoy."

"Good. So here's my plan. You slip over to the mercantile, tell Slater and McCoy what's going on . . ."

Lucky Ben Wong was getting real impatient, so you can forget about what I wrote down just a few minutes earlier about the Chinese being patient and polite and all that bunk.

"Why me?" he interrupted. "Why not you?"

"You've staked how many people in this town?" He didn't answer, because I didn't give him time to. "Slater and McCoy will trust you a lot quicker than they'd trust me." I mean, I'd blowed a fellow through the window on the top floor of the bank building, which meant they'd have to replace that window—at Calico prices—before they could rent it to somebody else. And I'd been in the middle of that shoot-out that left eight men dead, and even if Mr. Slater's brother did run the undertaking parlor, I didn't think the citizens of Calico would find me the kind of stranger they'd trust. Besides, the story I'd just told Lucky Ben Wong was mighty hard to swallow, without some Irish whiskey or London porter to wash it down with.

Lucky Ben Wong didn't say nothing to that, which I figured meant he saw my reasoning. So he went back to puffing on that cigar, and I went back to my plan.

"Have Slater and McCoy round up some of the best guns in Calico. They sneak over to that canyon near the water hole, and they ambush Whip Watson. Tell them not to give Whip no chance. Just open fire and shoot down them dogs. Well, maybe they don't have to shoot Mister Clark. If they can help it, that is. Hit them hard and fast. Then the girls are saved, and Watson and his blackhearts are dead, and I . . . no, you . . . you are free to marry Jingfei and live happily ever after in your"— I wave my hand around his cans of coal oil—"your . . . palace."

I sniffed. Damn place stank like coal oil.

Lucky Ben Wong wasn't smiling. Fact is, his face had turned to stone, and got even harder the more explaining I done. Hell, I thought it was a great plan. The vigilance committee would lead the attack. I'd just stay here for a while, drink tea, maybe sleep a bit, perhaps see how the Chinese played poker. Here, in Chinatown, I wouldn't be as likely to get killed as members of the vigilance committee.

"That is your plan?" Lucky Ben Wong asked.

"Yeah." I frowned. Lucky Ben Wong was grinding out his cigar in an ashtray, and he was really destroying that cigar till there wasn't nothing left of it but shreds of tobacco in the remnants of ash.

"Is it your wish to have my Jingfei killed? And thirty-seven other young American women?"

They wasn't all American. I mean, I knowed at least one of them was a portly Hun. And there was a Welsh lady. Probably one or two straight off the boat from Ireland, and that don't include the two Lannon twins from Savannah, Georgia, by way of County Cork.

"No," I told him. "That ain't my plan at all." My plan, if that damned Chinese mercenary had been listening at all, was to get Whip Watson and his gunmen killed, excepting, if at all possible, Mr. Clark. And saving all thirty-eight girls.

"How many girls were killed when Crutchfield attacked Watson?"

"Well . . ." There was six. I knowed that. I'd helped Jingfei pull the bodies from the wreckage.

"And how many girls were killed when Watson attacked Crutchfield."

"A . . . couple . . . or four."

"Do you think Crutchfield wanted to kill those girls?"

My head shook.

"Do you think Watson wished to see four other girls killed?"

"No." My voice become real quiet.

"Of course not. That would cut into their profits. Ricochets kill. Bullets have no conscience. If Slater and McCoy and the vigilantes were to attack the camp of the outlaws, even if Watson's men were wiped out—"

"But maybe not Mister Clark," I cut in. "Unless it just couldn't be helped."

He didn't care for my interruption, but got right down to his point. "There would likely be women hurt, killed. By stray shots. Or, as mad as this Whip

Watson is said to be, he might begin shooting them down. To spite the vigilantes. To spite us."

He was right, the little Chinese peckerwood. Whip Watson would definitely shoot down Jingfei. Because Jingfei wouldn't be huddled behind some Columbus carriage's back leather seat that smelled like fresh wax. She'd be right in the midst of things.

I stared at my tea.

"Well," I muttered.

"We must have all of the girls out of harm's way when we attack Whip Watson," Lucky Ben Wong said.

"All right," I agreed.

Lucky Ben Wong got right down to it, and, the more he talked, the more my head nodded, and the more I agreed that his plan was still a bit better than mine.

We would let Whip Watson go through with his original idea, let him parade the girls right down Main Street in those Columbus buggies. The mail-order brides would be escorted into The Palace of Calico, and once they were inside, then we'd open fire and gun down Whip Watson and all his boys, excepting, if at all possible, Mr. Clark. Behind the walls of The Palace of Calico, which Lucky Ben Wong assured me was built like a damned fort, those thirty-eight women would be safe from stray bullets.

"Yeah," I said when Lucky Ben Wong fired up another cigar to wait for my critique of his battle plan, "but that's a long wait, ain't it?"

"What do you mean?"

"Well, Watson's bordello ain't finished yet."

"Not quite," he said, "but there are beds in the upstairs rooms, and the back bar is in the saloon. For what you tell me, that is all Whip Watson needs."

I looked perplexed. "He has beds in the room . . . already?"

"Yes." Lucky Ben Wong's head bobbed rapidly. "One room has two beds in it. My cousin cleaned all the sheets and pillowcases for all of the beds yesterday."

I sighed, then thought about the room with two beds, which, the way I thought, would be for the Lannon girls from Savannah, but quickly tried to put such wicked thoughts outside my head, and shifted the Winchester in my lap.

"It'd be better to wait until the place is all dolled up, though, don't you reckon? With more than beds and fresh linens?"

Lucky Ben Wong's head shook hard. "Whip Watson doesn't have the luxury of time anymore. He has lost too much money already. He'll want to start earning money now, rather than spend more."

Made sense. I shrugged, then done some studying on more of Lucky Ben Wong's plan.

"Well," I said, "wouldn't Whip Watson have some boys inside The Palace? When the girls started coming in?"

"Yes. He is no fool."

"So . . . them boys . . . they'd have to get . . ."

"Killed," Lucky Ben Wong finished my thought.

That tea didn't taste so good about then.

"Listen, my friend Micah Bishop, Whip would have four men inside. Maybe five." Lucky Ben Wong's reassuring tone didn't comfort me at all. "We could overpower them before they knew they were dead. Then ambush the men outside when the last of the brides are inside. It is simple. It is flawless."

Maybe, I thought, but something else had begun to trouble me.

"When you say *we* . . . you mean Slater and McCoy and the vigilantes, don't you?"

His head shook even before I was done finishing my question.

"We cannot trust Slater or McCoy," he told me.

"Why not?"

"You mentioned that the late Rogers Canfield and Whip Watson and Candy Crutchfield had a silent partner in Calico, did you not?"

I allowed how that I'd likely mentioned that.

"What if McCoy is that partner? What if Slater is the villain? If we tipped the partner off, we would put your life, and more important, the life of my Jingfei and the lives of those other poor girls, in jeopardy."

Now my tea was curdling. Running fingers through my wet hair, I asked, "So who'd we have inside the building?"

"You."

"Against four men?"

"Perhaps five."

"And outside?"

"Me."

I couldn't recollect how many men Whip Watson had remaining, even if I didn't include Mr. Clark.

"That's it?" I didn't ask Lucky Ben Wong if he didn't have no friends here in East Calico who he could trust.

"Kill Whip Watson is like cutting off the head of a rattlesnake. Kill him, the others are as good as dead. They will leave town at a gallop."

It didn't sound like nothing I'd bet on, but I kind of rubbed the rifle in my lap.

"What do you think of my plan?" Lucky Ben Wong asked with boyish enthusiasm for what struck me as a dumb plan, but, I had to admit, it was better than mine.

I shrugged. "Might work." Although my plan, even if it meant having to trust Slater, McCoy, and the vigilance committee, would, in theory, mean that I'd stand a better chance of not getting killed.

"Good." He held out his hand. "You will need more bullets, I imagine, for your long gun."

Standing on weak knees, I somehow pitched the rifle to him. He nudged it into the crook of his arm, then his right hand disappeared behind his black silk shirt, and when it returned, it held this fancy-engraved .41-caliber "Swamp Angel" pocket revolver, and I thought he was about to shoot me dead for no good reason when the chimes outside his front door started singing.

CHAPTER TWENTY-FIVE

He swung around, dropping the rifle, heading to the partition that separated his coal-oil-can building. Right before I blew out the light, I saw him swinging back toward me, but then it was too dark to see nothing except streaks of light coming through the sides of the tarp.

The chimes sang again.

Quiet as I could, I crawled along the floor, fingers out searching, finally touched the fore-stock of my rifle, which I snatched into my hands.

"Micah?" Lucky Ben Wong whispered. "Where are you?"

"Right here," I told the darkness.

I could hear him breathing, and the chimes sounding again.

"Could be," I told him, "the girl with my duds."

"No," he said. "Not her."

"Well, I got the rifle. Want me to start shooting?" I knowed how easy it was to shoot through what he had for walls. Doors, too.

"No."

Another sigh, then Lucky Ben Wong slipped

through the tarp and moved toward the rubber tarp. I found myself a better position, sidling over to where Lucky Ben Wong had been, sticking the Winchester's barrel through the slit between canvas and coal oil cans, and drawed a bead on Lucky Ben Wong's front door.

Soon as that chime-ringer stepped inside, I'd shoot down the cur without a call.

Lucky Ben Wong slipped the gun behind his back, but kept his right hand on the grip, then moved carefully to the tarp, put his left hand on the cloth, called out. "Yes. Yes. It late. Very late. Come back tomorrow." He had slipped into that bad English again.

I couldn't hear what the person outside said, but it was something that staggered Lucky Ben Wong. His hand come off the grips of that "Swamp Angel," and he was pulling open that front tarp as fast as humanly possible, and a figure stepped inside, and the front door closed.

Me? I almost dropped my rifle, then I come through the partition.

"Jingfei!" me and Lucky Ben Wong cried out at the same time.

"Micah!"

Made me forget all my aches and injuries and wounds that was going to leave some remindful scars. Jingfei run right past her betrothed and greeted me warmly. "I knew you'd make it out of that desert. I just knew it."

I give her one of my awkward shrugs.

"I didn't know if I could trust Mister Clark," she said.

Now my shrug wasn't just playacting awkward, it was for real. "Mister Clark?" I asked.

"Yes." She turned back to Lucky Ben Wong, who wasn't looking none too happy at the reception I'd gotten and he'd missed out on. I mean, Jingfei didn't kiss me or nothing, but you'd expect her to greet the man who'd paid good money to get himself a wife a little better than brushing him aside to come hug a stove-up gambler dressed in a robe that was too small for him.

"I bribed Mister Clark one hundred dollars." Back at me, she said, "For not killing you."

He hadn't killed me, and now I knowed why. I also knowed that he was not a man to be trusted. He'd told me that I owed him, but I didn't owe that swindler nothing. He'd been paid a lot of money for not killing me. Hell's bells, the law in Las Vegas, New Mexico Territory, had put up only seventy-five dollars for my capture—and that was for murdering (it was self-defense, I swear) a fellow and busting out of jail before they could hang me.

"My Jingfei," Lucky Ben Wong said, and she faced her husband again. They spoke in Chinese, softly, and done some bowing at each other. Then they approached each other, studying the other's features. Jingfei was a good four inches taller than Lucky Ben Wong. Prettier, too. They spoke some more Chinese, then Lucky Ben Wong was looking past her and at me, and it wasn't no friendly look.

He said something in a most unpleasant tone.

She said something right sharp back at him, which caused him to step back toward the wall of cans.

"Maybe I should leave." Actually, I had no intention of going nowhere.

"No." Jingfei looked back at me. "We haven't much time."

"How did you escape Whip Watson, Future Wife?" Lucky Ben Wong asked.

"I bribed Mister Clark with another hundred dollars," she answered, "but I must go back to camp."

That caused my heart to jump. Lucky Ben Wong's, too. He sang out, "Why?" I cried, "No!"

"If I'm not back, the other women will be in danger," she said. She give Lucky Ben Wong one of them soulful stares, and turned to me with my own personal pleading look that nobody could resist. "I must be back before morning. I just came to find you, Future Husband, my savior." No, she wasn't talking to me. Back looking at that little dude in his black silk with his head shaved except for that queue. "They will be bringing the girls to town . . . tomorrow."

I cussed.

"What time?" Lucky Ben Wong asked.

She sighed. "I do not know. Afternoon would be my guess. But it could be morning. They have been very busy getting the girls . . . *ready.*" The last word she spit out like poison.

"Then we could get the vigilance committee and have them ambush the camp." I come back to my original plan. "Where is Whip's camp?"

She give me a look that wasn't soulful, and wasn't incredulous, nor pleading, but was kind of, well, horrified. Her look had me deciding that Lucky Ben Wong was right all along, so I changed my tune in a hurry.

"No, no, that's a bad idea. Women could get killed. We'll have to think of another plan."

Which got me an evil glare from Lucky Ben Wong.

"I have a plan," Jingfei announced.

A wave of exhaustion overtook her, and she had to sit in a wicker chair in the corner by me. Lucky Ben Wong hurried to the teapot and poured her some tea, and I dipped back behind the tarp, fumbled my way through the dark, found a washcloth that I hoped wasn't too dirty, and brung it back to the other room, wringing it out as I walked, catching another one of those mean looks from Lucky Ben Wong. Hell, the floor was dirt. Wasn't like I was ruining some fancy rug or nothing, dripping water, and maybe some blood on it.

I handed the cloth to Jingfei, who stared at me, then smiled. Then set the rag on the table beside her, and sipped some tea.

That's pretty much when she saw where she was. She looked around this part of the room, Lucky Ben's personal quarters, and then she looked at the walls, and the doors, and she handed me the teacup, then turned to her betrothed, and she said, "*This* is where *we* will *live?*"

"How many gunmen will be with Whip Watson?" Lucky Ben Wong asked.

By that time, we was all sipping tea again, in the front parlor room. From a pocket in my robe, I pulled the watch I'd taken off one of the dead men—kept real good time—and seen that it was 12:25. Jingfei said it had taken her two hours to get from Watson's camp in the canyons to town, and another half hour to find Lucky Ben Wong's place in the dark.

"Seventeen," she said.

"Is that including Mister Clark?" I asked.

"No, he's on our side."

Which likely had cost her another hundred dollars, and that got me staring at her suit of *moiré,* and I figured she had to have a money belt. I mean, I didn't think Mr. Clark would take a letter of credit or nothing like that. Most men of his poor upbringing and low morals dealt in cash.

"And Doctor Kent," Jingfei said, "he will help us, too."

Wasn't sure I trusted either of them sidewinders. If she mentioned Juan Pedro as an ally, I'd have to speak up.

"Whip Watson will be in town first, to get the people ready," Jingfei told us. "They plan on parading us up the street, one at a time, in those dreadful carriages. Do you know what he plans to do with us?"

We both did, but she didn't give us time to answer. "He says the contracts you"—she nodded at Lucky Ben Wong—"and all the other husbands signed had a clause that if the matrimonial agent died before delivery of the brides, the contract was null and void."

"So the husbands would be out of the money," I said.

"Yes." Her tone got real steely. "But we women will be out of something much. . . ." Her lips and eyes tightened.

Which meant that Whip Watson was going to force twenty-five of them—the twins from Savannah sharing a room—into prostitution at The Palace of Calico. The others, the more homely ones, I figured, would be auctioned off as brides.

"That is not the contract I signed," she said.

"Invisible ink," I said.

"And Watson likely has a copy of that contract," Lucky Ben Wong.

"It wouldn't hold up in court," I said, having some experience in courts and trials and things of that nature.

"There is no court in Calico. No law. Not even a jail." Lucky Ben Wong had to remind me of all the bad things about this burg.

"But I made a copy of the contract," Jingfei said. "I had my attorney look at it. It's in his office in Trinidad."

"You went to an attorney?" Lucky Ben Wong turned pale.

"Of course," she said. "I am no fool, Future Husband."

"But this . . . is America . . . it is . . . the West . . . A man's word is his bond."

"I am no man." She might have had to remind Lucky Ben Wong of that, but not me.

I got smart. "So, all we got to do is get a copy of the contract you signed. Show it to a circuit judge. Then when they see the contracts with the invisible ink, Whip Watson will go to prison for a good long time. That's your plan?"

Lucky Ben Wong spoke up. "It will take weeks to get that contract to Calico."

"Then we must fight," Jingfei said. "Tomorrow."

Now, I wasn't keen on that fighting idea, not with the odds we faced, but Jingfei . . . well, all she had to do was look at me, and so I dealt myself in the game. That's when Lucky Ben Wong rose, bowed toward his beloved, and turned to me. "Your rifle, Micah Bishop. I have cartridges."

I stood, give him a real formal nod, and tossed him the Winchester. He caught it like he was used to catching rifles, and bowed at Jingfei one more time. My mouth dry from the thought of what might happen come daylight, I taken the teacup in my right hand. While I was sipping tea, Lucky Ben Wong tossed the rifle behind him, and his right hand come up with that "Swamp Angel" in his fist.

The little pistol was aimed right at my belly.

"Future Husband!" Jingfei jumped to her feet. "What are you doing?"

But I knowed. I'm slow, but every now and then I get struck with genius.

"It's you. You stake everybody," I said. "Including Rogers Canfield."

He smiled. "And Whip Watson."

"Candy Crutchfield, too."

The arrogant little peckerwood grinned even wider, and I felt sick. Hurt even. Hell, I'd told Jingfei that her Future Husband was a good man. Turns out, he was a real peckerwood.

Jingfei took a step toward him, but I reached over with my free hand, and grabbed her shoulder, reined her in. No, I did not use her body to shield my own. I eased her to my side, but she was still mad, so angry she begun shaking.

"Future Husband," she said, "I agreed to be your wife. Not a . . ." I reckon she used the Manchu word for soiled dove.

"You will be my wife," he said. "All of the women who will work in The Palace of Calico will be married. To me. To Whip Watson's men. And you know, as brides, you must do as your husbands command."

That caused me to snort. He didn't know the women I'd knowed. Especially Jingfei.

"You're mad," Jingfei told him.

"But this is America, Quiet Not," Lucky Ben Wong said. "Ask him. Ask Micah Bishop. Ask him if not many gamblers have concubines who also sell their bodies to strangers. It is America. Capitalism. The Gilded Age. It does not mean that the husbands do not love their wives less. It is all for . . . money."

She was going after the cad, and once again I had to pull her back.

"I won't be a prostitute," she said. That was in English, and Lucky Ben Wong cringed, but he didn't lower the .41.

"Tell her what I say is true!" He raised the gun at my head.

Of course, what he said was true. Not that I'd ever had no concubine, or any "wife" who worked the tenderloin, but, sure, there were men who done such things. Women, too. But I told Lucky Ben Wong, "Only a son of a bitch would do such a thing."

He sighed. Shook his head. Give Jingfei one of those loving looks. "You are a beautiful woman. The Americans would find you exotic. The Chinese would—"

"I don't want to hear it."

I'd heard enough. Jingfei yelled at him in rapid Chinese, and when Lucky Ben Wong dropped his head at the insults, that was all I needed. Since my left hand gripped Jingfei's shoulder, I jerked her back, and she fell—right through the tarp. Still holding the China teacup, I flung it at Lucky Ben Wong, who flinched, the craven coward, and rushed his shot. I was also moving, through the partition, and into the dark bathhouse.

A bullet punched through the tarp. Banged off one of the coal oil cans.

"Micah!" Jingfei called out.

I reached toward her voice. Grabbed her hand. Another bullet sliced lower, banged off the tub. By then we was up and running right toward the new wall that had replaced the one I'd torn through during my last visit to Lucky Ben Wong's.

Hit hard, smelled the kerosene, and the cans give, and dirt was falling and we went through, bouncing off the ground in the moonlit night. Behind us, still in his home, Lucky Ben Wong cussed, screamed, and shot.

Rolling over, I saw light from the hole in the wall. Lucky Ben Wong had grabbed a lantern, was holding it in his left hand. There was a flash, and a bullet zipped past my ear. Jingfei screamed—not out of fright, but anger—she was cussing her Future Husband in English and Chinese. All around us, dogs barked, hens squawked, roosters crowed, and Chinese men, women, and kids yelled.

I could make out Lucky Ben Wong, behind the dirt pouring from the roof, and the cans scattered around him. I had no gun. All I could find to defend my person—and Jingfei's life—was an empty can of coal oil. So I grabbed it and flung it, and it sailed like one of them baseballs hurled by a ballist, and struck Lucky Ben Wong somewhere on his person.

Don't exactly know where, and I'm still not certain what happened next. Well, I do know. Because once the *Calico Print* got things in order and could publish newspapers again, it had this little notice, which I clip and paste inside this journal.

DEADLY FIRE
Hurls Chinaman into Fiery Hell
In Blaze in East Calico

Lucky Ben Wong, the renowned Oriental who ran a bathhouse and barbershop in East Calico, was killed in a tragic fire that destroyed his place of business during the early morning hours of the 24th inst.

This conflagration, of course, was much smaller than the one everyone is talking about, but it does deserve notice in our newspaper.

The Celestial businessman lived where he worked, and manufactured his place with empty cans of kerosene. Having recently repaired his walls with new cans, he was apparently emptying a can to repair his abode when tragedy struck. The fuel was ignited by a lamp that stood near his body. An explosion followed, as kerosene is as explosive as gunpowder, and the burning oil consumed his body in a most shocking manner.

Perhaps the Celestial had smoked some of the opium, which was also available at his bathhouse. That might explain this act of folly, which resulted in tragedy and an agonizing death.

The entire establishment was destroyed, but the Chinese neighbors prevented the conflagration from spreading. Jasper Wiggins, barber in Calico, however, said he will be open for business in two weeks and welcomes all of Lucky Ben Wong's former customers. Wiggins, however, wants to make it clear that his barbershop will not have opium.

That ain't exactly how it happened, but I have yet to write a letter to the editor of the *Calico Print* to correct his report.

We shielded our eyes, Jingfei and me, and heard some more explosions—apparently the remaining rounds in the little hideaway gun Lucky Ben Wong was holding went off from the heat. People started gathering around, a few pointing, some looking like it was a Fourth of July fireworks show, and quite a few battling the blaze with wet blankets.

"Oh," Jingfei said. "My."

I figured it was time to get away from there. So I helped Jingfei up and led her toward the steps in the rocks and the ladder.

We didn't say nothing for a while. I mean, it had to be a shock. First she learns that the man she was betrothed to was a heel. Then she watches him burn like bacon. She'd come all this way, from Trinidad, Colorado, and now there was a fire consuming what was to be her home—not a loss, I can assure you—but she was a strong woman with a strong mind and strong will.

There wasn't time for mourning, and, well, criminy, it ain't like Lucky Ben Wong had courted her or nothing. They'd exchanged a few letters is all. Hell, she hadn't even laid eyes on the dog till an hour earlier. A son of a bitch like that ain't worth tears or grief.

When we reached the ladder, I asked, "Are you all right?"

"Yes."

A sigh escaped her throat, and she leaned on me. "I was a fool."

"No." I lifted her chin, looked into her face. "He was the fool."

She pulled away from me, and I figured she'd let

me have it for being disrespectful about the dead, especially since the dead had been her betrothed.

"If Whip Watson learns that his silent partner is dead . . ." she began.

I finished for her. "He'll figure it means more money for him. He ain't gonna fret over Lucky Ben Wong's demise. And you shouldn't, either."

"I won't. But this means you have only yourself and Mister Clark. And perhaps Doctor Kent."

"You don't have to go back to that camp," I told her, but I knowed what she'd say, and she said it.

"I must."

I said, because I'd read a few of those half-dime novels writ by that Colonel Wilson J. M. Drury, even though in his stories it's always the woman saying this to the hero: "I know."

"I have a plan," she said.

Then the sky behind us lit up. Another can had exploded. I could hear Chinese men directing the wet-blanket brigade.

"They'll be able to see this fire from the canyon," she said. "I need to get back now."

"Be careful." Which is what the girl always tells the hero in Colonel Drury's dreadfuls, too.

She started toward the ladder, but turned, come to me, and kissed me. On the lips. It was a hard kiss, because she had thin lips, and they was all dried and she sort of smelled like coal oil and dirt, but it was a fine kiss. I kissed her back. Then she was starting down the ladder when another can boomed.

"What happened?" she asked.

I shrugged. "Reckon he should have washed out them cans first before using them for walls."

"What a stupid peckerwood," she said. "And I almost married that idiot."

CHAPTER TWENTY-SIX

I held the ladder steady, and she hurried down into the canyon, then hitched up her skirt and took off running, but it didn't take long till the darkness swallowed her. Unable to move, I just stood there, smelling smoke, feeling the wind at my back, staring at the darkness, wondering if I'd ever see Jingfei again.

For a moment, I cussed myself, telling me that I never should have let her go, but that spell didn't last long. Hell, I had to admit, I couldn't have stopped her. And, well, there was other lives at stake.

People were gathering across the bridge in Calico proper, pointing at the blaze, so I decided it would be a good idea for me to skedaddle. Down the ladder I went—with only the moonlight and the glow from that ever-growing fire over at the late Lucky Ben Wong's place to see by, and no one holding the ladder steady for me—and found Yago sleeping where I'd hobbled him.

"All right," I told that horse after I'd woke him by removing the hobbles, and tightening the cinch.

"It'll be a busy day this morning, boy. But that's all right." I taken the reins, and swung into the saddle. "Jingfei has a plan." We rode back toward the Calico cemetery. "The problem is," I told the Arabian, "she didn't tell me what that plan is."

But that was all right, too. Because I was coming up with one myself.

The sign above the door read:

SLATER & McCOY
Purveyors in Implements & Sundries

The fellow underneath the sign held one such implement in his right hand, another .41-caliber "Swamp Angel," which I guess is where the late Lucky Ben Wong had procured his.

"We're closed," Mr. McCoy said. He wore brown pants, brown boots, and a brown vest. The shirt was white. No tie. No hat.

I didn't move.

"We open at eight," he said. "Now stop banging on this door and come back then. We're doing our books."

"I ain't here to buy nothing," I said.

Which made him take a step back inside. "You must be."

That's when Mr. Slater, also dressed in brown, come to the door and peered over his partner's shoulder. "Maybe he always dresses like that," Mr. Slater said.

All right. I didn't have nothing on but that Chinese robe, which didn't fit too good, and certainly didn't come close to feeling comfortable in a saddle. No boots. No socks. Not even a hat. The little Chinese girl had never returned with my duds, and knowing now that Lucky Ben Wong had planned on murdering me, I don't think she was really a laundress or ever planned on washing those clothes.

"I'm here," I said, "because of the vigilance committee."

The two businessmen looked at each other. One of them said, "There's gonna be need of some vigilancing today. Real soon."

Mr. Slater stepped around Mr. McCoy, who lowered the little pistol. "I've seen you before," Mr. Slater said.

"Yes, sir," I told him. "I was—"

"With Whip Watson," he interjected.

I nodded.

The two merchants give each other a glance, then Mr. Slater was nodding at his pard, and the .41 disappeared into the brown pockets, and Mr. McCoy motioned me inside.

I followed them two dudes past shovels, pickaxes, post-hole augers, folding sights, levels and transits, compasses, measuring chains, pans, buckets, canteens, barrels, and a rack of Beadle and Adams five-penny dreadfuls, and to the counter where I saw some duck trousers and shirts behind the glass panels. Mr. Slater walked into an office, and Mr. McCoy held open the door for me. Mr. Slater sat behind a desk, and Mr. McCoy stood at the door. Mr. Slater offered me a chair, but I didn't feel right sitting down in nothing but a bathrobe, so Mr. McCoy taken the chair instead.

"What's this about?" Mr. Slater asked. "You sure you don't want to buy some pants?"

"Business first," I said. And I told them. Everything.

I talked. They didn't even interrupt.

When I'd finished, Mr. Slater pulled a cigar from a box on the top of his desk, bit off the end, and fired it up. I guess he felt sorry for me, so he slid the box, and I got myself a Jersey cheroot. He slid the box of Lucifers to me, and soon I had my own cigar smoking. To my left, Mr. McCoy coughed in his chair.

"So Whip Watson is bringing twenty-four whores to town, eh?" Mr. Slater blowed a perfect ring toward the tin ceiling. I'd never been able to blow rings myself.

"Twenty-five," I said. "The two twins."

"Yes," Mr. McCoy said dreamily.

"But they ain't whores," I had to remind them. "They're being forced into this business."

"Yes," Mr. Slater said. Then, in a tone I didn't much care for, "So you say."

I removed my cigar, didn't try to blow no ring, and leaned forward, pointing my cheroot at a framed photograph of a handsome woman holding a baby girl. "You're married, ain't you?"

He smiled at the photograph. "Indeed I am. Twenty-three wonderful years."

"Fourteen myself," Mr. McCoy said. "My second wife. My first one died. Typhoid."

"Sorry to hear that. Well, the way I figure it, we can post vigilantes on the roofs. Let Watson parade his girls right down Main Street, right to The Palace of Calico. Then when the last of the girls is inside, y'all cut loose. Shoot them dirty dogs down like the dirty dogs they are."

"Twenty-four ladies of the night." Mr. Slater whistled.

"Twenty-five," Mr. McCoy corrected. "Here. In Calico."

"No more Betty," Mr. Slater said.

I stood real straight, all indignant. "You want prostitutes in town?" My voice, however, sounded weak.

"Those twins," Mr. McCoy asked. "You say they're Southern and Irish? And they'll be in one room?"

"They ain't prostitutes," I snapped. "They're good women. Come here thinking they were mail-order brides."

"Mail-order whores." Mr. Slater sniggered.

"I wonder if the post office is aware of this." Mr. McCoy giggled.

"I don't think, Jeddah, that the Pendleton Civil Service Reform Act covered this subject at all." Mr. Slater and Mr. McCoy had a raucous belly-laugh that got Mr. Slater coughing from his cigar, and Mr. McCoy was wheezing so bad, he laid the pocket pistol on the top of the desk, had to fetch a handkerchief from his vest pocket, and dabbed his eyes.

When the laughter died down, Mr. McCoy was about to make another comment, but I said first, "Y'all won't do nothing to help those poor girls."

"At Calico prices," Mr. Slater said, "they won't be poor for long."

"They'll be richer than Lucky Ben Wong is," Mr. Slater said.

"Was," I corrected.

They wasn't laughing now. They was staring hard at me. I give them a grammar lesson that would make

Kermit of the Calico Water Works . . . Incorporated real proud. "*Is* is present tense. *Was* is past tense. Lucky Ben Wong is dead."

They blinked.

"Y'all didn't see that fire last night, early this morning rather, in East Calico?"

Their heads shook.

"Home and business burned down. With him in it."

"And his records?" Mr. Slater asked. He wasn't looking at me. He was staring hard at his pard.

Everyone was silent for a moment. Then one of the Dover clocks begun to chime. And the Regulators. And the Seth Thomases. And the Monarchs and the Recorders and the Kings. It was 7 A.M.

When the echoes faded, Mr. McCoy said, "If Wong's records burned . . ."

"Then there's no record." Mr. Slater smiled.

"We don't owe that damned Chinaman anything!" Mr. McCoy jumped up and pumped his fist in the air. "Especially since the yellow-skinned dog is *dead!*"

"The women!" I reminded both of them merchants.

Mr. Slater shouted something real indelicate about what I could do with the women, and it was something I had dreamed about, and thought about when I saw Jingfei . . . and maybe every now and then, the Lannon twins from Savannah by way of County Cork.

"We'll all be doing that!" Mr. McCoy yelled. "Probably starting tonight!"

It was a good plan. I still say so. If Jeddah McCoy and Max Slater had any decency flowing through their money-grubbing veins, my plan would have worked, and things might have turned out different. But they was peckerwoods. They was men. And

I was mad as hell. So while Mr. McCoy was dancing a little jig, and Mr. Slater was making vulgar displays with his cigar, I snatched the "Swamp Angel" off the desk and broke Mr. McCoy's nose with the barrel.

Down he went, wailing, trying to keep the blood from spraying the desk, and I aimed the .41 between Mr. Slater's eyes.

"I can't leave you two here," I told them. "We're going for a walk. If you talk, yell—shut up, McCoy, and be a man—if you do anything I don't like, I'll kill you in the streets. And remember them eight boys that got buried here week or two ago. Remember what I done to that assassin and the second-story corner window of the bank."

Mr. McCoy stopped whining. Mr. Slater nodded his pale head.

I said, "We're going. But first I need a pair of pants, any color but brown. A shirt. Some undergarments. Socks. Boots. Vest. Bandanna. Nothing brown. Bring anything in this room brown, and you'll rue your mistake. A hat. A Winchester rifle. Box of cartridges. Better make that two—no, six boxes. A Colt revolver. Some extra bullets for this peashooter." That sounded like all I'd need, but then I saw that box. "A box of Jersey cheroots. And some Lucifers." Recalling the recent chiming of the store's clocks for sale, I realized I must have lost my pocket watch when I'd crashed through the wall of coal oil cans. "A Seth Thomas pocket watch. Hunter's case if you have it, but open face will do." That sounded like enough. "No." I stopped Mr. McCoy from going out to fetch my plunder. "You'll bleed all over my clothes. You go." Mr. Slater got going. "A deck of playing cards if one's handy. Two decks." Mr. Slater was behind the counter, fetching my clothes. I looked at Mr. McCoy. "Put it on Lucky Ben Wong's bill," I told him.

The sign below the sign that read SLATER AND McCOY, PURVEYORS IN IMPLEMENTS & SUNDRIES said this:

> *Closed Today*
> *Out of Respect*
> *For the Late*
> **LUCKY BEN WONG**
> *Rest in Peace*

Mr. McCoy had real nice handwriting, and his nose had stopped bleeding, so there was no blotches or stains on the piece of paper Mr. Slater tacked onto the door.

"Let's go," I told them two birds, and we walked down the boardwalks, where there were boardwalks, and dirt, where there was dirt.

Now, I had no respect for Lucky Ben Wong, but leaving that sign would let Whip Watson know that Lucky Ben Wong was dead. That would likely cause him to relax, maybe get a little overconfident, and it would explain, I hoped, why Mr. Slater and Mr. McCoy wasn't around when Whip come in to rouse up everybody and parade the women down to The Palace of Calico.

My Seth Thomas watch—open face, but that was fine, and lever set, and the biggest size the company makes—told me it was 7:42. Most businesses in Calico opened right at 8:00, but the cafés was already serving, so town was coming to life. I looked toward the schoolhouse, which got me to frowning.

Smoke still rose over the roof, the last traces of Lucky Ben Wong.

"Is there school today?"

"It's Sunday," Mr. Slater told me.

"You don't observe the Sabbath?" I asked.

"You're asking *me?*" He shook his head, then said, "There is no Sabbath," he said. "In Calico."

"No school today, though." Mr. McCoy's voice was all nasal, as his nose had swollen up to the size of an Idaho potato and I was certain it was broken. "Miss Flint, the schoolmarm, won't allow it."

"She'll be singing at the services over at Sioux Falls," Mr. McCoy added. "No real preacher. Just singing and reading the Bible. Followed by a picnic. Starts at ten."

"They even let Betty attend," Mr. Slater said.

"Won't end till sundown," Mr. McCoy said.

"All right." That relieved me some. Women and children and Christians and Betty would likely be in the Upper Calicos, so they'd be out of danger from gunfire that was likely to commence this day.

"Smile," I instructed the two men walking in front of my new Winchester. "Tip your hats."

They done what I said, and I give one of the ladies who run one of the boardinghouses a friendly nod as we passed by the bank with the second-story window still boarded up. As we walked, I kept looking behind me, dreading the sight of dust or of a Columbus carriage heading into town. I also had my companions slow down as we passed any saloon, none of which observed the Sabbath, either, and looked through the windows or open doors.

Luck remained with me. Still no sign of Whip Watson or his boys.

"Cross the street," I ordered them.

J. M. Miller's store was already open, with some husky fellows loading boxes of blasting powder from the Giant Powder Depot into the back of a wagon with "Silver King Mine" writ on the side in handwriting much cruder that Jeddah McCoy's.

We stepped onto the boardwalk, the scent of fresh-cut lumber real strong and sawdust still on the planks. The plate glass windows were already installed, and stenciled in real pretty script, in gold with blue outlines, was THE PALACE OF CALICO.

Through the windows, of course, I could see the insides was real spartan. But there was a back bar. With liquor bottles on it. My throat was a bit dry.

"Open the door," I told Mr. Slater.

He jiggled the handles on the twin fancy doors.

"It's locked," he said.

I cussed.

Was about to suggest we go around back when I heard some spurs jingling inside the building. The handle jiggled from the inside, then there was a snap, a click, and a belch, and the door pulled open.

"Is that you, Whip?" Bug Beard asked.

He answered the question when he seen me. "You ain't Whip. You're dead."

I could smell the whiskey on his breath, and see the red in his eyes, and the bloodstained bandage covering his ear that had gotten shot off. Then he got wise, and started for the gun in his belly, but I smashed him right across the face with the stock of the Winchester, and he went flying back, turning over a table, breaking a bottle of whiskey—Scotch, though, never cared much for the taste—and rolling over in a bloody heap.

"You killed him!" Mr. McCoy cried out in that nasal wail.

I shoved him inside, told Mr. Slater to follow real quick. Right behind them I followed, pulling the door closed, hearing a voice upstairs say, "Julius, what the Sam Hill is going—"

A fellow had come out of one of the upstairs rooms, scratching his head, but when he saw me, and Bug Beard Julius lying on the floor, he started to bring up the shotgun he was holding loose in his arms.

The last thing I wanted to do was shoot off a gun this early in the morning. That would alert the folks in town, and Whip Watson if he was near Calico. So I brung up the Winchester quick, taken my aim, and said, "Drop it."

He didn't drop it, but he sure didn't bring it up into a firing position. Instead he smiled.

That's when I heard someone upstairs to my left say, "No, you drop it." He punctuated that thought by earing back what sounded to be a right powerful rifle.

"I thought you was dead," the man with the shotgun said. "Hey . . ."

His expression changed, and I heard a crunch I'd heard many times before. It's the sound of a gun barrel slamming into a skull. There was a moan, a crash, and the sound of a rifle falling onto the floor to my right. Then the man with the shotgun lost his grin, and his shotgun, and raised his hands.

Slowly, I turned around, looked up, and saw Mr. Clark beaming at me, another man in buckskins lying like a sleeping baby at his feet.

"Good morning, Mister Bishop," Mr. Clark said. "Glad you could make it."

CHAPTER TWENTY-SEVEN

Mr. Clark come prepared. He had wrist and ankle irons, and plenty of rope, so I made Mr. Slater and Mr. McCoy drag them vermin to the storeroom behind the bar, where we trussed them up with irons and rope and gags. The two merchants got real cooperative, but that's because Mr. Clark said he'd kill them if they acted poorly.

My heart pounded against my ribs, the hole in my forearm ached, I sweated, my belly felt like it was full of crashing waves against the side of a whaling ship. I leaned against the bar, laid my arsenal atop the mahogany, and checked everything. A long-barreled Colt and a Winchester rifle and that "Swamp Angel" .41.

"What do we do now?" I asked Mr. Clark.

"We wait."

Waiting ain't my best trait, but there wasn't nothing else to do. Turning, I spotted my reflection in the mirror, and shaken my head at my battered appearance. Then I noticed something else on the back bar.

"Hey," I said to no one in particular. "Is that Jameson?"

The morning bracer of Irish whiskey made me feel a mite better, and then we gathered at a table—a fancy one, with a top of green felt—by the big plate glass windows, and I dealt a little poker with the cards I'd purchased from Slater and McCoy's store.

While I dealt—not even off the bottom, and I didn't pocket any card, it being a friendly game of passing time—Mr. Clark revealed his plan.

Later that morning, Whip Watson would arrive, and, like a snake oil salesman, would begin his preaching and shouting and advertising. Next, the ladies would come up Main Street in the Columbus carriages, the brides-to-be first, then the girls Whip had designated as courtesans of The Palace of Calico. The wanna-be husbands could bid on the brides as they rode down the street. The bachelors could see what temptations awaited them in Calico's newest brothel.

"I'll help the girls out of the carriage," Mr. Clark said, "and then escort them in here. The carriage driver and his guard will head back to the edge of town to pick up the next girl. Once the girl is inside, we'll guide them out the back door."

A tall wooden fence ran behind the alley separating The Palace of Calico with Miller's store. A few adobe privies beyond that would also keep the girls out of view from the street.

"Have the girls run straight across the bridge into Chinatown. Have them hide. They'll be safe there."

"What about us?" Mr. McCoy asked in his nose-busted tone.

Me and Mr. Clark, and even Mr. Slater, glared at the coward.

"And when the last girl is outside?" Mr. Slater asked.

Mr. Clark grinned. "We open up."

"But . . ." Mr. McCoy hesitated. "Won't there be a lot of innocent people on the streets."

"The innocent people," I told him, "will be at Sioux Falls reading Scripture and singing 'Rock of Ages.' Who'll be left on the streets is a bunch of swine bidding on brides like they was at a cattle auction."

Those boys looked across the table and stared hard at me, like they couldn't believe I'd said that. Well, my dander was up. I dealt the last cards up for our five-card stud.

"You'll be outnumbered," Mr. Slater said.

"Nope." Mr. Clark looked again at his hole card, snorted, and flipped his cards over. He couldn't beat what nobody else was showing. "*We* will be out-numbered."

Mr. Slater folded his hand, too. "We?" He turned pale again.

I bet a bottle of gin. Mr. McCoy looked at the bet, then at Mr. Slater, then at Mr. Clark. "But we're not gunmen."

"You are now," Mr. Clark told them, which got Mr. McCoy to fold his hand, and allowed me to win with a jack high.

"What happens?" I filled everybody's tumbler with two fingers of the gin I'd just won. "What happens if Whip Watson decides to come inside here? While the girls are still on the streets?"

"Let's hope," Mr. Clark said, "that doesn't happen."

* * *

Waiting ain't no fun, especially when you know
that when the waiting's over, things will become
dangersome. I didn't drink too much gin or Irish,
didn't even really focus on playing cards. Wasn't
no clock on the wall. Who keeps time in a brothel?
Every last one of us would stand, move to the
window, peer outside. Nothing. Nothing at all.

Until . . .

Wasn't no mistaking that sound. A whip cracking
in the midmorning air, followed by some shouting.
Even a pistol firing off a round or two into the air.

All of us went to the windows. Whip Watson
stood in the street, flanked by a couple of his
gunmen. He'd be explaining some things, and what
he was explaining rankled some of those husbands
who thought they'd already paid for their wives. A
tall fellow took umbrage, but one of Whip's
gunmen cured him of that by buffaloing him across
the skull with a pistol barrel. After that, most of the
menfolk nodded their heads. A few—not husbands,
I figured—even looked excited.

Mr. Clark sneaked away, went to the storeroom,
and a few minutes later come out with two of the
guards. He unloaded their pistols, shoved them
toward us. Bug Beard wasn't one of the men, likely
on account that I'd smashed his face, and his nose
was swole up, lips split, some teeth busted, and
where there wasn't no dirty beard was fairly bruised.

"You two will stand at the door." He give them
two boys shotguns he'd also unloaded. "Just like
Whip expects. You give any warning, make any
move, do any fool play, and you'll be dead."

"Whip Watson will kill you for this," one of the
fools said. "He'll see you in Hell."

"You'll both be in Hell long before we get there.

Don't forget that. Now . . . outside. No words. Just look tough, and ugly."

He nodded at Mr. McCoy, who got the hint, and held the door open for our two guards. When they was outside, standing on either side of the door, Mr. Clark tossed Mr. Slater and Mr. McCoy a Winchester each.

"If they move . . ." he begun.

"Kill them!" Mr. Slater had gotten over his fear and was practically giddy with what was about to happen.

"Not so loud," I told him, and moved down the room to the corner, looking out through the glass.

We waited. . . . Waited some more. Kept right on waiting, sweating, nervous.

Finally, I spotted the dust, shifted the Winchester, leaned closer to the window to make sure them two guards wasn't trying nothing suspicious. The carriage went by Whip Watson, who was now standing atop a cracker barrel in the center of the street. One fellow run toward the coach, but Whip whirled, snapped his whip, and popped the dude's bowler hat off. He scurried back amid hoots and heckles, and got whipped on his buttocks before he reached the boardwalk. I sort of felt sorry for him.

Later, the editor of the *Calico Print* told me that embarrassed fellow had been Jürgen Baader, who had lied to the late Maud Fenstermacher of St. Louis, and helped get her killed, and I didn't feel sorry for that peckerwood no more.

Two men rode in the front seat, one armed with a double-barrel shotgun. Whip was shouting something, but I couldn't hear it.

"Do you know her?" Mr. McCoy whispered.

"Not by name," I said. It was one of Candy

Crutchfield's gals. She wore a nice silk dress, had a parasol. The carriage turned wide at the edge of town, and the driver reined in his matched pair of black horses. Mr. Clark stepped outside, off the boardwalk, helped the girl down. Said something to the driver and guard, who laughed a bit, and as soon as Mr. Clark was leading the girl inside, the buggy was heading back down the street. Already, I spied another carriage coming our way, and there stood Whip Watson on his cracker barrel, yelling, popping his whip, having a fine old time.

Once Mr. Clark escorted the young woman inside, he closed the door and urgently steered the woman, whose face was streaked by tears, red with shame, into Mr. McCoy's arms.

"Get her out of here," Mr. Clark said.

Mr. McCoy obeyed, whispering to the woman, now sobbing so hard she was shaking. I heard the back door squeak open, slam shut, and Mr. Clark was stepping outside again, and the second Columbus buggy was pulling closer.

So that's how things went. Right according to Mr. Clark's plan. We taken turns, me and Mr. Slater and Mr. McCoy, leading the women out the back door, behind the buildings, to the bridge that led to East Calico.

I'd just taken the big German gal, pointed to the bridge, then run back to The Palace of Calico. We was growing shy of women. Once the last was gone down that bridge, I knowed Whip Watson would be coming, and things would turn ugly. So I wiped my sweaty palms on my new denim trousers, come through the door, and moved the Winchester to my other arm so I could wipe the sweat off my right hand.

Then I seen Mr. Clark bring Jingfei inside, and

Mr. Slater taken her into his arms, heading right toward me. I stopped him.

"I'll take her," I said.

"No," he said. "It's my turn."

"I insist," I said.

"But . . ."

"Thank you," Jingfei said, and she turned and bowed slightly at Mr. Slater, who sighed, shrugged, and returned to the front door.

"How many more women are left?" I asked Jingfei as I led her to the rear.

"Four," she said.

Four more women. Then hell.

I was telling her what to do, where to go, warning her not to cross that bridge back into Calico proper until everything was settled. She didn't say nothing. She hadn't been crying. No, her face didn't show no tears, no lines, nothing but rigid determination.

I opened the door, stepped outside, and felt something slam into my head, crushing the brim of my new black hat.

Down I went, dropping the Winchester, yelling, rolling over, and hearing some wild cussing. I pulled myself up, holding my aching head, and, shaking off the pain, I reached for the Colt on my hip.

"I'll kill you! I'll kill you! Nobody betrays—" That was a whine I'd recognize anywhere. Through blurred vision, I saw Candy Crutchfield, her face fried from the sun, gaunt and pathetic and even more hideous, and she was wielding that little knife with the big handle at Jingfei.

But not for long.

I ain't rightly sure if I saw all this or imagined it. I mean, there stood Jingfei, between a trash barrel and the door, in her fine dress, not doing nothing, not moving, just watching Candy Crutchfield come with that sticker.

Then all I saw was a blur, but it seemed that Jingfei was jumping, and I mean real high, and not from no running start. Spinning like a ballerina or a real rank, unbroken mustang, and her foot caught the side of Candy Crutchfield's hand, and I heard a bone pop, and seen the knife sail against the wall. But Jingfei wasn't done. She kept spinning in the air, and her foot caught Candy Crutchfield on the side of her jaw. Bones popped. Teeth and blood flew. The old hag slammed against the wall, and swallowed her plug of tobacco, juice and all.

Once Jingfei come down, she kicked that woman four or five more times, then slapped her upside the head with about a half-dozen blows, kicked her twice in the belly, then grabbed her frayed, dirty, stinking clothes and pitched her right beside me.

Hadn't even worked up a sweat.

I just sat there, blinking, and then Candy Crutchfield climbed to her knees, shaking her head and sending blood onto my new pink shirt. Just like that, she snatched my Colt, and staggered off, slammed against the fence, and the whole shebang come crashing into the alley.

That brought me to my senses. I heard a shout, and come to my feet, finding the Winchester. Peered around the corner, and saw Candy Crutchfield hobbling toward the street. The driver of the Columbus carriage had reined to a stop. He was shouting something, and then the guard was leaping out of the buggy, thumbing back the barrels of the Parker twelve-gauge.

The guard, I noticed, was Juan Pedro.

That's when Candy Crutchfield shot him in the belly.

Damn good shot. I mean, Candy Crutchfield had shot him with her left hand, since Jingfei had just broke her right wrist. She was also bleeding considerable, and was staggering. Juan Pedro groaned, dropped to his knees, and then Candy Crutchfield fired at the driver.

That shot wasn't so good. The driver dived out, and the horses took off running, taking the empty buggy behind them.

"That tears it!" I shouted, and drawed a bead on Candy Crutchfield's back, but before I could kill her, she'd rounded the corner to the Miller store.

"Come on!" Jingfei grabbed my shoulder, yanked me around. She was heading right back toward the door, and I was shaking some sense into my head, telling her, "You need to get to Chinatown."

Mr. McCoy was escorting the two Lannon twins outside when he stopped.

"What the hell is going on out here?" he said.

He got his answer when a cannonade of gunfire rocked the streets of Calico.

CHAPTER TWENTY-EIGHT

If you've happened to have read *Massacre in the Mojave; Or, Whip Watson's Duel With Death,* likely you recall that, the way Colonel Wilson J. M. Drury seen things, the battle that commenced went like this:

Oh, the horror; oh, the eternal shame. Women lay huddled in the streets, leaden bullets tearing through the air.

"Must we die like this?" one poor girl cried out, clutching the cross that hung over her bosom.

"Help us!" yelled another young mistress. "Save us. We are defenseless against these ruffians!"

At that moment, Michael Bishop turned to his faithful comrade, crying out, "What shall we do, Whip Watson? What will become of blessed womanhood if these poor damsels are killed?"

Captain Whip Watson, however, was already answering that question. There would be none of the fairer sex killed. Not on this day. For Whip Watson charged, leaving his trusty bullwhip behind, and filling his hands with his weapons.

"Fear not, ladies," he cried, and the guns boomed in each hand. "I shall save the day."

Didn't happen that way at all. It went like this:

I was yelling at Jingfei, who wasn't listening. Mr. Slater had thrown open the front door and knelt on the floor, levering round after round into that Winchester, which barked and sent thick white smoke all around his head.

Mr. Clark hurried upstairs, taking three steps at a bound.

Jingfei had fetched Mr. Clark's rifle, smashed out the glass and the pretty stenciling job on one of the front windows. She cocked the rifle, aimed, pulled the trigger.

The Lannon girls raced by me, one of them carrying Mr. McCoy's long gun, the other grabbing a Colt from one of the guards we'd captured who was lying on a poker table.

Bullets blasted through the glass that hadn't already been shattered, then Mr. Slater slid out of the smoke, fishing cartridges from his coat pocket. I swear, the merchant grinned. He spied me and Mr. McCoy, just standing like knots on a log, and he waved over his pard.

"Come on, Jeddah!" he yelled. "This is not only exhilarating, it's damned fun!"

A moment later, the whole world shook.

If you believe the *Calico Print,* and it's probably as accurate an account as we'll ever know, this is what transpired: After mortally wounding one of Whip Watson's gunmen (Juan Pedro) and scaring the driver across the street, the wild woman rounded the corner and snapped a shot at Whip Watson, who, of course, stood well out of pistol range.

Whip's gunmen, many of whom had been posted along both sides of Main Street, opened up at Crutchfield, who fired a couple more shots, then darted into the only open door she saw. Which happened to be the powder house. What happened inside won't be known. A stray shot? Did Crutchfield strike a match to see as she reloaded her revolver? Did she just decide to end it all right there?

Well, she did. Even if it wasn't her intention.

The powder depot blew up, taking Candy Crutchfield with it, and sending flaming wood and cinders and stone and rocks and dirt and wood and parts of Candy Crutchfield all across Calico. The concussion alone blew out every window that wasn't already shot out in The Palace of Calico, and flames erupted on the near wall.

Smoke billowed. Men skedaddled. Calico, California, become a forest fire in a dry year, the flames jumping from building to building. The two carriages bringing the last two girls overturned, and some brave souls darted into the street, rescued one of the women (Donna Shaw) in her fine *moiré*, and taken her out of the path of bullets and flaming bits of wood and cloth.

The other gal (Betsan Priddy) lay unmoving, but a fellow charged out from Whip Watson's gunmen, run right to her. That fellow turned out to be Dr. Franklin Kent, and I got to give Mad Dog John Milton credit. He taken care of that girl, who'd gotten a nasty bump on her head, and after he let some two boys carry her across the street, Doc Milton went from body to body, wounded to dead, treating those he could. It was a brave thing to witness.

Of course, our concern focused on Whip Watson

and his boys, marching right down the street, right toward the already burning brothel he owned.

My ears was ringing. I knowed I was lying on the floor, but I also knowed I wasn't dead. I sat up, already spotting flames lapping through the wood on the wall next to what just moments ago had been Miller's store. I coughed, picked up my Winchester, and headed toward Jingfei.

Upstairs come a familiar sound, and I knowed what had sent Mr. Clark to one of them bedrooms.

"Hooray!" Mr. McCoy shouted. "That's a Gatling gun!"

Bullets dug up all around the marching gunmen in the street, and they scattered, started firing up at Mr. Clark and his Gatling.

There was another noise that penetrated my ears as I slid next to Jingfei, who was reloading her Winchester.

"Damen! Angriff! Damen! Angriff!"

I looked through the busted glass, and saw women—women in all colors of *moiré,* calico and silk—pouring out that alley, around the inferno that was Miller's store and Giant Powder Depot. Leading the way was the big Hun, and it was her doing most of that shouting. I don't know what those words meant, but she was acting like a sergeant, and a bunch of girls was following her orders.

Don't ask me where they got the guns. The *Calico Print* said they picked up rifles that had been blown out of the store when the powder house was destroyed, but even in Calico, merchants don't keep loaded weapons in their stores for sale. It ain't safe. I heard one story that said the women begun hauling out boxes of weapons from the back of Miller's store at the very beginning, because they always planned on a good fight. But make no mistake, those women had rifles, Marlins and Winchesters, and they had revolvers, two fowling pieces, a shotgun, and one Sharps .50-caliber buffalo rifle with a fancy brass telescope sight.

Here's something I learned that day. Mail-order brides ain't damsels. They sure as hell ain't defenseless. Think about it. Them women had left their lives and all the comforts they had knowed behind, they had traveled maybe a thousand miles, maybe even two thousand, one of them all the way from New York City, across country they didn't know to a town they'd never seen, to meet a fellow they'd never met except through an exchange of posts.

That don't take guts?

They had endured Whip Watson and Candy Crutchfield and the vermin they hired. Had made it through the scalding Mojave, through dust storms, thunderstorms. They had seen ten girls, just like them, die. Die for nothing. Die because of scum like Whip Watson.

No, women like that, they ain't defenseless. Colonel Drury ain't only a liar, he's a damned idiot.

"*Küss mein Arsch!*" the big woman yelled, and she shot a rider out of the saddle. "*Hure Nie!*"

Which become the battle cry for all the brides. Even those who didn't speak German, they was shouting, "*Küss mein Arsch! Hure Nie! Küss mein Arsch! Hure Nie!*" Shooting down Whip Watson's boys.

Even when something inside the orange-and-black ball that had been the Miller store popped or boomed, those women didn't flinch and sure didn't retreat.

Let's see if I can't paint you a picture. The women, those mail-order brides, lined the street behind one overturned wagon, two wrecked Columbus carriages. They pressed against buildings that weren't totally engulfed by flames. They knelt in the streets, behind water troughs or water wagons, or lay on their bellies. They waved their fists. They shot their weapons. The girl who'd been rescued by two men after the buggy wreck even come charging out of the smoke on the other side of the street, taking guns off dead or wounded gunmen, joining the other brides. The two Lannon sisters jumped through the busted out window, and begun shouting, "*Küss mein Arsch! Hure Nie!*" I swear, that intriguing mix of Georgia, Ireland, and German, that was something sweet to hear. Even if my ears was ringing, something was exploding next door, and bullets was peppering the brothel.

Even Doc Milton put away his scalpel and flask, and picked up the now dead Juan Pedro's shotgun, and started blasting.

I brought the Winchester up, saw one of Whip Watson's boys up on the rooftop of the bank, and was about to shoot him dead with that façade got chewed up by bullets from the Gatling gun upstairs, and that fellow was falling over the splinters, and crashing down right near the water trough where I'd sent some bad guy just weeks before.

Then I couldn't see on account of smoke. Mr. Slater run outside, and took a knee behind the screaming Hun, and Mr. McCoy went right after him. I don't know where the two boys we had acting like guards got off to. Maybe they run away. Maybe that got blowed apart along with Candy Crutchfield.

Then the noise of the Gatling stopped, and a few minutes later, I saw Mr. Clark coming down those stairs. "We got to get out of here!" he said. "Or get roasted alive."

That's when I noticed all the firestorms on both sides of the building. Flames danced out of three of the upstairs bedrooms. No wonder them two merchants had run into the street.

"I'll get Bug Beard!" Mr. Clark yelled, then coughed and, lowering his head, run into the storeroom.

Jingfei's rifle jammed, and she threw it onto the floor, leaped through the busted glass, and I started right after her. "Hey!" She turned, and I pitched her my Winchester. She caught it, grinned, and found a spot beside one of the Lannon twins.

I pulled out my "Swamp Angel." Which would do absolutely no good from where I was. Then I saw him. Whip Watson. Running across the street, into the smoke. I knowed where he was going, and I, like a damned hero in one of Colonel Wilson J. M. Drury five-penny dreadfuls, went after him.

On that east edge of town, there wasn't no place for Whip to go. The canyon dropped straight down, and although I reckon he could have fled down to the Hyena House or Applewhite's livery, got hisself a fast horse, and flown the coop, I knew he would run back our way. He wasn't no quitter. He'd come to kill whoever had taken over The Palace of Calico and robbed him of his brides and his profit.

I started for the back door, but all I could see was smoke and feel heat. My boots crunched the glass along the boardwalk. Eyes burning, I run around the other side, shielding my face and neck from the flames consuming one of the privies. Sprinting across the back, coughing from the smoke, I stepped over debris and one flaming piece of wood, and seen him, Whip Watson.

He slid to a stop when he spotted me, and I stopped, too.

We stood in the smoke and heat, the bridge between us, staring at each other.

I said, "I owe you one." It was a damned good line, something worthy of even Colonel Drury to write, only if he'd put it in his stories, when his hero pulled the trigger, he wouldn't have heard just a heartbreaking metallic *click*.

Whip laughed, and pulled one of his Colts. His gun went *click*, too.

Both of us now cussing, we hurled our guns at the other, missing, and then we charged, and met in a numbing collision. I bounced off to my right, landed on the bridge. Rolled to the edge, missing one of Whip Watson's spurs. Tried to get to my feet, but Whip kicked, caught me in my really hurting ribs, and I landed on the bridge's rope edge. Almost flipped over.

Tried to straighten, but Whip had me, fingers clawing at my eyes, his thumb splitting the corner of my lips. I gagged. Tried to bite him. Felt myself almost slide over. We grunted. We pushed. We done our best to kill one another. The rope burned my back, and then I slid down onto the flimsy planks. I come up, and that's when I felt Whip Watson's blacksnake whip slash across my shoulder.

Down I dropped again, trying to shield my face, watching Whip Watson come at me, his whip barking, him seething, eyes burning from smoke and hate. And then something drove him past me, and he dropped his whip, and spun around.

Jingfei walked right down the bridge, working the lever on the Winchester rifle, aiming from her hip, firing. Whip staggered back. Now I couldn't see him, could only see Jingfei, and smoke from the Winchester.

Being a card player, I counted. A Winchester rifle, fully loaded, will hold fifteen .44 rounds. Jingfei was at ten when she stepped over me. I rolled over.

"Eleven," I said.

"Twelve."

The last three she was placing the barrel on the back of Whip Watson's head and simply pulling the trigger. She was still pulling the trigger, still jacking the lever, when I got to my feet and walked to her. I took the empty rifle from her, turned around, didn't even look at what was left of Whip Watson, and led her the few rods down the bridge.

We hit solid ground. The Palace of Calico was nothing but furious flames. Something again popped inside the ruins of the Miller store. I looked through the alley Main Street, but didn't see nothing but smoke. However, I didn't hear no more shooting, no more Hun cussing. What rose above the roaring flames and the squawking fowls and barking dogs over in East Calico was women . . . singing. The Lannon girls was leading this one, not the Hun. It was an Irish war song, or love song, or drinking song. But . . . hell . . . ain't they all?

So I put my arm around Jingfei. Figured we could join the celebration a several doors down, where it wasn't yet burning too hard. Then we'd march out of Calico before we all burned to death.

Her body trembled a bit, but then she leaned against my shoulder, and, for once, didn't boss me or nothing. She just let me guide her to safety.

She stopped once, whirled abruptly, and looked back toward the bridge, but the wind had changed direction, and she couldn't see Whip Watson because of the smoke.

"Is he dead?" she asked.

Didn't answer her. Just leaned over and kissed her softly on the forehead, then I escorted her through the heat and smoke to the part of Calico that wasn't yet burned to the ground, but soon would be.

EPILOGUE

Well, that's pretty much all there is to my story, which is much truer, for the most part, than that pack of lies Colonel Drury proclaimed was his wildest but most truthful story ever penned.

After Calico got wiped out again—even them rammed-earth adobe buildings didn't stand up too good to that fire—the citizens got busy rebuilding. They do that in silver towns, especially when silver's selling for 96.59 cents per ounce fine.

Seems that Lucky Ben Wong's contracts with brides and grooms had likely been destroyed in the strange fire that consumed his home and his life, but most of the girls wound up wedding the men who'd they corresponded with. None of them become prostitutes, which must have made Betty, if not Calico's miners, thankful.

Far as I know, the mail-order brides and their grooms all is busy living happily ever after.

Even Jingfei. Now, her betrothed was one dead criminal, but a nice Chinese family taken her in, and me and Mr. Clark would pay them a visit, sip tea, chat about the weather and laundry and things of that nature. We never brung up Whip Watson or the fifteen bullet holes that ended his wicked life.

After word got out about all that had happened, a bunch of deputy U.S. marshals arrived with those prison wagons and plenty of iron manacles and John Doe arrest warrants, but Calico was cleaned out by the time they set up headquarters at the Hyena House. Only was a few wounded boys left to be arrested.

Dr. Franklin Kent, who had teamed up with Calico's doctors to help those injured in the fire, was questioned by one of them law dogs. "Aren't you Franklin Kent?" the lawman asked. "The mad killer from Bodie?"

The doc said, "No, old chap, my name is John Milton."

And the deputy let him go. I seen the old doc ride out later that day, and the peckerwood was on my old horse, Lucky. Another deputy wound up with Yago, saying I didn't have no bill of sale or nothing. And the law calls me a criminal!

Ever the gentleman, I taken credit for sending Whip Watson to his eternal rest. Didn't want Jingfei to have to go through that ordeal, and I also figured that there might be a reward posted on Whip Watson. That's what I was doing that abysmal afternoon, sipping a hot beer in the sun—the saloons hadn't got rebuilt yet—with Mr. Clark and telling the editor of the *Calico Print* how I had gotten the best of Whip Watson in that legendary gunfight that Colonel Drury got all wrong.

"He was shot fifteen times," the editor said.

"It was a fair fight," I said.

"At least five of those rounds came at point-blank range."

"He was a tough man to kill."

"But you killed him?"

"Damned right."

Which is how I wound up here in Folsom.

"Well, that's right interesting," this fellow nursing a hot beer behind me says, and I turned. First I seen the barrel of a .45 Schofield in his hand that wasn't clutching the pewter stein. Then I seen the badge. Finally, I looked at the face.

"What son of a bitch would give you a badge?" I asked, but I already knowed the answer. It was pinned on his lapel. The United States marshal for whatever district we was in had sworn in Corbin, the double-crossing snake who had damned near gotten me hung in Las Vegas, New Mexico Territory.

Still, all things considered, my luck changed a bit.

Corbin, for instance, didn't mention to his bosses or the judge, jury, or prosecutor about the fact that I was an escaped convicted murderer from New Mexico Territory. And the state of California agreed to reduce the charge from murder to manslaughter upon learning what a nefarious soul Whip Watson was. The prosecutor even said I probably would have gotten off scot free if not for the fact that Whip Watson had been shot fifteen times, most of them bullets coming at right close range and several after he had already terminally expired. Those arson charges also got dropped.

Most importantly, Mr. Clark and me never let Jingfei hear about anything that was going on. I figured it made me a hero.

Or a damned idiot.

Here at Folsom, the guards rarely put me on the

rock pile, and a few will even sit in on a few hands of stud poker when the warden's at church. The lady from that hifalutin society does a fine job, and despite what folks say about food, the chow here ain't all that bad.

Ain't heard nothing from Doctor John Milton, but last week, I got a wedding announcement from Mr. Clark and Jingfei. He's taking her to Seattle, Washington, and I wish her a long and happy life, preferably as a widow.

(Clark . . . Corbin . . . I need to avoid future partnerships with gunmen whose last names begin with C.)

Thusly, I close this factual narrative of my adventures in the Mojave Desert and the town of Calico, California. Bug Beard just dropped by my cell to say that the lady from the hifalutin society will be in the library to read to us this afternoon. Bug Beard says it's a thick book, might even be bigger than *Moby-Dick.*

I told him, "As long as it ain't *Massacre in the Mojave; Or, Whip Watson's Duel With Death* by Colonel Wilson J. M. Drury."